Smoking Ruin

I0550140

A Mystery by

D. R. Martin

Published by Conger Road Press

Minneapolis, Minnesota

Cover Illustration © 2011 Doug Oudekerk

ISBN-13: 978-0-9850196-0-0

For Susie, who makes it all happen.

Chapter One

My phone jangled once, twice in the pitch black. And Rick didn't pick it up.

It took me two beats to remember that he'd stormed out of the house on Sunday. So no Rick snoozing next to me.

Blinking in the dark, wrestling with flannel sheets that stuck like glue, I managed to roll over to the far side of the bed and grab the phone.

"Yeah," I croaked like a frog, "whozat? Rick? I'm really—"

"Marta Hjelm?" a man's voice purred. "Is that you, Marta?"

My heart skidded to a stop and I woke up real fast.

"Is this," I said with a little, embarrassing quaver, "who I think it is?"

He laughed—a chuckle like pricey champagne—and I knew. *The bastard.*

"Depends who you think it is, Marty."

"Terry," I said dully.

"The one and only."

Suddenly the charming voice—it had always been charming, right up to the end—came oozing over the airwaves. "It's so fantastic to—"

"Why the hell," I growled, "are you calling me in the middle of the fucking night? After seven years? *You fucking asshole!*"

"Just fine, thank you," my ex-husband burbled with annoying equanimity, "and how are you?" Then he glittered another intoxicating laugh at me.

You notice here that I didn't hang up.

Could've.

But didn't.

Still don't understand why.

Big mistake.

"Always the smooth character," I said, feeling like a mouse suffering the attentions of a "friendly" cat. I sat up in the dark cross-legged, where Rick should have been sleeping.

"Too smooth for my own good sometimes," my ex confessed.

"No shit," I agreed. "Where are you?"

"Right here in Minneapolis."

I pronounced a little, inaudible "Oh crap," then forged a-head. "Why Minneapolis? You hate Minneapolis. Snow in the winter, mosquitoes in the summer."

"Yeah, I do. Hate it. Too God-damned cold. I'm on a big project."

"What kind of project?"

"I'm still in advertising, Marty, with a major consumer goods company. In the *Fortune* 200, in fact."

"Hurray for you. Who?"

"Amfoodco."

"So you work with Happy Pops Cereal, then, Terry?"

"No, Marty, the tobacco subsidiary. Bertram Tobacco, Cigarette Division."

Perfect, just perfect, I thought to myself. He couldn't be doing something wholesome? Like rotting out little kiddies' teeth? Adding inches to America's waistline? Something a little less noxious?

"Anyway," he continued, totally missing my mood of dis-approbation, "I'm here in town trying to finalize a contract with a local agency. I have corporate approval to do a test market with them, if we can iron out some stuff. A new cigarette brand. Hemo. Great moniker, huh? And there've been, uh, problems that need looking into."

"So?" I said. "Everyone has problems."

"Yeah, but not these kind."

Suddenly a light went on in my sleep-soddened head. "You need an investigator? Is that why you called?"

For some reason—another mysterious neurological occur-rence inside my thick skull—I didn't tell him I was planning to quit the business. I could have. But didn't.

"Uh-huh. I stay in touch with Chuck and Clarice and I heard through them that you were a licensed PI. Didn't see that one coming, I can tell you. And they said you're supposed to be pretty good. I mean, what's wrong with throwing a few bucks your way? Thought it might be fun to see you, too."

I know I ought to have told him to go to hell, and shut the manhole cover after himself. I can't tell you how many times I've daydreamed about telling the guy to go screw himself if he ever came crawling back. But I remembered what an old blues singer sternly told me once when I bitched about a tough investigation: "Honey, a gig's a gig, so long's the check don't bounce."

"So what's going on?" I said "What's the problem?"

"I'd like you to meet this morning with the agency VP, at your office. Downtown St. Paul, right? He'll fill you in, then you can decide if you want the job."

I stewed for a half minute, and figured it wouldn't hurt to listen to the man.

"Okay," I said. "What time is it now?"

"Five."

I moaned, grieving for the lost hour of shut-eye.

"This morning, you said?"

"Yup, I did," he chuckled. "By the way, the VP said he knew you from way back."

"Is that so? What's his name?"

"Denny Ryan."

Now didn't that just round out the *perfect* morning?

Good old Denny Ryan. The only person who'd ever fired me.

Chapter Two

Rick and I share digs on the third floor of the old Amalgamated Manufacturing Building in downtown St. Paul. World headquarters for Hjelm Investigations LLC and Mueller Images Inc. His and her companies. Sometimes he helps me with legwork, sometimes I haul gear and shoot for him.

I got there about seven that Tuesday morning and only had to wait ten minutes for the knock on the door.

Denny Ryan still had that barracuda look, out there under the sickly fluorescent hallway lights.

The same sharp, narrow features. Sharp, narrow canines. Sharp, narrow body wrapped in a sharp, narrow Italian suit and a gorgeous slate-blue trench coat. But he had a green tint around the gills, a sallowness in his cheeks, a worrisome vibration in the well-manicured hands. Raccoon circles half-surrounded the washed-out baby blues. Even the Shelby knot in his pricey silk regimental looked cockeyed, sloppy. There was a large, unmarked manilla envelope in his left hand.

He didn't look all that different. Pretty much the same, except he'd had a very bad night.

I wasn't self-deluding enough to think I looked the same. I was a little thicker through the waist and thighs, a little slower on the jog. My Norwegian grandma used to tell me that I was "handsome." Rick says I'm "gorgeous," but I don't believe him. "Handsome" just about does the job. As my dear old Dad used to say, it's better than a poke in the eye with a sharp stick. Beyond that, I'm five-ten, a little overweight. Not in bad shape, but not as good as I'd like. I have short, layered dark blonde hair—no gray yet, knock wood—and brown eyes.

My old boss stuck his hand out with salesman conviviality. "Hi, Marty, y' look great." *Really* sincere.

"Marta," I said evenly. "Only relatives and friends call me 'Marty.'"

He blinked, and the bags under his eyes quivered. "Sorry, forgot. Been a while."

I took the smooth millionaire hand and shook it once, eyeing the Rolex Oyster. "Understand you've done well."

"Yeah, I guess so. We had some good luck with those new publications after you left."

"Maybe you did yourself a favor sacking me."

"Yeah, maybe."

He followed me into the office, took a quick look around—dismissive, distinctly unimpressed. He blinked at the gray linoleum floor, the light table, the fire-proof cabinets where we keep old slides, negatives and camera gear. Rick's images covered the walls—wildlife, kids playing, scenics—and they didn't seem to impress him. He actually sniffed at our long-in-the-tooth Macs and hulking CRT monitors.

I sat at my work station and swiveled around as my old nemesis from newspaper days plopped onto the Naugahyde sofa. Without his jabber, he suddenly looked all shriveled up and frightened, like a tiny old man imprisoned inside a ridiculously chi-chi trenchcoat.

"Like some coffee, some donuts?" I said. "I can go down to the Ace Cafe—"

Denny shook his head. "Been up all night. All coffeed out."

No kidding. I could smell his rank, sour breath from several feet away.

"So why are we here, Denny? Why'd Terry call me? I do retail loss prevention work now, mostly. Silent shopping, checking up on clerks and cashiers and such. Frankly, I'm kind of phasing out of the private investigator routine."

"Then it's a good thing I got here in time, isn't it?" Denny said brightly. "You went to California after you left the *Bugle*. Right?"

I nodded and sat down behind my desk. "Yeah, that's where I met Terry."

"Do you know what happened with the company?"

"I did, but refresh my memory."

"I sold the *Bugle* and the magazines." Denny dallied with the big diamond ring on his right pinkie. It made him look like a two-bit gangster from central casting. "Got close to nine million for them. I thought I was going to take the money, play golf and sail the rest of my life. Had a timeshare in Vail, bought a condo on Sanibel."

"Nice," I said, and meant it. I adore Sanibel—even after the big hurricane stripped out a lot of the trees. I was jealous.

"But after six months I was going nuts, absolutely crazy. I didn't exactly make it easy for Jessie. She said I'd damned well better find something to get me out of the house or she'd have to think about taking the kids and four-point-five million off my hands."

I laughed.

"No, seriously, she was this close." He held up thumb and forefinger, holding them a fraction of an inch apart. "I coulda started a new book. But shit, Marty— 'Scuse me, *Marta*. I didn't want to do the same thing all over again. Then the phone rang. Christ, the timing was incredible. It was Herb Gottwaldt."

I riffled through the chaotic Rolodex I keep in my head. "The advertising guy?"

"Yeah, *the* advertising guy. At least around this town. Awards up to here, one of the savviest, most creative ad men outside of New York and L.A. Like a dynamo."

"You always were an ad man," I said. "I mean, you could hustle the ad lineage. Drove me nuts with all those late ads, re-doing the layouts all the time. It took me a while to figure out you weren't really in the newspaper business."

"I never could understand why anyone'd want to write in-stead of make money." Denny cracked his first, lopsided smile, as if savoring that thought. "Writers are saps. They give it away. Always have, always will. Look at all those millions giving it away on the internet. But it worked out good for me. There were always plenty of writers and editors, and they were happy to take peanuts."

"They're useful, too, when the publisher's illiterate," I observed.

Denny laughed and jabbed a finger at me. "Hey, I read a book last year."

"Schopenhauer?"

"Naw," Denny replied with a perfectly straight face, "don't

know about him. Harvey MacKay." Then he grinned at me: *Gotcha!*

The last time I'd seen him had been more than a decade earlier, on an August evening that resembled a steam bath. I remember it because I'd just put to bed what turned out to be my last issue of the *Bugle*, a free weekly. I was the managing editor—a great job for a music nerd a few years out of college. Unfortunately, Denny Ryan was the owner and publisher.

The writer and I had sweated bullets, doing a cover investigation on a guy who owned a regional media empire, with a reputation for suing the bejesus out of any detractor. We had some brave folks go on record about the shit this guy pulled, but Denny got cold, cold feet. He and the copy editor spent a couple of hours hunched over the monitor, snipping out everything but the least controversial sections.

I chewed him out in the main office, with half a dozen witnesses, addressing him as "you yellow, fucking asshole troglodyte." Or words to that effect. After I stormed out I had my supper—the famous chicken special at Peter's Grill at Eighth and Marquette in downtown Minneapolis. When the place closed at eight, I wandered down to the bus stop. A few minutes later a bistro up the street disgorged three young men in suits, all roaring drunk. One of them was Denny Ryan. He saw me and zigzagged over.

"Hey there, Marta," he slurred, peering at me for a moment with goggle eyes. "Whadja call me that shit for, front of everybody, y' stupid bitch?" He came right up to me, nose to nose. "You're gonna haveta 'pologize in front of the staff."

"You tore the guts out of a great story," I growled, backing away from the fumes. "You don't even have the balls to pretend you're in the newspaper business. *So fuck you!*"

He stared at me for a couple of beats. Then he hooted. Literally hooted. "EEE-EEE-EEE!" Like Cheetah the Chimp in the old Tarzan movies. He ran a circle around me and scampered three feet up a lamp post, screeching away. I'm not making this up.

I turned and walked.

"You're fired!" he shouted after me from the lamp post. "You're fucking FIRED!"

I hadn't seen or talked to the little Irish shit since then. That was a dozen years ago and Niagaras of water had passed under many bridges.

He'd become a millionaire ad man. I'd bounced through a series of careers—including private investigator. Lately I'd been trying to help my boyfriend build up his business, a photo agency. We needed fifty grand for computers, photo gear and operating budget, and we couldn't find a bank that would float a loan to a funky business like ours during the "Great Recession." A nice payday would be welcome.

That was my rationalization for seeing Denny and not telling my ex-husband to take a flying leap. Besides, I have to admit I was plenty curious to see both these prize specimens from my ancient past.

"Anyway," I said, blinking at my old boss in the early morning gloom, "you got connected with Herb Gottwaldt—"

"Herb owns a substantial majority of the agency. I have about 10 percent and the rest belongs to some of his relatives and investors. We have a dozen, give or take, regional accounts. There are three national accounts—Hamburger Shack, Chippewa Motorcycles, and Honeymoon Cruises. Minneapolis Mutual Insurance is a kind of super-regional. Major player in the car insurance business in the Midwest and Mountain states. Until a year ago we had Trans National Airlines and Big Mart discount stores. They're gone. We're doing in the neighborhood of about 90 million a year in revenues."

"Dollars?"

"Yup."

I was impressed. "Nice neighborhood."

"Terry Rosen's the product marketing manager for Hemo, which Bertram wants to start test marketing here in the spring. He's picked Herb to do the campaign, and his bosses think it's a great idea. Not just anybody in our shop, mind you. Herb himself. We just have some extra details to iron out before it's official. It's a fantastic opportunity."

"Hemo? That's a weird name. What's it mean?"

He grinned broadly. "'Hemo' means blood. It's the new, gotta-have cigarette for all the young adults who are into those vampire books and movies. Incredibly hot these days. Black cigarette, red filter, lots of potential for fun creative stuff. Huge potential market. You should see some of the concepts we've come up with."

"You're going after kids? I thought you couldn't do that anymore."

"No, Marta," he said, waving me off. "We're targeting young adults 21 and older. Not kids."

I didn't really believe him—they'd be happy to hook all the kids they could—but nodded tiredly. "Okay, whatever. So tell me why you're here at 7 o'clock on a sub-zero morning."

Chapter Three

"Some really dangerous shit is happening relating to Hemo," Denny said hoarsely, "and we need to find out who's doing it. Last night our Hemo team—" He shook his head, as if the thing he had to recall made him queasy.

"I better begin at the beginning. The test market involves five upper-Midwestern states. Print, point-of-purchase, promotions, events. Basically, everything that the big tobacco settlement of '98, '99 allows us to do. We've actually started working on it, even though it's not a done deal. If it goes well—and Herb has some fantastic ideas—we have a very strong chance to do the national rollout next year. That would be unprecedented."

"What do you mean?"

"Usually tobacco companies go to New York or Chicago when they pick ad agencies. So an agency like ours has to provide added value. And ours is our creativity. Herb comes at you out of left field, when you least expect it. *Bam!* That's why Bertram wants to take a chance with us."

"Sounds hunky-dory to me," I opined.

"It was, until about a month ago."

I raised my eyebrows in the interlocutory manner.

"Someone must've seen in the trade press that we were in the hunt for Hemo. We started getting threatening letters, saying Herb—Herb personally—would be a murderer with blood on his hands if we actually got the contract. Then they started getting *really nasty.*"

"How's that?" I asked.

"These letters said if we didn't drop it, Herb might have an accident."

"Extortion, Denny. You don't need a PI. Call the cops."

He held up one of those well-maintained paws of his: Whoa, girl!

"Our initial Hemo team— Herb had something else to do. Meg LaGrange was there, the copywriter. Harry Litzky, art director. Sue Hewlett, traffic. Archie Gottwaldt, Herb's son, who's working with Sue. And me, I'm account exec. An intern was there, too. Sue's little sister Michelle.

"We were working last night about eleven, on point-of-purchase and contest concepts that'll kick off the test market." Denny rubbed his eyes and ran a hand through his unsettled coiffure. "We sent out for pizza. Chez Pizza, a real good place on 394, west of Ridgedale. Not the usual crap. The owner's a friend. Sue went down to the lobby about midnight for the food. Couple of pizzas some cola in paper cartons. We had some wine, too. Pinot Grigio, I think. But that came out of the fridge downstairs. We spread the stuff out on the table, grabbed a few paper plates.

"I took mine back to my office. Had to call Tokyo. Before I had a chance to dial, all hell broke loose. Someone started screaming. I ran out. Sue Hewlett had spit her cola out all over the floor, and she was running for the water fountain. She looked like she'd just eaten shit."

"Something in the cola?" I twisted from side to side, to loosen the knot between my shoulders.

"Uh-huh."

"Do you know what it was?"

Denny made a fist with his right hand and gently punched his left palm. "Yeah."

"How'd you get it analyzed so quickly?"

"We didn't. But we know what it isn't."

"Do tell," I said, suddenly quite curious.

Denny opened his manilla envelope and fished out a sheet of paper folded in quarters. He carefully unfolded it and heaved himself upright. "Here," he said, walking over and handing it to me. "Anonymous e-mail."

The printout, from nosmoke354@hotmail.com, read:

You people all deserve to die, Herb Gottwalt, and this is a warning that you should stop working for Bertram. Next time it's real nicotine in your soda, a real poison. Or bullet or knife or bomb. The product you plan to sell contains nicotine that adicts others and is responsible for millions of

deaths. Stop now or you all die.

I stood up, and went over to the old warehouse-style window wall. The moonless night was just giving way to the crystalline light of the early-February coldsnap, the sky midway between black and Nordic blue. Stars still twinkled. Feathers of steam wisped off the tops of downtown St. Paul's office towers and condo highrises. I could just barely catch the enticing, sausagey perfume of the Ace Cafe down below. It called to me, as always. A newspaper, a cup of dense java with cream and honey, a short stack of sourdoughs, and a couple of Cajun sausage patties. Yessir.

"What do you say, Marta? Do you think these, uh, people are really trying to kill Herb? Is this some kinda hoax, maybe?"

I turned around and looked at my old boss. "Herb wasn't there, was he? So they couldn't have gotten to him. And they imply the stuff in the cola isn't really nicotine, isn't poisonous. We'll need to test it. So no, I don't think they want to off anyone. Not yet, anyway. This was a demonstration."

"I don't understand."

"The woman who sipped the cola spit it out, didn't she? They wanted someone to taste it. Unless I'm mistaken, nicotine doesn't have much flavor at all and in sufficient quantity it shuts down the nervous system, or something like that. They just wanted to scare the sap out of you guys with some goop that tastes bad. Symbolic, too. You know, extort nicotine peddlers with faux nicotine."

Denny squirmed at my description of his "team." "Yeah, that makes sense."

"You want me to look into it, right?"

Denny nodded, and hunched forward, elbows on knees.

"Yeah. I want you to document what's happened, interview our people, help with their security, just in case someone tries something again."

"So you don't want the police involved?"

"No, we don't want *any* publicity. Zero. Nada. Nothing that could embarrass Bertram. We could lose the account. That's what Herb wants, what Terry wants, what I want."

"Are you going to do what they say?" I asked.

He shook his head energetically. "Herb says fuck 'em. He's rarin' to go with the project."

"But why me? Hell, I don't even—"

I almost gave him my spiel about how tired I was of interviews and tails and surveillances. How sick I was of bad, bad shit hitting the fan. How I was almost ready to "retire." But it never does to tell a potential client that you dislike the thing that he's prepared to pay you good money to do. Would you hire a surgeon who confided that she hated the sight of blood? An accountant who couldn't stand numbers?

Still, it sure sounded like a job worth keeping the shingle out for. I figured there were three reasons to do it. One, 75 bucks an hour for maybe a hundred hours. Two, I still had my license. Three, plain old nosy-parker curiosity to see Terry and Denny in action again.

He peered at me, waiting for the end of the sentence.

"Sor-ry," I said. "Why me?"

"It's a small-world thing, for sure. But Terry brought your name up, and I sure remembered you. I mean, we got along pretty well before that last blowup, right?"

No we hadn't. Not even close. Because I'd thought he was a greedy asshole and he thought I was a snotty socialist bitch. But I nodded just the same.

"So anyway, Marta, Herb knew that you'd worked for me and I always thought you were a sharp gal. Besides, he wants someone off the radar, someone discreet. Why not you?"

I shrugged. He was definitely bullshitting me. I'd never heard him compliment anyone. So why now? A change of personality?

"So will you do it, Marta?"

"Two conditions," I said, returning to my chair.

"Yeah?"

"First, you owe me eight-hundred bucks plus interest."

He almost snarled, but caught the lip-curl just in time. "What the hell do you mean, I owe *you?*"

"When you fired me," I grinned, "I had two weeks vacation pay coming. And you wouldn't cough it up. Your letter said, more or less, 'I'm not paying vacation money to anybody who doesn't work for me anymore. So sue me.'"

Denny's expression of perturbation softened and shifted toward amusement. "Okay, Marta, I'm in a short-hair situation here. I owe you eight-hundred plus interest. What's the second condition?"

"I gotta clear a couple of things off my calendar before I can accept. I'll call you this afternoon. Just hang onto the evidence, okay? Letters, e-mail, pizza, cola. Make sure your people keep their traps shut, even with the other office staff. If it's a go," I concluded, "it's 75 bucks an hour plus expenses."

"Right," Denny said without blinking. I grabbed my calculator, did some figuring, and he wrote me a check for my old vacation pay plus interest—a good deal over $1500.

• • •

I slathered the last crescent of pancake with faux maple syrup.

The Ace was noisy, crowded, a haven from the windchill outside. Young to middle-aged waitresses, squeezed into tight jeans and tighter tops, scurried around good-naturedly, dispensing humongous sticky rolls and seasoned comebacks to tired, old joking come-ons. There were at least a half-dozen cops scattered around the booths and tables, mostly big, heavy men in big, heavy blue jackets. Police headquarters was around the corner. Some of them I knew from retail work downtown, and we nodded companionably at one another when we made eye contact.

Back upstairs, I saw a message in my voicemail. Maybe another big job. Maybe a good excuse to not go to work for shills for a tobacco company.

I rewound the tape. It was Terry again.

"Hi, Marty," Terry told the machine. "I hope the meeting with Denny went okay. Maybe I'll see you out at the agency later." The creamy timbre of his voice still tugged at me, still evoked some memories. Dammit.

"Anyway, Herb here got some court-side seats for the Timberwolves game tonight, and he couldn't use 'em, and I wondered if you'd like to go. Freebies, kiddo! I'll even pop for dinner, okay? Call me whenever." Then he gave the number.

"Shit, Terry," I said under my breath. "What the hell are you up to?"

Chapter Four

Sammy Davis, Jr.'s one good eye twinkled out from beneath a jauntily angled bowler. Jimmy Carter held a dusty, beat-up Skil saw in his well-calloused hands and smiled that Alfred E. Newman smile of his. Eudora Welty sat, gnome-like, grave, in some humid Southern glade.

I went up and down the main gallery of the St. Paul Photography Museum, past the ranks of portraits. My toes and nose were numb from the subzero walk down from our office. At least I'd had the sense to wear jeans and layer like crazy—silk undershirt, turtleneck, blouse, sweater, brown silk blazer, parka, and a stocking cap that guaranteed a bad hair day but saved my ears from frostbite. When that spot between your eyebrows hurts from the windchill, you know it's *cold*. Well, it hurt that morning. I rubbed it with icy fingers, hoping Rick would show up for work ASAP. He pulled duty here quarter-time, doing PR. He also got to use their darkroom for free. Rick mostly shoots digital these days, but he still had a deep affection for old-fashioned chemical dark room work.

I stopped in front of Leonard Bernstein—the elderly, disintegrating maestro of his later years, not the young lion of the '40s and '50s. A smoldering cigarette dangled from his lips and I could almost see him dying in front of me, the rabbinical spark fading in his eyes. The photographer was Herman Brush, a star of post-WWII fashion photography, turned portraitist. He'd caught Lenny's luminosity just before it winked out.

"Marta?"

I turned around and saw the young guard who'd let me in.

"It's almost like they're lookin' at you, isn't it?" he said. "Brush's the greatest since Karsh. No doubt about it. I like his Churchill even better."

"Yeah, Bob, it's almost like they're looking at you," I agreed. I gave him as much of a grin as I could. That minus-30 windchill sort of anesthetizes your face. "You said Rick was supposed to get in about nine-thirty?"

"Right. But he's pickin' up Mister Brush today. He might be

off-schedule."

I did some math in my head. "He's gotta be up in his nineties."

"Yeah, ninety-five. But still pretty spry."

"So it's okay if I just wait around?"

"Sure. They finished getting the show up last night. Enjoy." The kid strolled cheerfully back out to the main door, honored to working for poverty wages in the "A-R-T-S."

I was giving Keith Richards the once-over, when Rick came into the gallery at a quickstep. He saw me, caught his breath and proceeded on over.

"Howdy, ma'am," my lover and partner said. He gave me an un-lusty peck on the cheek. He smelled like Vienna Roast, good enough to drink.

"Howdy, sir. Stayin' warm?"

"Not particularly. Freezing my butt off, actually. How about you?"

I shook my head. "Except in bed, things are okay. Awful cold in there. Not much fun. Nice to have somebody to rub up against. You ready to come home yet?"

"I'd like to."

"Then do it.

He shrugged. "We've got some issues, you know. That was a pretty big dust-up on Sunday. You quitting the biz. Me not agreeing."

"The birds miss you, too," I said, dodging the subject

"No kidding? They told you this?" He flashed me one of his broad grins that, after several years of being together, still made my old ticker go pit-a-pat. What I missed most of all, though, was that first, sandpaperykiss of the day, and a long wakeup snuggle.

When we have serious fights—fortunately, only a few times so far—Rick thinks it's a good idea for him to go stay with his brother until the air clears. He says he prefers it that way because the duplex is mine. "The parrot's despondent," I confirmed, "suicidal."

"Give him potato chips, let him watch his *Cheers* reruns."

Rick looks kind of All-American wholesome—square-jawed, open expression, always ready with a smile, a truly good-natured guy. He's about six foot two, lanky but not skinny, with rapidly thinning blond hair and—you guessed it—eyes of blue.

I could sense his frustration, though. He stared down at the terrazzo floor, a clench-lipped stare. "Have you thought anymore about what I said?" he finally asked in a low voice.

My turn to stare at my toes. "Yeah, sure. But if I knew any better, I'd think you think I'm not a good photographer. I'd think you think I'd screw something up if I came into the business full-time."

"No, no, *no!*" He put a hand on my shoulder and cocked his head to the side. "You're good, plenty good. That's not the point."

"Then what *is* the point?"

"I think you don't really understand how good you are at what you do," he said. He took his hand back. "I think you'd really regret not being a PI. You're tired, a little burned out. That thing last summer—" He shook his head. "Take some time off. But dammit, Marty, why give up something you do so well?"

We stood staring at each other, uneasy with the notion of another argument. We seldom shout at each other, just raise our voices a notch at a time, until one of us gets steamed enough and leaves the room. Or leaves the house. Just like you'd expect from a stubborn Norwegian and a stubborn German. Mother Teresa, peeking benevolently over Rick's left shoulder, definitely didn't approve.

"Haven't we had this fight before?" I said.

"Yeah. Every week for two months. Same lame dialog, too. Gotta get a better writer." Rick took his parka off. He had on his best going-to-work clothes—a gray Harris tweed jacket, freshly pressed black slacks, dark blue Egyptian cotton shirt. He'd grabbed them on the way out the door.

"I guess maybe we'd better save it, huh?" I said.

He nodded. "I don't have a lot of time. I've got to pick up Brush at the airport about eleven."

"It'll go great."

"Yeah, I think so."

"The reason I came wasn't because of our, uh...debate. I didn't come to get you mad."

"I know."

"But I've got a dilemma."

He raised his eyebrows quizzically: *Yes?*

I told him about Terry and Denny Ryan, and the attempted extortion. I didn't have the nerve to tell him that Terry had, in effect, asked me out on a date.

He stood there and his jawline got tighter and tighter.

"What are you even talking to those assholes for?" he spat. I had never restrained my derision for the ex-husband who'd cheated on me, and the ex-boss who'd fired me. "Why would you even consider working for them?"

"The money's good, Rick," I said. "Our business needs the money. We gotta have the new iMacs, the new software, those new Nikkors, a big upgrade for the website—"

He waved me off with a waggle of the hand. "How could you work for a tobacco company? What about your Dad, Marty?"

That was something I'd hoped wouldn't come up. I'd kind of pushed it off to the side all morning, ever since Terry called. Leave it to Rick—Mr. Conscience—to hone right in and zing me on my tender spot. Lord knows I didn't need him to remind me. Neither of us could ever forget the gaunt, bespectacled figure who shuffled around our lower duplex, puffing away on "low-tar" weeds, watching game shows, waiting to go to the hospital one last time.

"Anyway, didn't you just say I was so damned good at this stuff it would be a crying shame if I quit?"

He cracked a little smile. "Yeah, I did say that, didn't I?" He took a step over to me, bent down a scootch, and lightly kissed my cheek another time. I returned the favor.

"Do what you think is right," he said. "I'll talk to you later." And he marched off down the gallery.

• • •

I headed west in the big, gray Mercury Marquis that my Dad had bought new, not long before the Big C got him. I got the car and the equity in my duplex that Dad had helped me with, while my sister got the big old house in Duluth. We both own the cabin up off the North Shore of Lake Superior, near Grand Marais—but I hardly ever get up there.

Owning the Merc was like having a little piece of the old fart, who spent 35 years driving similar land-yachts around the Midwest as an insurance company field rep. Always Fords and Mercs. The car still had the dusty smell of ancient cigarettes, a reassuring aroma from childhood. Dad's faded bumper stickers—"Hug a Norwegian!" and "Geezer On Board"—still regaled passers-by. The recycled ah-oo-gah horn he'd installed had long since ah-oo-gahed its last, but his remote control starter still worked.

I got lucky. It took me only 45 minutes to get out beyond Ridgedale shopping center. Then off 394 and a quick southward jog through Wayzata, past toney shops filled with Louis Vuitton and Prada and Coach.

I curved left out of the village, following the undulating shoreline of Lake Minnetonka, much slower now. You have to respect the capacity of that ice to kill you if you break through it. Except for evergreens and brown-leaved oaks, every tree was barren. The mansions up off the lake shore looked anything but homey. Like citadels, fortresses.

The ad agency offices were only a few miles down the winding road, a sprawling neo-Prairie-Style office building set in a hilly grove of full-grown oaks. They had a tastefully small, Prairie-school sign in wrought iron that simply said, "Gottwaldt and Ryan." I'd seen Chez Pizza on the way out, on the north service road west of Ridgedale shopping center, in a strip mall. It couldn't have taken their driver more than ten, fifteen minutes to get out here that time at night. And somewhere along the way someone was waiting who knew what to expect and what to do.

Chapter Five

The Prairie School look didn't extend inside. The inner lobby was clean as a Bauhaus hound's tooth, all chrome and black leather and furniture out of a modern art museum. Advertising awards, Clios and so forth, covered the walls. I even recognized some of the prize-winners in frames and on video loops.

The famous boxing kangaroos, for a headache-pill company. The motorcycle encased in a block of ice, then thawed and run. The upside-down, bungee-cord-jumping young couple happily managing not to upchuck their Burger Shack gut-bombs.

The receptionist—with her neo-Carnaby Street do, clad in a tie-dyed designer sweatshirt—announced my arrival into a chrome speakerphone, then took my Thinsulate jacket and down vest and cap with an unspoken note of disapproval for my sense of couture.

I barely had time to sit, when Denny Ryan came charging out of nowhere. He grabbed my hand, muttered a "Thanks for coming," and towed me into a labyrinth of offices. I kept my mouth shut, as we marched past cubicles filled with account executives, designers, copywriters. They stared at us. They knew something was up.

Going by one doorway, Denny stopped and peered in.

"Hi, guys," he said to someone I couldn't see. "Introduce you to somebody?"

"Sure," said a deep, velvety woman's voice.

"Marta," Denny said, "I'd like you to meet Sue Hewlett and Archie Gottwaldt."

We strolled in and found the Hemo traffic manager and her assistant looking like they weren't working very hard at all. A blues tune—Buddy Guy doing "Voodoo Chile"—was thrumming quietly out of a CD boombox on a shelf. Herb Gottwaldt's son had perched on the edge of the desk, facing his superviser, who lounged in a Miller Aeron chair behind the desk. Master Gottwaldt hopped off as we came through the door and pivoted to face us.

"Guys, this is Marta Hjelm. Marta and I worked together

back when I had the *Bugle*."

Sue was thirtyish, a head-turning woman of color, approximately *café au lait*. Her ebony-black eyes gave the impression that this woman knew all, saw all. She had fine, chiseled features and a sharp looking page boy. It should be illegal to look so good in a cream silk blouse and black wool trousers.

Archie looked a lot like a Kirk Douglas clone—the incendiary young Douglas. Except his eyes didn't spark that much. A sturdy kid, strong, preppie-looking in jeans, a green cotton sweater, and $400 Mephisto shoes.

"So you're the gumshoe," Sue said in a mock conspiratorial whisper. She stood, smiled broadly, and offered her hand, a good, firm grip. "I'm *really* pleased you came. 'Cause this is getting a little too hairy for my taste. Frankly, I'm kinda scared."

We said bye for now. Denny steered me into a stairwell at the end of the hallway, and up. We emerged in an open, quiet space under a huge stained-glass skylight, with more pricey, modernistic furniture. Across the way I saw a huge meeting room behind glass, with one of those teak tables that goes on forever. Two big plasma screens—50-inchers, anyway—were mounted in the meeting room's ceiling, tilting down. One at each end of the table. There were also some glass office doors, but I didn't see anyone behind them. Nonetheless, a pretty young blonde woman in olive-drab cargo pants topped with a blue linen blazer emerged from one of the doors with a sheaf of manila folders, heading for the elevator that we hadn't taken.

"Down here," Denny said, pointing at an office door next to the meeting room.

Along the way I noticed the splatter of a cola stain on the natural-colored wool carpet, beside a small table. The scene of the crime, I supposed.

We went in through a small, windowless outer office. Terry and two other men were waiting for me in the inner sanctum. A tall, distinguished fellow stood by a broad picture window that overlooked a frozen duckpond. The other—a rosy-hued bald guy—riffled through an advertising trade magazine on a mile-long art-moderne couch next to Terry.

Terry winked at me as I came in, and my heart did a little two-step. The first time I'd seen the man in almost eight years, and some old, forgotten hormone ignited. I beat it down fast and nodded to my ex.

Had to admit he did look super in his dark-gray suit and Italian shoes. He still had the short, dark, straight hair and big brown eyes; the full, inviting lips; the comely tan; the lean swimmer's build and easy muscularity. All that had changed was his new, neatly trimmed salt-and-pepper beard and mustache, and some fresh crows feet.

"Terry," I said, as coolly as I could manage.

"Hi Marty," he returned evenly. He had the good sense to not try to give me a hug.

The fellow by the window was also tan as a brick, and pencil-thin. He had a full shock of white hair, penetrating eyes, and his memorable features were the pre-echo of his son's. In other words, the old Kirk Douglas—the gladiator in retirement. Tired, a bit stooped at the shoulders. He didn't have a suit on. Instead, a pair of beautifully tailored gray flannels and the most gorgeous Aran sweater I'd ever seen.

"Marta," Denny said reverently, like someone introducing his priest, "I'd like you to meet Herb Gottwaldt."

I grabbed the ad mogul's expensively manicured hand. His fingers felt bony, sharp; his skin like worn silk. His grip was strong and his gray eyes penetrating. "Good to meet you, Herb," I said.

He nodded, as if to say, of course it's good to meet him. Then, remembering his manners, he said, "Likewise, Marta."

Denny took my left arm and turned me around to meet the other man on the couch. "This is Harry Litzky, our art director. He'll be supervising the design work."

We exchanged howdies and I pumped his hand, more on the order of five cocktail sausages. He was a stout little fellow with close cropped red hair and a ruddy complexion. The brownish herringbone sportcoat and red bow tie were perfect on him. But the thick-lensed, flesh-toned glasses made his washed-out blue eyes look tiny.

"Glad you could help us, Marta," Gottwaldt said in a voice like Drambuie. He went over behind his grantie-topped desk and sat down. He gestured to the couch and I plopped down next to Litzky. Denny leaned against the door frame.

"This is a bloody little mess," said Herb, "and we need to get it cleared up pronto. On the QT." He raised his eyebrows to accentuate the point, and stared at me like I might've stared at my plumber. No question who the servant was. "Terry and I are letting Denny handle it. Understand you used to know both of them."

And how. "That I did, Herb."

"This investigation's important because the Hemo test market is riding on it," Denny said, telling me what I knew already. "If we get the test market from Terry here, we have an inside line on the national rollout next year. That'd be very big for G and R."

"Naturally," Herb put in, "I wanted to meet you and see just what we're getting."

Fair point. I would have felt the same way myself.

Terry gave a snappy nod. "Herb's absolutely right. A lot's riding on this. Because we really want Gottwaldt and Ryan on this rollout. Traditionally, tobacco marketing is pretty stodgy. But we wanted something audacious. And when you think audacious, you think Herb Gottwaldt. We can't go with Herb and Denny, though, if there's negative publicity attached.

"Being a tobacco concern, we understand that lots of people hate our guts. Doesn't matter to them it's a legal product that millions of folks enjoy." His voice uncharacteristically had taken on the timbre of an polished advocate and defender—speaking the piece he'd spoken many times before. "Bertram gets sued all the time, never lost a case. Never had any extortion attempts, though. And we're not going to tolerate it here."

Gottwaldt tugged at his left ear lobe. "We want you to interview people on the account but no one else at the agency. Gather the facts, get together everything we need to stop it. As I said, *on the QT*. Maybe we'll get lucky and it'll just peter out. Then we can all forget it ever happened."

"What if I have a suspicion about who's doing it?" I said.

"You let us know, and we'll take it from there," Gottwaldt said. "No Lone Ranger stuff, okay? Just the facts."

"Okay. Then what about security," I asked, "in case there's a real threat?"

"Of course it's real!" Litzky barked. "That wasn't pinot noir Susie Hewlett drank!"

"I think what Marta's talking about," Denny assuaged, "is the personal safety of the team members."

I nodded. "How they can avoid putting themselves in danger while this is going on. Off the top of my head I'd recommend they go home for a few days, see what happens. No one else on staff should get any specifics."

The big cheese looked at me, and I half expected he'd object. He tented the tips of his index fingers together in front of his face and rested his chin on his thumbs. He sat like this for half a minute, then pulled a cigarette out of a drawer and lit it with a battered, old-fashioned Zippo just like my Dad's.

He blinked at me, spewing smoke. "Yeah, okay. We'll have people stay home a few days, till things settle down."

"Of course," I warned, "all bets are off if anybody gets hurt."

"Then I suppose we have to go to the authorities," Gottwaldt agreed, nodding. "Bertram or not." He peered at Terry. "Sorry, buddy."

"But what if these terrorists, whatever they are—" I wondered out loud. "What if they start sending out press releases or something? What do we do then?"

"We can't control that." Gottwaldt stretched his arms up over his head and let out a subvocal sigh. "But we need a plan, just in case. Denny'll do a contingency on that. Okay?" Denny nodded. "And he'll give you all the help you need, Marta. All you gotta do is ask."

My once and present boss, my ex, Litzky, and I ambled out into the top-floor common room. Litzky peeled off, and Denny took Terry and me into his office suite, opposite Herb's. It was only slightly less grand. I met his personal secretary—Margie Polish-name, with auburn hair in an untidy bun, wire-rims and beady falcon eyes—and he told her to give me a hand with any-thing I needed, any time. *Anything.* She looked suspicious as hell.

Inside Denny's inner chambers, I lowered myself onto yet another piece of black leather furniture—I hated to think of how many black cows died to furnish this place—while Terry stood by.

"You were there last night, Terry?" I asked

Terry shook his head. "Nope. Denny called me at the hotel."

"Harry was here, though."

"Uh-huh," Denny said. "He really freaked when Susie gagged on that stuff and spit it out."

"How did Herb react when you told him?"

He shrugged. "It pissed him off. But he's cool under pressure."

"Where's the food and cola now?"

"I put it all in the fridge in Herb's office," Denny replied.

"Good. Is there anything rumbling in the office rumor mill yet?"

"It's bound to get out," Denny said, "but not yet."

I nodded, not liking it. "The people from the pizza place?"

"The owner's a friend. We work out at the same gym. I told him we had some problem with the food, and could he come over to talk about it."

"Yeah, absolutely. I want the driver to come, too."

Denny looked me up and down a couple of times. "So, what do you think, Marta?"

"What do you mean, what do I think?"

"Do you have any theories or anything?"

"Well, Denny, you got several options. Some genuine radical types on the outside, like the bozos that spike old-growth tim-ber. It's not a for-profit criminal venture."

"Meaning some kind of idealistic thing," Terry opined. "They think they're doing something noble."

"Yeah, I guess. They think they don't like people dying of lung cancer and emphysema and second-hand smoke and shit like that."

Terry gave me his little-boy-hurt look—I remembered it well.

Denny scowled. But at that moment I didn't give a damn.

"Then you got your inside-outside job," I continued.

The two of them looked puzzled.

"You have someone outside the agency working with some-one inside, who feeds information. After all, they had to know a lot to pull off this cola scam."

"Anything else?"

"Yeah, totally inside, someone who's working here now."

"That's a depressing thought," Denny moaned.

"Isn't it?" I took a beat. "I assume it happened out there, where the stain is on the carpet."

"Right," said Denny. "We were in here, brainstorming. But we usually eat out in the common room."

"I'd like to see your security footage from last night."

Denny groaned. "Sorry, Marta. No can do. Our entrance camera's in the shop. No coverage there. And I think the guy dodged the cameras out in the parking lot. He had to have come in through the snow and the bog. He knew what he was doing."

"Meaning he or she has cased the joint pretty thoroughly. Or has up-to-date access to some inside knowledge."

He nodded dismally.

"Okay, then. I'd like to talk to Sue and Archie, if I can."

Denny nodded. He picked up his phone, punched a number, and listened. He repeated the process.

"Sorry," he said, "they seem to have taken off."

"Then I'd like to take a peek at your personnel records. Discharges from the last two, three years. Let's see if anyone who worked here has a reason to be really PO'd at you guys."

Denny said he'd arrange for me to go downstairs and look them over.

Back out in the common room Terry and I were alone for the first time. I'd played out my revenge fantasies over the years, lovingly plotting how to make him feel like complete, utter garbage. I'd murdered him a few times in my daydreams. But here he was, and I almost felt like thanking him.

Weird, I know. But consider this:

If Terry hadn't gotten it on with three other women—that I

27

knew about—I never would have filed for divorce. Never would have left Santa Barbara. Never would have had my unusual first encounter with Rick Mueller on a foggy street near the University of Minnesota.

"So, Marty," my ex said, cranking up the old charisma, "do we have a date for that roundball game tonight?"

Just then Denny emerged from his office and gestured that I should follow him.

"No we don't, Terry," I said. "I've got work to do."

Chapter Six

Denny installed me in a vacant office next to Sue Hewlett's. I pored over a stack of personnel records, and as far as I could tell no one had recently parted ways in the manner of a wild-eyed postal employee. Nothing even approaching acrimonious.

I also had a good look at the five extorting letters, addressed to Herb personally, and the e-mail sent the night before. No clues in the venom, alas. Any fanatic nutcase might have written them. They began with vague but unexplicit vituperations against Herb's desire for the Hemo account—merely grumpy, profane, and anonymous. The next to last, a letter, stated that Gottwaldt would personally regret it. The e-mail suggested (correctly, in fact) that the perpetrators could and would act on their threats. Unless the agency publicly quit its effort to secure Hemo's test-market campaign.

A little later Margie Polish-name fetched me the dubious pizza and cola. The one discovery I made were the needlepricks in the corner of the open cola carton as well as the corner of the unopened container. I had no way of knowing if the pizza itself was "kosher." I knew a good lab off in St. Paul, and made arrangements to drop the items off later that evening.

At about six I supped on a granola bar and Sprite, which I was savoring when Margie came to get me. The pizza men had arrived.

Denny and his gourmet pizza maven were shooting the bull, sprawled on the modernistic sofa. As if nothing had happened. Old buddies, indeed. Pizza man had on one of those sweaters that looked like the colored endpapers of a fancy book. Underneath it seemed he had on football pads. Only he didn't. The guy pumped iron seriously. The delivery driver—a stringbean post-adolescent with wispy, blondish beard and 'stache—sat nervously on a straight chair next to the wall, fidgeting with his blue ski gloves.

Denny caught sight of me, and hopped up. Pizza man did too.

"Marta," said Denny, "I'd like you meet George Ramnath.

George, this is Marta Hjelm."

He said hi, I said hi.

"And this is?" I gestured at the kid.

"Tom Peterson," said Ramnath. "He drove last night."

The kid said it was nice to meet me.

I didn't believe him.

Propping myself up on the edge of Denny's desk, I fished a pen and a narrow reporter's notebook out of my jacket.

"So, Denny," I said when the two of them settled back down on the sofa, "have you explained to George what transpired last night?"

Denny nodded earnestly. "Yeah, and he thinks whatever happened happened after Tom left the delivery in the outer lobby."

I perked up. "Could you elucidate, George?"

"I'd be happy to," he replied with a half-smile. "We were really short-handed last night. My evening manager has the flu, and my Monday night driver quit." He frowned. "Got a job paying eleven bucks an hour. "

As I scribbled, I resisted gasping, *ungrateful wretch!*

"Tom was able to come in."

"What time did you get Denny's order?" I asked.

"About eleven," he said. "Two cartons of cola, a large proscuitto/artichoke and a large Granny gorgonzola."

I blinked. "What is *that?*"

He almost beamed. "My creation. Gorganzola cheese, Granny Smith apples and pecans. One of our most popular."

Such an affront to pizza secretly appalled me. I have a deep and abiding faith in a crispy thin crust, a smattering of sausage, a modicum of mozzarella, and mucho zippy red sauce. Call me a old-fashioned. "Blue cheese, green apples," I said. "Okay. How long does it take to fix an order like that?"

"Twenty minutes," he said.

"So the pizza's done," I said. "Tom takes it out to the car. Right, Tom?"

"Truck," Ramnath corrected me. "His Dodge pickup. All my people drive their own vehicles."

"Who called in the order, Denny?" I asked.

"Meg LaGrange did," he replied. "She picked it up from downstairs, too."

"Meg told me," Ramnath said, "to just leave the stuff inside the outer lobby. That's what Tom did. We've done that a hundred times. No big deal. Denny pays on PayPal."

"Meaning the pizza and cola were in there for a few minutes before Meg got it," Denny said.

"Tom," I asked, "when exactly did you drop the pizza off?"

The kid screwed up his nose and scratched an acne-scarred cheek. "About 11:35."

"You sure?"

"Yeah, I had to write it down in the delivery log."

"So our bad guys," I essayed, "had maybe twenty minutes to taint the cola when it was in the outer lobby. 'Cause Denny said Sue went down to get it about midnight. Plenty of time."

I squeezed the bridge of my nose with my thumb and index finger, and shut my eyes. This makes me look like I'm ruminating very deeply indeed. At 75 bucks an hour, the client deserves the appearance of deep rumination. "Could anything have been injected in the cola cartons in your kitchen, George?"

"Ab-so-lutely *not*," Denny's pal boomed. "I made the pizza myself, I filled the cola cartons. Nothing went into that order but good food and soda."

"You're quite sure."

"Damn betcha I am."

"Why cardboard cartons? Why not bottles?"

"It's retro. Like at old drive-ins. People like 'em."

"Would it be possible to talk to the others who worked there last night?"

Now Denny jumped in. "I told George that wouldn't be necessary. At least not yet. Like I said, Marta, this has to stay close to the vest. I only called George because we know each other, and he wants to get to the bottom of it too."

I turned to the kid. "Did you notice anything unusual when you drove the pizza out here?"

He mulled on it for a moment. "Well, I dunno. There was a

31

car followed me part of the way."

"Tell me about it."

And he did.

A dark-color, older-model Escort had come up behind him after he'd left Wayzata. Dark color. Wasn't sure what color. Followed him all the way. Made him a little nervous, in fact. He saw it when he headed back to Chez Pizza, pulled over on the side of the road a couple of hundred feet before the entrance to Gottwaldt and Ryan. No one was in it. He thought that was a little strange.

"You're sure? No one kneeling down, checking out a flat on the far side of the car? Someone you couldn't see?"

"I'm sure."

"Can you show me where?"

• • •

Ramnath and Denny took a pass while the kid and I bundled up and headed out into the windchill—it was another nasty one, that night. Worse than my morning stroll down to the photography museum. I picked up a flashlight out of the Merc's trunk, and pretty soon we were soft-shoeing along the side of the road, avoiding ice patches, swinging the beam from side to side so oncoming traffic could see us clearly.

The pizza delivery kid told me again how he spotted something in his rearview mirror. A small car zooming up behind his pickup. With a dead headlight. The two vehicles rolled together through the dark, with the icy, sinuous lakeside road all to themselves. He snuck another look, thinking the car would spin by behind him when he pulled into the parking lot.

But the other vehicle never came.

"Weird," the kid mumbled through rapidly numbing lips. "Their outer lobby door was unlocked, as usual. I put the pizzas on the stone bench, along with a brown paper bag with the cartons of cola. Then I hustled back to my truck. Out on the lake road I spotted the Escort, pulled over. No one was in it. No one was walking the road."

We soon figured out why: Tom found the spot where the little Ford had stopped. A sweep of light through the ditch and the scrub brush beyond it revealed two sets of footprints in the icy, dirty snow, where none should have been-one set heading in, one heading out. Fresh and crisp, not weathered by a week or two of wind and grit. About a size 11.

The "perp"—as we in the biz like to call our bad guys—had tramped in through the underbrush between the road and the advertising agency. The path taken had been plotted to avoid coverage by two parking lot cameras. Someone knew just where to go. It's easy to infer that he or she opened the brown bag, neatly punctured the top of one of the cola cartons with a hypodermic, and injected part of the contents of the syringe. The process was repeated with the other carton. And no functioning security cam witnessed this strange event.

It was too late and too cold to go mushing through the woods, so I sent the kid back inside and went over by the north end of the parking lot, which was closest to the road. Sure enough. I found the same set of tracks just beyond the icy blacktop, crunching through a couple of feet of old snow, out on to the edge of a frozen bog, and back in by the side of the main building.

• • •

Back in the vacant office next to Sue Hewlett's I made a few calls. First, to Deb Brown, my old college roommate. A mother of two teenagers, Deb does most of my computer legwork—license plates, criminal records, that sort of thing—from her split-level in Woodbury. She's cheap and good and, best of all, a buddy. I promised I'd e-mail her a list of names on the morrow for background checks.

Then I got hold of Meg LaGrange and set up a meeting for the next day. She sounded drunk, and who could blame her?

My voicemail had two new offerings for me.

Rick's voice came on first: "Hey, I'm sorry if I wasn't real helpful this morning. I've been thinking. If you really have problems with working with some crummy tobacco company, you shouldn't do it. Don't do it just for the dough. We'll be okay. I know you'll do the right thing, babe."

"Too late, Rickie," I said.

I barely listened to the next message—a reminder that I had root canal coming up next week. I'd probably have to cancel. Darn.

Chapter Seven

Denny hadn't examined the evidence very closely. So he looked genuinely astonished to see the punctures in the corners of the cola cartons. He settled in behind his desk, put the carton down in front of him, and stared at it balefully.

"So they really must've gotten to it after the kid left," he finally said, slumping in his chair, "before Meg went down to pick it up."

"Somebody came in from the road, Denny, right in that time frame. Mushing through the snow to avoid showing up on your security cams. So yeah, I think so. But how'd this person know your lobby camera was out? How'd this person know about cardboard soda cartons?"

Denny pulled up out of his slouch. "Good question. How?"

"It's what we were talking about earlier. Someone outside did some very thorough homework is possibility number one, as we discussed earlier. Number two, someone outside gets tipped by someone inside."

He shook his head emphatically. "Nah, I don't buy that. I don't buy that he had inside help. I know everyone in this building, Marta. I trust them, Herb trusts them. They like their work, they're all making *real* good money. Why in hell would they screw the pooch, huh?"

"Then there's option three. It's pure inside job. One of your trustworthy employees was out there last night tip-toeing through the underbrush."

He shut his eyes and shook his head emphatically. I was surprised he didn't stick his fingers in his ears and start loudly singing, "LA-LA-LA-LA—"

Time, I thought, for a soupçon of diplomacy. "You're probably right, Denny. It's probably not an inside job. But you hired me to ask the tough questions and find some answers. Right?"

"Yeah, of course, of course."

"So it's something we have to consider. If your people have nothing to hide, nothing's going to come up in interviews and background checks. Everything'll be copasetic."

He nodded slowly.

"But what if one of them has some affiliation with some fringe group? What if one of them has some personal beef with you or Herb, something long forgotten? What better way to get back at you than mess up a potential major account?"

"Okay," he averred, "I see what you mean."

"Who do you think inside would have had opportunity?" I asked him. "Let's not even talk about motive."

"Almost everyone in the agency knows we're kicking ass on Hemo," he said. "Everyone knows that we have an account with Chez Pizza, and they know that midnight munchies are SOP. Hell, thirty people could've made a good guess that we'd send out for food last night, and they'd know just where it'd come from."

My turn again. "On the other hand, as I said, if somebody outside did it, they did some damned meticulous homework. They had to know you were working late. They had to know which place you order pizzas from. They had to know you order cola in paper cartons. They had to know the territory."

"You think one of our people did it, don't you."

I put my hands up, palms forward. "I honestly don't know."

"So what do we do now?"

I blinked at my Swatch. It was about eight. "I'm going to take this chow—" I nodded at the pizza boxes and cola cartons on Denny's desk. "—to a lab I work with, and we'll find out what kind of junk they put in there. Then tomorrow I start interviewing people, check out those tracks out there in the daylight."

Denny nodded once, but not a happy nod.

We sat silently for a moment or two, staring at our laps, while I knawed on a rubbery cheddar bagel Denny had found me in Herb's fridge.

"What's the deal with Archie?" I said. "He really deserve his job?" I raised my eyebrows with a trace of prejudgment, and Denny caught it.

"Yeah, I know what you're thinking," he said. "The boss's kid gets the break. He's worked here a year and a half, ever since he got out of college. I wouldn't have hired him. His sister's even more spoiled. Eight or ten years older. Jennifer. Don't call her 'Jenny,' though, or she'll have your head on a platter."

"She work here, too?"

"Nah, thank God. But she and her kids own a decent piece of the company, and she's on the board. She's pissed off about Bertram. She's into this social responsibility crap. Says we'd be killing people."

"Nasty stuff, social responsibility," I said, deadpan. I caught another whiff of his coffee breath.

"No shit," he replied in all seriousness. Denny never did get irony. He usually knew a joke when he heard it, and laughed because he figured he was supposed to, but didn't exactly know why.

"I'll be talking to everyone as soon as I can. I'm seeing Meg in the morning. And I'll prep them on how to take care of themselves till this blows over."

I threw on my coat, tugged on my cap, put the food in a shopping bag and said goodnight to Margie, who was still hammering away on her iMac. The sooner I got the samples to my lab guy, the sooner we'd find out what sort of grunge our anonymous poisoner had put into them. If I didn't arrive by ten, he told me, he was out of there.

The Merc hunched low and sad in the blasting, arctic wind, alone in the lot but for two other cars. I unlocked the door, set the bag over on the passenger seat, and hopped in. The hurt between my eyebrows told me the windchill was at least minus 30, maybe minus 40. A bad night to start a car that's been sitting out on the tundra.

The Merc agreed. I cranked it ten, twelve times, and it just growled at me. *RAOWWW-RAOWWW-RAOWWW*. Translation: "Tough shit, baby."

I didn't have jumper cables. My upstairs tenant had borrowed them. And my Dad's remote car starter wouldn't have made any difference, even if I'd had it with me.

So back inside I marched into Denny's office past Margie, muttering "Dead car," and picked up Denny's phone. The automobile club said they could have someone out to start the Merc in three or four hours. Everyone needed a jump that night.

It took some effort, but I sweet-talked Denny's secretary out of the keys to an agency car down in the basement garage. She fussed that she ought to ask him, but he was in his shower—man, I wish I had an office shower—and she couldn't possibly stroll in and present my request. Would I wait?

No time, I said. Didn't Denny tell her to help me any way she could?

Yes, he had.

I doubted that he would appreciate bureaucratic concerns slowing things down.

No, he wouldn't, she agreed, and fished a set of keys out of a drawer in her desk.

I said I'd return the vehicle first thing in the morning.

Snuggled tight in the heated basement garage, the agency's Lexus started like a charm. I touched the button on the remote door control, and drove up and out into the brutal January night. I turned right, through the back parking lot, and right a-gain, around the end of the building, into the front parking lot, past my frozen Merc.

A minute later I was curving north and east at a good clip, toward Wayzata, feeling like a rally driver. The sky was a deep azure, clear as glass and full of the stars you don't often see in the city.

It was the first time that day I'd felt relatively on top of the situation. Sure, plenty of things were screwed up.

Rick needed calming down and getting home, where he belonged. I'd had to go to work for people I didn't like, for a cause that gave pause. And my reaction to seeing Terry again made me a little queasy. What's up with that? I asked myself. But clear them all up—and I had no doubt that I would—and things looked a lot better.

I tooled over a narrow bridge, went left, then right, the lake only a dozen feet away. The headlights caught the glitter of ice on the road. I lightly tapped the brakes, but didn't feel them catch. No anti-lock kicking in. Doing something wrong, I thought, as my heart accelerated and my gloved hands squeezed the wheel harder.

I feathered the brakes again—a reflexive, fluttery tapping of my right foot, from teen driving days—as I came onto the ice. I was going way too fast. Again, nothing happened. The Lexus kept rolling.

Turning the wheel left, I could feel my heart coming up into my mouth.

The tires refused to find a purchase on the ice and the car began to yaw sideways.

I kept feathering the brakes, then pressed hard. The pedal went to the floor with a forbidding "thunk."

The road curved left again, but the Lexus kept going straight.

A puny steel-cable guard rail came up fast as a shot and the front of the Lexus sheared through it with a percussive roar.

I was briefly airborne over eight feet of steep shoreline, starting to scream, when the car nosed down.

The frozen lake rushed toward me, brilliant in the headlights, like a wall of dirty, corrugated granite.

Chapter Eight

That's all I remember.

When I came to, I was flat on my back by the side of the road, with a cop and two well-bundled-up businessmen squatting down next to me. For half a second, they looked like cartoon dragons, with gushers of steam coming out of their mouths. Don't ask me why, but I thought if the dragons had any brains they'd make a joke. Something like: "She ain't a vestal virgin, but she'll have to do!"

Pretty soon they started looking like human beings, and they weren't cracking wise. They gritted their teeth in the cold and shivered. Funny, though. I didn't feel too bad. Just chilly.

I rolled my head to the left. A parade of headlights went slowly by. Wide-eyed, pale faces stared out the car windows. They were probably wondering if they'd seen a real stiff. I would have.

With what must have seemed like bone-headed pluckiness, I mumbled an incoherent "Than-oo-beryuch" and started to pull myself up. The cop gently restrained me by the shoulders. His grip was delicate but firm. He wore Old Spice, like my Dad used to in the weeks after Christmas—long enough for his two daughters to get as sick of it as he was. The officer had a bushy, sandy moustache, just like the one Rick used to cultivate.

"Not a good idea, ma'am," he said. "Let's wait for the paramedics."

"'S cold," I wheezed.

"I know, ma'am, just be patient."

"Wha' happen'?"

"You had an accident, ma'am," the deputy sheriff said.

"No shit?" I replied with no irony intended.

"You seem to have lost control of your vehicle, ma'am, and it plowed off the road into the lake ice," the deputy said. "I've gotta ask you a couple questions, okay?"

"Sure."

"You name, ma'am?"

"Marta J. Hjelm," I replied.

"Do you remember going over the edge, Ms. Hjelm?"

I nodded. "Like it was yes'erday."

"What's the day of the week?"

"Tuesday," I said, trying to rub the ache out of my neck. This little contretemps would play havoc with my back, you could bet on it. Already I could feel my nerve endings and muscles concocting ever more baroque forms of pain.

The deputy smiled a little. "How many fingers am I holding up, Ms. Hjelm?"

I squinted at the deputy's gloved left hand. "Seven."

The officer's smile disappeared.

"Okay, sorry," I said. Nobody likes a smart-ass, especially when you're trying to rescue her. "How 'bout two squared?"

There came the merest hint of a smile, a nice smile. "Do you have double vision, Ms. Hjelm?"

I shook my head.

"Would you mind taking off your cap, ma'am? I'd like to see if there's any bleeding from your ears."

The officer didn't see any. Then he told me how the gentlemen next to him—one on the pudgy side of middle age in a quilted down overcoat, the other taller and younger and substantially hunkier, in a tan parka—had been behind me, and saw the accident. They stopped, scampered out on the ice and managed to haul me out of the car, then called 911. The ambulance was on the way, and I was going to the hospital for a CT scan and full workup.

I protested. I'd only run into the seatbelt, since the air bag for some reason hadn't deployed. I had work to do, malefactors to catch. But the deputy said the paramedics would be there in a minute. And you shouldn't mess with potential head and neck injuries, potential concussion, ma'am. Guess so, I said, sick of being "ma'am-ed" all over the place. Best just to agree and get him to shut up.

The paramedics arrived, in a flurry of flashing lights and clangor. After they got me on the backboard, I thanked the Samaritans. I told them to call me sometime and I'd pop for drinks and steaks, whenever they found themselves washed ashore in downtown St. Paul.

Truth be told, I didn't feel real good as they hoisted me into the ambulance. Woozy. Headachy. Nauseous.

• • •

My phone rang about 9 a.m., and I wanted to cry like a baby.

I hadn't gotten home until two that morning.

The accident had happened a little after eight. It had taken three hours for the doc to give me an all-clear. Then I had had to call Denny and fill him in, and he ended up retrieving the pizza and cola from the Lexus, which had been hauled to a nearby garage for analysis of the non-functioning brakes and airbag. Miraculously, the cola in one carton hadn't spilled entirely—plenty left for analyzing. He said he'd courier all of it to my lab first thing in the morning. I called my renter, Grace Corelli, who got out of bed and came to fetch me. She offered to stay up with me. In case I should keel over. I gently declined, and sent her back upstairs. She's like the big sister I wish I had, that girl. Somehow, I got to sleep without the codeine-laced acetaminophen the doc gave me for what he predicted might be an uncomfortable night.

Denny kind of touched me, really. He seemed a good deal more worried about me than his Lexus. We'll pay all your medical costs, he kept repeating, as if I was somehow too delicate to ask for it. Fat chance.

I did my best not to roll over on Rick when I grabbed for the ringing phone. Only Rick, *the ingrate*, still wasn't there to roll over on.

I muttered an inarticulate greeting into the receiver—something like, "Hurow, whoozat?"

"It's Denny, Marta." He sounded like he'd plugged a finger into a wall socket. "You doin' okay?"

"Yeah," I said. "More or less."

"You're not going to like this, Marty—"

I didn't even bother to remind Denny again that I let only fathers, mothers, sisters, husbands, and boyfriends call me that. "Yeah?"

"I called my mechanic last night."

"Uh-huh."

"Had him look over the Lexus first thing this morning. I wanted him to see it before the insurance adjustor checked it out." Denny did some serious inhaling and exhaling. "Someone tampered with the brakes when it was in our garage. Must've drained out most of the fluid, cause there's none on the floor. They disabled the airbag."

"Nuts," I said. It seemed like the appropriate response. "Anything else?"

"Yeah. Herb got an e-mail."

I tried to cut my heartbeat back from a tap dance to a mere fox trot. "What's it say?"

"It just says, 'We're glad, once again, that we made our point without serious harm to anyone. We still expect you to de-cline—'" Denny stopped, he sounded like he was hyperventilating.

"Take a couple of beats, Denny," I said. "Chill out. Won't help to get all cranked up."

"Right," Denny panted. "Right." He took a breather, and continued: "'We still expect Herb Gottwaldt to decline the Hemo account.'"

"Denny," I said, hunched over on the edge of the bed, "they've gone after you guys twice in twenty-four hours. Seems they faked a poisoning and clipped your brakes. They're really good, these kiddies, really dangerous. We gotta tell the police."

"Just a minute," Denny said, "just a minute. Nobody has to know what happened. You weren't hurt, right? I'm paying any of your medical expenses. We're not filing a claim on the car. We'll cover it ourselves. I'll give you a bonus. You didn't tell the cop that the brakes went, did you?"

"I don't remember, I was too woozy. But it's in a police report. Lexus goes out of control. I'm at fault, the road's at fault, or the car's at fault. Or some combination. The cops'll want to know which it is. You can't stonewall this, Denny. The cops are coming and that's okay. I mean, someone could really get hurt."

"Marta," he snapped, "you gotta keep 'em off our—"

"Just a minute," I barked back.

I stood, a little wobbly, and put the cell on the bed. My head throbbed like a well-struck timpani. I was stiff as a two by four, too. Back, ribcage, arms, neck. Everything hurt but my eyeballs and my feet. But I guess it was better than the alternative.

The phone yelped a tiny, tinny protest, from a great distance, as if Denny had turned into a munchkin. He could squawk for a while.

I shrugged my shoulders, opened my mouth wide as a window, and it helped. I looked around the bedroom in the dim glow of the hallway nightlight. The heavy-duty gray ragg wool cardigan Rick's mom gave him lay in a heap on the chair in the corner. Right where he'd left it Sunday afternoon. The radio, which came on when I was asleep, was flogging some obscure Central American folk music.

When I picked up the phone again, I asked Denny, "How *big* a bonus?"

He told me, and I said that wasn't big enough. He tried again, and it sounded like just enough to buy a Nikkor 300mm f/2.8 lens. And that's no cheap piece of glass—four or five grand.

"Deal," I said. "I shouldn't, but I'll try to hush it up. One more incident, though, and I go to the local constabulary. Got that, Denny?"

He said he did.

"But I want you lay low, like I said yesterday. Now more than ever I want everyone to lay low."

There was a long, stunned silence on the other end of the line. Denny Ryan didn't like being told what to do, especially by a mere peon.

"I also want Herb out of circulation, got it?"

He almost shouted. "Listen, Hjelm—"

Whenever he really got steamed Denny called me by my last name. He always did that back at the *Bugle*.

"—I'm willing to hide out, so's most everyone else. But Herb's never going to go for it."

The only thing to do was outshout him. "Dammit, Denny!

44

He'd better, or he's going to end up dead!"

Denny didn't say a word. The grim reaper, after all, respects not even advertising moguls. All I could hear were his furious gusherings of breath.

"Have Herb tell everybody he's got the flu real bad," I continued. "Needs total bed rest."

Denny sputtered a few more complaints, but agreed to try to move the great man to safety. He promised again he'd make arrangements for Margie Polish-name to get me any information I needed, as well as to access people at the agency. And I told him I expected that bonus check, next time I visited Gottwaldt and Ryan.

After he hung up, I threw on my bathrobe and ambled down the hallway into the living room. I could hear Grace padding around upstairs, making the joists creak. She's a tall, overweight woman with a heart bigger than herself, an academic Gypsy filling in as a sociology instructor at the university.

The birds were starting with their early-morning cheeps and twitters, so I went over and uncovered all three cages. Jo, the hen cockatiel and senior bird from Rick's pre-me days, looked displeased to see me—her dreaded rival. She hadn't given up on her chances for laying Rick's egg. Chuck, the male cockatiel, scampered up to the corner of his cage for a look-see. Taco, my blue front Amazon, greeted me with the customary half-sung, half-spoken "Strawberry fields forever." I fed and watered them, then grabbed the paper off the front porch—my breath still geysering white in the cold air. But I had no time to read it.

Rick's touch was all over the place. He had all the style. He'd arranged the furniture kind of catty-cornered, diagonal. To "break up the geometry of the room," he said. "Sounds good," I said.

The pieces were mostly traditional. Lots of dark maple and mahogany. There was a maroon-hued Persian rug in the center of the room, also diagonal. Rick had one wall covered with Chinese fans. Cheap, but handsome. On another wall antique prints mixed amiably with copies of cubist etchings. Above the fireplace he had his treasure—an original Cartier-Bresson,

"Banks of the Marne, 1935."

I nearly jumped out of my skin when the door ding-donged at me.

Looking like the bathrobed, fuzzy-slippered housewife of sitcom yore—sans curlers and mudpack—I shuffled over to open the door, not even bothering to look in the peephole.

There stood Terry Rosen, in a ridiculously quilted red ski jacket, holding a white paper bag and two paper cups in a cupholder. I can't deny it: My heart skipped a beat, and a hormone or two kicked into action.

"Marty, I heard what happened," he jabbered. "Are you okay?"

"Yeah, more or less."

"I feel absolutely like shit, getting you involved in all this," he said in a rush, meaning every word. "I had no idea it would be, well, this, this—" He blinked at me.

"Dangerous?" I said.

"Yeah," he said, and smiled anxiously.

"Me neither."

We looked at each other half a moment.

"I think you should just tell Denny you don't want to work on the case anymore."

I shrugged and shook my head. "Sorry, Terry. I just told him I'd stay on it."

The fear on his face seemed like something even good old Terry couldn't fake. Fear that something would happen to me. I felt flattered. But I wish I hadn't read that in him.

"I really don't think you—"

"*No*, Terry," I said a little more emphatically that I needed to. "I gave Denny my word."

"Denny's on my nickel, Marty. I can—"

"Will you let me handle my job, Terry?" I growled. "*I do know what I'm doing.* And I'll do my best to not get killed."

It was his turn to shrug. "You're sure you're not hurt?"

"A little dinged up is all," I allowed, shivering a bit.

"Can I come in? I brought some fresh *petits pains* and French strawberry jam." He held up the bag like a record-weight fish.

"Remember? *Le petit déjuener?* Sunday mornings with the *L. A. Times* and two big *café lattés*. I got lattés here, too."

In hindsight, a simple "No" would have sufficed, with or without a lame excuse. A straightforward "Scram, Terry," would have been infinitely smarter. But what did I go and say?

"Yeah, sure. Come on in."

God help me, I remembered why I fell in love with the guy in the first place. He was gorgeous, smart, funny. Fantastic in the sack. Back in the day I was incredibly flattered that he found me attractive. What I didn't know was that he found *many* women attractive, and they him. That he did a lot of his decision-making somewhere south of his belt.

I sat Terry down in the living room after he fussed about taking his boots off, and I told him not to worry about it. Everybody fusses like that, and every time I tell them to keep their damned boots on. Though not in those exact words. Then, as he peeled off his ski jacket, he gushed about how great the place was, and what super taste I had. I pointedly mentioned that my *boyfriend* had done it all. He remained unfazed.

We went to work on the bread and jam and lattés, and he actually made me laugh a couple of times. Never had I doubted his allure. I just knew the burn marks that came with it.

He told me why he'd quit the record store chain—the internet had slapped the handwriting up on the wall. Music on discs was doomed. He got into an ad agency in L.A. for a couple of years. A friend of a friend told him about an opening at Bertram, and he got the job. A bump or two up the ladder, and here he was, birthing a new line of cancer sticks.

It seemed important that he find out my Dad died of Bertram cigarettes—the old man had fumigated the house in Duluth with Top Peak cigs ever since I could remember. But before I got the words out I heard steps on the front porch, and a key turning the in the front door lock.

And in walked Rick, his big, gray camera bag on his shoulder. He had on a smile that died like a ruptured duck the instant he saw Terry and me—achingly sexy in bathrobe and fuzzy slippers.

"Hi Marty," he said, like a crew member wanting Scotty to beam him out of there.

"Hi, hon," I answered with exaggerated cheeriness. What else could I do? "This is Terry Rosen."

"Yeah, I know," Rick said, chilly as the great outdoors. "I've seen pictures."

"And Terry," I continued, "this is my boyfriend Rick Mueller."

Terry hopped up and over, ready to glad hand my significant other. "Good to meet you, Rick," he said.

Only Rick was in no mood to glad hand him back, and kept his right paw clasped firmly around the camera bag strap. "Yeah, hello," he said, as if greeting Typhoid Mary.

Terry ground to an embarrassed halt in front of the Chinese fans and had the good sense—for a change—to keep his mouth shut.

"How was the Herman Brush thing?" I ventured to Rick, hoping desperately to get some small talk going.

"Fine," he said.

"Get a lot of people?"

"Yup."

"Have a good time?"

"Uh-huh."

"Did he enjoy himself?"

A single nod.

So much for that.

"I just came for some extra memory cards," Rick finally said, glaring at me.

"Why don't you stick around?" I pleaded.

"Naw." He shook his head. "Don't want to butt in."

As he headed down the hallway without another peep, I thought I saw a little smirk on Terry's face.

I chased after Rick, scuttering along in my slippers. "He just showed up at the door," I whispered to the back of his head, loud as I could. "He didn't spend the night!"

"Good to know," Rick replied *sotte voce* over his shoulder.

I winced, trailing behind him through the kitchen and into

the back vestibule. "It isn't what you think."

"What is it I think, Marty?" he growled, clomping down the stairs, leaving a trail of melting snow.

"That I'm getting a little too cozy with my ex?" I said as I followed him down.

He growled a bit more, wordlessly, meaning I'd hit the mark.

"I'm after the money, Rick, that's all. You know, the money that'll help *our business!*"

Down in the cold, dank basement, under a dim 40 watt bare bulb, Rick grabbed several Compact Flash cards from his storage cabinet. He slammed the door shut.

"I've already made enough to buy that 300 Nikkor," I blurted, avoiding mention of the fact that I could have gotten killed earning it.

Rick—who loved his toys as much as any boy I've ever known—surprised the hell out of me.

"Screw the fucking lens!" he spat.

I didn't even have a comeback, but just stood there slack-jawed.

"What has gotten *into you?*" he asked, calming himself down by force of will. "What is wrong with you? You let this man back in your life who treated you like *shit,* who broke your heart. Not only that, you go to work, *again,* for one of the major assholes you've ever known. Not only *that…*"

He was getting steamed all over, and he took a slight pause to collect himself. "You go to work, indirectly, for a tobacco company. I remember some choice words about tobacco companies when Don was dying. *I was there, too, you know.*"

He was absolutely right.

But not only had something gotten into me, I thought, following him back upstairs, something seemed to have gotten into *everyone.*

Chapter Nine

I made Rick promise that we'd rendezvous in the next twenty-four hours. No matter what.

He took off—after a grudging hug and kiss in the kitchen—and I managed to shoo Terry out of there on the pretext of getting to work. I can't say that I liked the self-satisfied look on his face. I could almost read his mind: "There, that was a pretty good monkey wrench to throw in the works!"

With my Merc marooned out in the Gottwaldt and Ryan parking lot, I had to taxi down to Loring Park to visit with Meg LaGrange.

The lead copywriter inhabited a high-rise aerie a ten-minute hoof from the heart of downtown Minneapolis. From her floor-to-ceiling windows she could clearly see the giant, warped, weirdly reflective box that is the Walker Art Center. Further to the north stood the somber, Baroque façade of the Basilica. LaGrange apparently took recent events seriously. First, she checked me over via the fish-eye peephole, apologizing through the steel door. She asked me, almost shouting, to hold up my ID. I showed her my soon-to-expire detective's license. Then she unlocked two deadbolts and a couple of chain locks—*snap, snap, click, click*.

The door swung open and we exchanged greetings. A frosted-stainless 9mm sat on a teak side table a few feet down the hallway. A Smith & Wesson Ladysmith. A serious handgun for the lady about town.

"Don't worry," she assured me, noticing that I'd noticed the weapon. "I've had training."

"Good to know. Is it loaded?"

She nodded.

"More useful that way," I said.

"You know," the copywriter confided, locking the door and leading me down the hallway, "a year ago I got mugged. Right down in front of the building. Some kid. He hit me in the face and grabbed my purse. Didn't make a NRA member out of me or anything." She hooted, turned, and flashed a grin. "But next day I signed up for shooting lessons. Never in my wildest did I think I'd do something like that."

"Why's it out?"

"Seemed like a good idea, after night before last. Things got serious all of a sudden. I mean, Jesus, *terrorists!*"

Normally I don't get to hang out in places like Meg's condo. It was straight out of *Architectural Digest*—sleek, but plush and comfortable. She had a couple of pure white recliners and a cream leather sofa long enough for a pro hoopster to stretch out on, with a pair of sheepskins draped over the back. A triptych of sizable abstract paintings hung on the walls. Color field, Rothko-like, if my college art history served me—luminous, orange- and blue-colored lozenges floating in who knows what. No magazines or papers laying around. None of the mess you expect of a normal human being, let alone a writer.

She had herbal cachets around the room. Not that sickly/spicy sweet "country" smell ubiquitous in cutesy-ootsy giftshops. But subtle and aroma-therapeutic, like one of those pricey shampoos you buy at the salon.

I eased myself into a recliner, reclined it, and my back thanked me. Though it hadn't forgiven me yet for the car wreck.

"Sorry," Meg apologized, plopping down on the sofa, "but let's get cracking. I have only about half an hour. Have some stuff to do out at the office."

I nearly scowled my "don't-be-a-fucking-idiot" scowl. But I caught myself just in time, and merely frowned. "Not a good idea," I said. "I'm asking everyone to lay low, for the time being."

"Are we getting bodyguards or something?"

"Not yet. I just want people to understand the security issues."

She cocked her head to one side, and I could see the sassy, know-it-all, twentysomething tease lurking inside the middle-aged woman. "Like not wandering around the lion's den with porkchops hanging out of my pockets?"

"Yeah," I laughed, "more or less."

"Drink?" she asked, picking up a crystal cocktail glass from the gray marble coffee table in front of the sofa. "I'm working on a Manhattan. We have time, if you'd like."

"Eleven in the a.m.'s a little too early for me, Meg. But thanks."

She took a slow draw on her drink, staring at me all the while, like a cat eyes a bumptious canine. "Denny tells me you're a regular Miss Marple. So what's going on—" She affected a limey accent. "—in St. Mary Mead?"

I told what I knew, but omitted my little misadventure with the Lexus. No reason to frighten the natives any further. Word on the cola and pizza hadn't come back from the lab yet.

Meg LaGrange was lanky, taller even than me. She had a square jaw. A noble prow of a nose. A thick, short cascade of shiny black hair. Out of a bottle, I suspected. Intimidating blue-gray eyes. Now, though, with gravity starting to work, there were hints of jowls and dewlap, well-etched crows' feet.

"So you think this is more than a hoax?" she asked when I finished. She had another sip of her Manhattan.

"I'd take it seriously," I said. "That's why I asked all you guys to lay low."

She nodded nervously, put her drink down on the gray marble. Then she pulled her green cardigan tightly around her shoulders—as if donning armor.

"Meg, was Denny's version of what happened pretty accurate?"

"Yeah. He has a good way with details." She screwed up her face, and shivered. "I can still smell it. Like industrial waste, or something. Organic. Repulsive! I don't know why Sue didn't throw up."

I debated asking her how she liked selling something "repulsive," as well as addictive. But I held my tongue—I mean, I'd sold out, too—and asked her to reprise her part in the affair.

She confirmed that she had indeed called Chez Pizza about a quarter to eleven, after polling her colleagues about the kinds of pies they wanted—a proscuitto/artichoke and a Granny Gorganzola. The teenaged intern, Sue Hewlett's little sister Michelle, had wanted pepperoni and mushroom, but got outvoted. All they needed in the way of drink was some cola. They had beer, wine, and mineral water in the lunchroom fridge.

"It takes them about half an hour to get out there," Meg said. "Usually they just leave the food in the lobby. No one's ever ripped it off. Hell, who'd be out there that time of night? And it was frickin' cold, too."

"Yeah, tell my chilblains," I said. "So you went downstairs when?"

"Probably about midnight."

"Was it still nice and warm?"

"Warmish. It had cooled off. How could it not cool off?"

I wondered if she'd seen anyone else handling the cola, as if they were trying to hide something. She hadn't.

"Sue poured herself a cola first thing," Meg continued. "She took a sip and, like *instantly*, spit it out all over her desk. She started screaming bloody murder."

"Did she say anything?"

Meg shrugged. "You know, 'Yuuuuukk, icccck…' Stuff like that. She pulled out a handkerchief and stuck it in her mouth and tried to wipe it out. Weird, how the first thing I thought of is how this girl'll sue the pants off the damned pizza place, putting shit like that in their drinks. Or the soda company. Like, she drinks poison, and the first thing that comes to mind is her attorney Bernie. The *first* thing!"

Meg's wide, magnetic smile burst out, and didn't look out of place. She was one of those women who, depicted in the newspaper or online, would look like a gargoyle. But see her in person, see the smile and the spark and the animation in her features—it gave her a kind of electric sexiness that no beauty queen could match. Somehow I could see her getting the guy a good percentage of the time.

"When something like that happens—" She trailed off. "For all you know you're dying, and you just want to nail some stupid bastard." She crossed her legs Indian-style, then pulled her right calf up over her left thigh—an offhanded half-lotus. "Anyway, we were all real pissed off. But Denny got us calmed down, and he read us the e-mail, and sent us home. You know the rest."

"I guess the e-mail came in afterwards."

She nodded at my brilliant deduction.

"How'd the other people react?" I put to her.

"Sue was mad as hell, naturally. Michelle got kind of freaked, crying. The kid's an intern with us this school year."

"Wasn't that pretty late for her to be working?"

"Actually," said Meg, "Sue was basically babysitting her. Their mom was out on a date or something. Michelle's usually around an afternoon or two a week. Anyway, they left right after the, uh, incident."

"Archie?"

"Archie looked like he was gonna faint."

"He's kind of an apprentice?"

"An assistant. Working in traffic under Sue. Actually, I think he'd like Sue working under him, if you get my drift."

I have as dirty a mind as anyone's, so I indicated that I did.

"He finished college a year ago last summer, but I can't see him getting anywhere in the business. Too lazy, spoiled. Trust fund baby. When he and his sister inherit the agency, they'd better have enough brains to let Denny run it. That is, if Herb doesn't sell it."

I grabbed the handle and shifted the recliner upright. "Tell me about the others, how they reacted."

"Harry Litzky. Gay as a three-dollar bill, but clever as hell, great to work with. We all love him to pieces. Got into the business from newspapers in Chicago. He's got a shelf full of awards." She flashed me the big smile again. "Hell, I didn't think of the bungee-cord jumping couple for Hamburger Shack. Harry did. I just wrote the copy."

"'Bounce by for a MegaSuperShack today!'?"

She chuckled and looked flattered that I remembered it. "Yeah, that's the chap. People loved it. They sold a jillion of the things."

"So all the others— The couple in the big-wheel truck, the couple hooking the giant bass, the couple on the twin bucking broncos—"

She nodded. "All Harry's ideas. Herb and I just filled out the concepts, then the campaign."

"So how'd Harry react the other night?"

"Went white as a sheet. Didn't say much. He's down in Northfield, hiding out. We're still working, but remotely. Harry loves playing the gentleman farmer." Her eyes twinkled. "As opposed to *laying* the gentleman farmer."

Meg LaGrange must have mixed herself a hell of a good Manhattan, considering how pleased she looked with her little play on words. But I guess that's what she did for a living.

"So Herb's the key man with Bertram?" I stated.

"Damn straight." She clenched a fist and pumped it as I heard the subdued roar of an airliner overhead. The sound carried impressively in the winter air. "He's the only reason Bertram came to us."

"How long have you known Herb?"

She shrugged. "Longer than I care to admit."

That got my attention. "What do you mean?"

"I've known Herb almost since I was out of college, which means I'm not a foxy young babe anymore. That's about 25 years."

"Where'd you meet?"

"I grew up in Milwaukee, went to school in Madison." She drew the palm of her right hand down her neck, elegantly, then entwined her fingers in a kind of cats cradle. "Then I headed for California, San Diego to be exact. I worked as a production assistant at a TV station, then I got into an agency as a copywriter. Herb had a shop out there, and he hired me. A couple, three years later he had some kind of business reverse—he never would say what it was—some investment thing. And he had to lay people off. But he kept me. We've stayed connected ever since. Even when we aren't working together."

"So a friend, not just a boss?" I asked.

"Yeah, more or less."

I took a peek at my Swatch, and figured I'd pretty much used up the half-hour. But like any good interviewer or reporter will tell you, you keep asking questions until you get sick of the subject, or the subject gets sick of you.

"Meg, has anybody on the team—or anybody you can think of in the agency—had relatives, friends, colleagues die because of smoking?"

She nodded. "Sure. Off the top of my head I can think of four or five funerals. Including me. Smoking's a bitch, then they die."

I did my facial question mark—raised eyebrows, pursed lips, tilted head.

"My dad died eight years ago," she stated matter of factly. "It was a Bertram brand, even. Freshaire. Is that a bullshit name, or what?"

"Lung cancer, emphysema?"

"Emphysema. He suffocated."

I nodded. "My Dad, too. Big C."

"So why are we working for these bastards, Marta?" she asked familiarly, looking burnt out now, her face blank and tired.

I held up my right hand, palm up. I rubbed my thumb over my forefinger and middle finger. *Hush money. Payoff. Bribe.*

"Bingo," said Meg. "But I didn't put shit in any soda pop, and I don't think anyone there did. We're family. Dysfunctional, maybe, a little fucked up. But family. We wouldn't hurt each other."

I didn't believe her, but I didn't say so. Wherever big bucks and big egos intersect—like at Gottwaldt and Ryan—things can go *boom*.

"Do you know about anyone with a grudge, maybe a former employee?"

"Well, we've been together— We, meaning the people working on Hemo. We've been on projects on and off for years. Archie and Sue's sister are the only new people. Besides, in the ad business, folks come and go all the time, accounts come and go. Nobody goes postal over it. You get sacked, you go job hunting. Like any business."

Meg muttered a few words of deep and quite insincere regret, and told me that she had to get dressed for work. I tried to dissuade her from going in, but she cordially told me to buzz off. On the way out I peeked at her frosted-stainless 9mm, and earnestly hoped that she'd put the thing away.

Writers packing? *A very bad idea.*

Chapter Ten

Down in the lobby of Meg's building I called Triple-A and arranged to meet one of their trucks out at Gottwaldt and Ryan. Time to jump-start the old Merc. I felt naked and helpless without it. I flagged a taxi cruising by and on the drive west checked in with my lab. My original hunch was right: No nicotine had gone into the cola. My lab guy had no doubt that Sue Hewlett— to explosive effect—had laid her taste buds on something brewed from the wild yeast that occasionally infects home-brewed beer. "A really disgusting taste," he put it. "A strong dose. Might've been distilled down, concentrated. But it wouldn't have caused any harm if someone had swallowed it. Other than maybe nausea."

My computer gopher and bookkeeper Deb Brown was hard at work, and I heaped a bit more on her plate. What's out there on the worldwide interwebs pertaining to anti-smoking terrorist groups or any unsolved blackmail/extortion/terrorism aimed against tobacco companies or their ad agencies?

I got to my old man's Merc five minutes before Triple-A's truck. After the guy got it started, I let it heat up nice and toasty. I sat inside, dictating my first report on the case into an Olympus digital recorder—everything so far. Transcribing would have to wait for the weekend. Or if I got lazy I'd e-mail the MP3 to Deb.

Back in Gottwaldt and Ryan, I was fortunate enough to find Herb Gottwaldt in residence. And he could spare me a few minutes. "And I *mean* a few minutes," he said, striding ahead of me, into his lair.

I got the corner of the sofa nearest the desk. His sharp gray eyes did an x-ray number on me again—suspicious but maybe curious, too.

"First," he began, "are you okay? I heard about what happened last night, and I'm real sorry." He growled a little and shook his head. "Like Denny told you, you'll get a bonus right off the top."

"All contributions gratefully accepted," I allowed. "I should tell you, as well, that the substance that contaminated the cola was not poisonous. Some kind of yeast-based brew. The so-called terrorists weren't quite ready to murder anyone. It was a proof of efficacy."

"Whadaya mean?"

"They wanted to show you they could do it if they wanted to."

"Okay, Sherlock," he said, winking at me, "where does it go from here?"

Usually I don't laugh at Holmes lines, but he said it so unexpectedly, with that music-hall wink, that I did. And he smiled just a bit. This was one seductive guy, let me tell you.

"It strikes me," I began, "that this terrorism—if that's what it is—is addressed pretty personally against you. All the messages came to you."

"So?" he said quietly. "I'm the front man for this outfit, and I make the decisions. Why should that surprise anyone?"

"Okay, maybe it shouldn't. But what if we do have some kind of personal vendetta going? What if this has nothing to do with cigarettes and Bertram?"

He cocked his head and pulled a pack of smokes out of the inside breast pocket of his tweed sportcoat, extracted one, tapped it down. Top Peak, my Dad's brand. "What's your question?" he asked.

"Who might go to the trouble of setting this all up, just to get at you?"

"I won't bullshit you." He ignited the smoke with his old Zippo, then took a deep, gratifying drag, and wafted it back out in my general direction. "I've known enough people who ended up not loving Herb Gottwaldt. Competitors, girlfriends, my ex-wife, one or two business partners. But honest to God, I can't imagine anyone who'd pull crap like this. Anyone I know is gonna get right in my face."

I snapped open my reporter's satchel and took out my notebook. "Can you give me some names?"

He laughed. "The usual suspects, huh?"

I waited for him to say more, and he didn't.

"Well?" I said.

"Listen," he said, leaning over his desk toward me, "I don't want to put you on anybody's tail— *Yet*. You do what you can do with the people here, plus whatever the hell other resources you have, okay? No leaks, though, or you're done." He paused, not very long. "That all?"

"You realize the police are going to check out the car crash."

"I know, but our cooperation will be, ah, um, sluggish and inept. Okay?"

"One more question then," I said, "and I'll get out of your hair."

He nodded curtly, once.

"What's the story with Bertram? How'd you get connected?"

"It was your old boyfriend," he answered.

"Ex," I corrected him.

"Whatever."

"And?"

"Terry," he continued, breaking eye contact, "met Denny on some convention panel somewhere. Terry knows the agency's work pretty well, admires it. So when he got a bit of clout at Bertram, he came to Denny. Would we be interested in the He-mo test market? I have to admit, at first it didn't seem like a good fit. I could've taken it or left it. But there's some fun to be had with the vampire thing. And the test market could turn into a national rollout. Even if it didn't, Bertram might provide an entrée into Amfoodco."

"Bertram's parent conglomerate," I pitched in.

"Uh-huh." He stubbed out his cigarette in what looked like a Waterford nut dish. "Basically, I could see this alliance benefiting Gottwaldt and Ryan. It's a challenge, too, to do something special with a cigarette brand. Imagination, crea-tivity— They've never been the strong suit of cigarette cam-paigns."

"You don't seem that enthused, Herb."

"My enthusiasm will improve," he replied tiredly, "when this shit storm blows itself out."

I thanked him and started to leave. But I felt my stomach

growl and claw angrily. I turned around. "Herb, will you do me one big favor?"

"Yeah, what?"

"The next few nights, stay at a hotel. Go somewhere. Don't let anyone know where you are. I can even make a call to an ex-SAS guy I know—"

"SAS?" He looked startled. "Special Air Service?"

"Yeah, my old street-fighting instructor. He can bodyguard for you while this thing plays out. Called him on the taxi ride out here. He's available and very reasonable, too. Not a bad idea."

Herb chortled like it was a sick joke. "Isn't that a little melodramatic, Marta? I'm fine, I'm okay. Let's just get through this and then we'll all have a good laugh about it."

I shrugged, unsurprised. Alpha males usually don't respond well to such suggestions. "Say, Herb, anywhere around here I can get bite to eat?"

"Sure. Fridge in the lunchroom down in the basement. We keep it stocked with sandwiches and salads from D'Amico, sodas and water. Help yourself."

• • •

After wolfing down a foccacia chicken-salad sandwich with Orangina, I ran into Meg LaGrange in the warren of cubicles. She was trying ever so smoothly to not tell another woman—a youngish, perky kid with an upturned, pierced nose and a kind of snazzy brunette crew cut—what the hell had happened Monday night. The buzz had it, I overhead the young woman say, that someone suffered an epileptic fit during the late-night session. So *who* was it? Meg shrugged and said she really couldn't say. Kind of a confidential thing, you know, medical issues. Could get in trouble spilling the beans.

Meg's pal nodded politely at me when she strolled away, but her eyes said: And who the hell are *you* to be wandering around here?

"Anyone else here from your stalwart cigarette-slinging posse?" I asked when the crew-cutted one withdrew.

"I don't know if Denny's around," she answered, directing

me toward her cubicle a short distance away. "Herb's here."

She sat down behind her prodigiously cluttered desk. How could her house be so tidy? I marveled. "So anybody else in residence?"

"Sue Hewlett had some stuff to do, I guess. I bumped into her a hour ago. But I think she vamoosed."

I thanked Meg again and went to knock on Sue's door, but no one was home.

Next order of business involved my doing my celebrated impersonation of "Sergeant Preston of the Yukon," and mushing out into the scrub brush between the lake road and the agency parking lot. I followed the tracks back and forth, and took a few shots of them with the little Canon point-and-shoot I always keep in my satchel. If this case turned into a full-blown police investigation—not unlikely, in my opinion—the cops might find a fresh photo or two useful. After all, in a week the tracks likely would be obliterated by the blowing "snirt"—that is, snow plus dirt.

From the cell phone in my car I managed to nab Sue Hewlett's husband, Doug, who said he expected the missus home "any time now." He sounded jumpy. I didn't blame him.

If someone had just fed Rick a cocktail of rancorous fermented something or other, I'd have the willies, too. Still, Doug didn't like my little lecture about not letting Sue out loose at a dangerous time like this. But the gentleman in him prevailed and he reluctantly agreed to let me stop by chez Hewlett.

• • •

After a slow trek east across both Twin Cities, I arrived at the couple's gorgeously renovated house on Lincoln Avenue at about three. Just off Grand in St. Paul, it was one of those big turn-of-the-20th-century jobs. The signs said no one without permits could park on the street during business-and-restaurant hours. Grand was very popular with shoppers and diners, but the locals hated to lose their on-street parking. I decided to take a chance on a ticket and not park three blocks away with a nasty windchill blowing.

It pained me to think about all the elbow grease that went

into scraping the old paint off the Hewletts' house, and knowing the fashionable new gray with cranberry trim would be peeling again in two or three years. Rick and I put steel siding on our duplex. It cost a bundle, but I didn't regret it for a minute. I'd had it with the Sisyphean torture of scraping and priming and painting every few years.

I tapped the buzzer several times. As soon as Doug Hewlett opened the door, I knew I'd seen him before—a square, jocular WASP face, a shock of light brown hair, a many-times-broken nose ruddy with drinking. An incipient smile and observant eyes. The smell of barley and hops hung pretty strongly around him. He stood a good four inches taller than me, and he had the build of a linebacker.

"Hi, I'm Marta Hjelm."

"Doug Hewlett," he said in a raspy baritone, the potential smile coming into bloom. "Great to meet you, Marta."

I stuck my hand out, and he shook it gently, like a man who knew his own strength. It reminded me of the grip of a pro rassler pal my sportswriter grandfather took me and my sister to see when we were kids, an old gentleman who always played "heels"—villains. The "Duke of Doom" had mitts big as shovels. He delighted us two little girls by saying, "Charmed, I'm sure, ladies." Then he delicately shook our little hands. I remember us giggling wildly in the dressing room, as large, ugly men padded around in bathrobes and wrestlers' shorts.

"Wanta come in?" He gestured that I should follow him. "Like a beer, maybe? I'm trying a new micro-brew out of Chicago, for my bars."

Suddenly I remembered the name and the face.

He'd been a hockey star for Duluth State when I was at the University of Minnesota. I'd seen him skate against my alma mater. A real tough guy, if I remembered right, an enforcer. He played pro for several NHL teams, until one of his shoulders went on him. Now he owned several sports bars around town, and he still popped up in the papers and on the tube—a demi-celebrity. "Glad to come in," I said. "I'll take a rain check on the brew, thanks."

I followed him into the vestibule. He and his wife or somebody had done a gorgeous job in here, too. The oak balusters had been stripped and varnished, as had the birdseye maple paneling leading upstairs. A choice Mahal Pakistan rug sat at the foot of the stairs, much finer than our Persian. An old stained glass church window, in the shape of a Gothic arch, hung over the window on the first landing, St. George standing over the dragon. George looked a little swishy, with his rosy cheeks, supple wrists and pursed feminine lips. But the worm had definitely kicked the bucket.

"We can schmooze in here," he said, pointing into the dining room.

It was more of the same—lots of gorgeous woodwork, antique furniture, another Mahal of a darker hue. There were some computer printouts and three open bottles of Lake Michigan Pale Ale on the table, all of them empty. What was left of the beer half-filled a Pilsner glass. I sat down at the table.

He lifted the Pilsner and tipped it my direction. "You sure, Marta? It's really smooth. I got plenty more in the fridge."

"I'm sure, thanks," I said. "When do you expect Sue back?"

Hewlett shook his head. "She went out shopping on the way back from work. She won't be here for another hour or two."

"Listen, Doug, it's not a good idea for her to be out alone. Chances are nothing's gonna happen, but just in case— With this extortion thing going on—"

A tint of anger briefly flashed across his face, then vanished. "Hey, you think I'm stupid?"

I started to assure him that I certainly did not, but he didn't let me.

"I tried to tell her the same thing. But she's one stubborn chick. And I learned a long time ago that *no one* tells her what to do. Least of all me. She's the top dog around here." The big smile came back.

I couldn't tell if he meant it or not. So I laughed politely— the prescribed reaction to a husband's joking reference to his wife "the boss."

"Doug," I asked, "can you think of anyone who Sue's talked

about who might have some grudge against her or Herb or the agency?"

"Man," he shrugged, sipping on his ale, "I wish I knew, Marta. I really do. But I'm not that interested in advertising. Except my own. Whatever keeps 'em comin' through those doors. Right?

"Right indeed," I enthused, and flashed him a thumbs-up. Somehow it seemed the thing to do.

"That's the ticket," he said, having another draw on his rapidly dwindling ale. "All I know is what she tells me, and she never said anything about anyone being pissed."

"So what do you think about her working for a cigarette company?"

"Fine with me," he leaned back, plucked up one of the empties, and regarded the fancy label. "The money's just as green. Smokers are some of my best customers, anyway. Can't smoke inside anymore, of course. But we have smoking patios outside. Cold as it is, there are always guys standing out there with their beers and smokes. Don't smoke myself."

He paused, trying to recapture the question, and succeeded: "But the agency doesn't have the account yet. Way I understand it, this thing with the extortion could queer the whole deal."

"True enough. Do you have any idea why anyone there, or outside, would want to?"

"Like I said, hell if I know. But don't you think it'd be crazy for someone in the agency to mess with a potential client like Bertram? You know they're owned by Amfoodco. They're fucking huge."

"You think someone at Gottwaldt and Ryan might try to screw the pooch?"

"Who knows? Sue says Herb and Denny are after the cigarette test market as a kind of audition. To prove that Gottwaldt and Ryan can do great, off-the-wall stuff, revolutionize tobacco advertising, and still be team players. But Herb can be difficult to work with."

"What do you mean?"

"If you tell him something's black, he'll say it's white. If it's up it's down, if it's tall it's short. If you tell him to not do something, he *will* do it."

I blinked perplexedly at the over-the-hill hockey star. "I still don't follow you."

"Herb's made his name, won all those prizes by being audacious. He does weird, funky stuff for his clients. And it works, too. Of course, nobody would let him do that shit if it didn't sell product. But he has to show Bertram Tobacco he's not some kind of loose cannon. If he does, he could have a clear path to the promised land: Amfoodco."

"Do you get along with Herb pretty well?"

"Well enough. Sue's known him for a long time. Ten years maybe. He hired her out of college."

"You like him?"

"Sure do! He's an asshole, Marta. Just like me!" He winked at me, and guffawed long and hard.

Before I left I asked him something I'd been curious about for a long time: Why do ex-jocks always end up owning bars?

"So," he said with twinkle in eye, and no irony intended, "the bullshit never has to stop."

As I went out the door, he said he'd have Sue call me when she got back. Puffing up his voluminous chest, the ex-hockey star promised me that if any goddamned terrorist touched his wife, he'd pound the pulp out of them. I know that would make *me* feel *a lot* safer.

Sitting in the Merc, I called Archie Gottwaldt and Litzky. No luck. Deb Brown hadn't tracked down much of interest. Just some DWI's by Herb and his son, and the fact that Meg La-Grange had had a proclivity for getting busted at environmental protests a generation ago. Rick I did reach, at the photography museum. He hemmed and hawed, but said he could meet me at the duplex at 6:30. Before he arrived, I barely had time to listen to my voicemail. My dentist and Terry checking on how I was feeling. By the way, he wondered, was I free that weekend? Red Hot Chili Peppers at the Target Center?

I called and got his voicemail. "Thanks, Mr. Rosen, but no can do," said I.

Chapter Eleven

Rick settled onto the big sofa, angled out from the wall in front of the Chinese fans. As if he'd never bombed out the door in a huff on Sunday afternoon. Right where he belonged.

My significant other looked pretty damned good, basking in the glow of our *faux* Tiffany lamp—a muted, reddish light. His long, blue-jeaned legs were crossed and stretched out, his horned-rims—for reading only—hunkered down at the tip of his nose. A mug of hot buttered rum steamed cozily in both his hands. The way he held his face reminded me of the Bhuddas he collected. Eyes serene, mouth imperturbable, brow smooth as porcelain. Not pinched and sour, like when he discovered Terry and me enjoying caffè lattes.

"You told me this was a business meeting," he said, blowing softly into his mug. "Like, *photography* business?"

"No," I replied from the plaid recliner, taking a sip of my first buttered rum of the winter. Rick mixed a great one, opulent, creamy, with both rum and cholesterol-kick. "*Investigative* business, darlin'. The case I'm working on."

"I thought you were getting out of *that* business. I thought that's why we had a big row just this Sunday. I thought that's why I went to stay with my brother." He gave me a half-scowl.

"I *am* getting out. Some day soon."

"I'd bet my last nickel you can't do it, Marta Hjelm. *Ain't gonna happen*. It gives you too much. You'd miss it something awful. Just because you had that *awful* case last summer—" He took a deep breath. "You did try to help that woman get away from her husband. But she wasn't ready to be helped, not by a long shot. All the king's horses and all the king's men couldn't've gotten her outta there. That's why she died. You can't blame yourself, you can't quit just because you think you didn't do enough. *You did your damnedest!*"

"You know, Mr. Mueller," I said, reddening in the face, trying not to sound mad, "this reminds me ominously of our little debate on Sunday."

"Sometimes the truth hurts, kiddo."

Whoosh! Score one for Rick, zero for Marta.

At first, becoming a PI just kind of happened. When I'd gotten back to Minnesota—post-Terry, tail between my legs—I punched the clock at Dennison's department stores, clerking in various locations, various departments. Pretty soon I transferred to loss prevention—as in anti-shoplifting and -pilferage. A year later a private detective named Tookie Peterson asked me to go to work for him. That was about the time I first encountered Rick and zapped him with pepper spray—a long story that I'll share some other time.

Back then my self-confidence hovered somewhere down around my toenails, my psyche resembled a puddle of melted Jell-o, my morale was a pile of smoking wreckage. I felt physically shitty—with grinding headaches and insomnia. And having put on twenty extra pounds, I looked ten years older than I was.

But after three years of working with Tookie—graduating from scutwork to the more interesting stuff, working lots of overtime—I'd not only accumulated the hours to get my own license and set up shop, I also managed to prove to myself that maybe ol' Marta Hjelm wasn't a basket case after all. I felt good. Lost most of the extra weight. I did good work. I handled interviews and surveillances, tails and skip traces. I liked finding out the truth of matters that people, or the years, managed to bury.

The fact that a few months before Terry's call I'd found out that a seemingly ideal husband and father was something much darker than he appeared, and it made no difference to the horrible outcome— That's when the photographic life started to look pretty good.

"Yeah," I said, after my long silence. "The truth's a bitch."

"Meaning," he returned gently, "let's not rip off the scab this soon?"

I nodded.

"Fine with me," he said. But his face didn't express that it was fine with him. "Tell me about your case."

I filled him in on everything. Omitting mention of myself, I described the Lexus's cut brake lines and the aborted airbag. I told him my impressions of the people I'd met, from fuck-up

Archie to masterful Herb to beautiful, nervous Sue.

"The upshot is," I said, "that I need a little help. Something only you, my darling honeybun, could possibly provide."

"Buuullshit," he growled amiably.

"No boo-shit," I said. "You know someone I don't."

He perked up, his blue eyes widened. He was curious, despite a determination to be hard-assed about Terry and about our little career kerfuffle.

"So what do you need?" he asked, putting down his buttered rum.

"You know Cal Bemis, right?"

He nodded. His eyebrows made a V above the bridge of his crooked nose.

Bemis wrote the gossip column for the *Herald*. He knew just how much celebrity X undertipped her waiter last night at La Belle Vie. How many K-notes she paid for her gown at the Dennison Circle Room. If a movie star came to town for a film shoot, and tried to grope every female he met— Well, Bemis sniffed the air, found a few trace molecules, and *knew* what the celeb had done.

"I'd like you to call him," I said, shifting in my La-Z-Boy, "and find out what he knows about the people on this list." I held up an index card that contained the names of all known persons with any connection to the "poisoned" cola affair. "Background," I said. "Who their lovers are, ex-spouses, old peccadilloes, connections between them, skeletons in closets, arrests and acquittals. Anything."

Rick hopped up and came over, stocking-footed, for the card. He peered at it through his reading spectacles. "I've only seen a couple of the names in Cal's column. Gottwaldt, Ryan."

"Yeah. But if anyone knows any dirty linen, Cal does."

"He'll want something back."

"Yeah, I figured he would."

"So?"

"Ask him if he wants the poop on a certain prominent, Bible-thumping state senator caught shoplifting lady's under-garments at a certain intimate-apparel store? Size 24. *The senator's* size. Not his wife's size. A size 24 thong! Gives me the queasies yet to this day. The rap's a little stale, but it has a certain piquant charm."

Rick hooted. "You're shittin' me!"

"Nope, I will never shit my honey," I drawled. "I kept a copy of the report. They settled it with the guy, under the table. But they stiffed me, bastards. Don't like them, don't like him. So I don't give a flying you-know-what if Cal prints it." I reached up and touched his hand, expecting him to pull back. But he peered down at me through his horn-rims, squeezed my fingers briefly, and let go.

"Why don't you stay for dinner?" I said. "Better yet, call little bro and tell him you won't be rooming with him tonight."

"Yes, to the former query," he answered. "Not yet to the latter."

• • •

Sitting in the breakfast nook in the kitchen, we worked away ravenously on parsley pesto over linguine, a micro-green salad and two big tumblers of zinfandel. As we munched and sipped, I told him more about the *dramatis personnae* of the Gottwaldt case. And how, for some reason, certain folks seemed out of character. Myself included.

"You gave me the idea yesterday," I said. "What's gotten into everyone? Why does Terry, who treated me like shit, come after me professionally?"

"And you, too, Ms. Hjelm," Rick said, a brief cloud shading his countenance. "You've gotten a little weird."

"Whadaya mean?"

"Marty, I'm not *blind*." He sloshed his zinfandel around a bit. "He wants you back. I saw it. And you've given him an opening."

"Can't have me," I spat.

"Better tell *him* that."

"I have, but Terry's tough to discourage, let me tell you."

"Yeah, so I gather."

He gave me this worried expression, almost a look of fear. "You're not tempted, *are you?*"

I scrunched up my face and growled: "Sometimes, Richard Mueller, you are such a fucking idiot!" And I lurched across the table, grabbed his shoulders and planted the loudest, sloppiest smacker possible on his sweet lips—and then hung on to him for a moment. An empty wine glass was tipped over and I got pesto smear on my sweatshirt.

"Getting back to character," I continued, returning to my starting position, "why does Denny agree to hire someone who he once fired and who he knows hates his guts? Why does someone like Meg LaGrange, with a background in environmental protest, end up shilling for a tobacco company? Why does Herb Gottwaldt seem so detached, so unenthused about this big, new project?"

"Damned good questions," my significant other agreed. "Maybe you should hire a detective."

I was about to heave my crumpled napkin at him when the phone rang. I scooted out of the nook and grabbed my cell from the kitchen counter. It was Denny and he'd rounded up both Sue Hewlett and Archie Gottwaldt for me, out at one of the sports bars Doug Hewlett owned. Could I make it in about 45 minutes or an hour? Sure, I said, thankful that I'd had only one glass of zin in addition to the hot buttered rum. It was about 9:30.

"I'd like to come, too," Rick said after I told him where I had to go. "I'll be a good boy. Won't break any china or anything."

"You'd only be wasting your time," I said.

"Just tell them I'm one of your operatives. I'll take notes."

"I don't know Rick—"

He pulled himself out of the nook—given his lankiness, a bit of a process—and came over to me. He put a hand on either shoulder, an annunciation of: "Listen up."

"I suggest we make a *quid pro quo*," he said. "You are welcome to work with me, as always. And if you love it and if you thrive and if you make money doing it, great. Likewise, I get to work with you on some of your cases. Under your direction, of course. You're the pro." He took a beat. "What do you say?"

He'd offered a way out of our little impasse, but he surprised me by asking to become involved in my work. We'd always talked over cases I had, and sometimes he did light legwork for me. But I wasn't so sure I liked him getting that involved in my stuff. And suddenly I could see things a little more from his perspective.

"I think we have a good start to our negotiations," I said.

Chapter Twelve

Hewlett's Sport Bar was out on the 494 strip, on the north side between Lyndale and Nicollet, one of three that Doug Hewlett owned.

Giant plasma screens were all around, blaring various NBA and NHL games. The noise level was brutal. The joint had a kind of buttery, rancid, popcorn stench, like the smell of an old dime store. What looked like five or six night-league basketball teams had descended like locusts a little after I got there.

It was about half past ten when I slipped out of my jacket and into the booth next to Denny.

Sue Hewlett nodded at me and said hi, with a sort of anxious expression. She took a few tiny sips out of a glass of Coors Light, then set it down. "I understand you had some trouble with the Lexus last night."

I saw Denny out of the corner of my eye and he very subtly shook his head: Don't tell her.

"Yeah," I said, "brake problem. Guess it's pretty much totalled."

"I'm glad you're okay," she said, reaching across and patting my folded hands.

Archie barely noticed my arrival. When he looked at me, his pale gray eyes—like his dad's, only skewed slightly to green—focused about twenty feet behind me, somewhere back by the jukebox. If he had been a cartoon character, little fizzy bubbles would have been coming off the top of his head.

A waitress had just brought him a fresh rum/cola. Denny—whose drunken antics on a downtown street still defined him in my memory—asked Master Gottwaldt if maybe four wasn't too many.

"Naw," quoth the scion. "I ca' handle it."

The waitress asked what I wanted, and I pleaded, "Just a cup of decaf, please." She scurried off.

With such a fine captive audience, I turned to the two young folks and delivered my little lecture on security. Never go anywhere alone, driving or on foot. Stay with a friend, if possible, until the nastiness blows over. Never answer the door. Use your common sense.

I'm sure Sue heard everything I said, because she nodded along the way. But she tapped her right index finger incessantly, and her bright black eyes didn't make contact. They surveyed the room, not me. Only natural, I suppose, for someone who'd sipped the befouled cola.

Archie didn't exactly scope the information I'd provided. He barely took his glazed eyeballs off the Celtics/Trailblazers game.

"If either of you would like it," I proposed, "Denny said the agency would pop for some protection."

"Rubbers?" Archie sputtered, and howled at his little funny. He peered woozily at us, and found not even a smile. "Get it? Rubbers. Protection, huh? Denny's gonna buy me some rubbers? Do they make 'em big enough?" He bobbed his head merrily, and returned that wispy attention span to the ball game.

Denny went red as a beet, and even Sue had a pinkish tinge as she did a slow, low burn.

"Speaking of protection," I asked Denny, "what's Herb doing for security?"

"I talked to him, like you asked," he sighed with a desultory shake of the head. "He's too fucking stubborn. He's driving himself, he's going places alone. Seems like he's itching for a fight."

"He sounds like a man who doesn't expect to lose," I observed.

"Damned fucking straight!" spat the younger Gottwaldt, suddenly veering back to earth. Well off the beat, he slammed a fist on the table. A few b-ball fans blinked at us, then wafted back to their game. "Dad's a pain in the butt sometimes. But man, he really goes after the brass ring. And he'll tromp on you to get to it. No 'stortionists're gonna mess with him, no way. He's goin' for Hemo."

I frowned and took a slow drag on my decaf, which had just arrived. I hadn't really gotten that impression, but I didn't know the man that well.

"I hope he understands," I put in a gingerly way, "that sometimes the sword *is* mightier than the pen."

Junior shrugged his shoulders, and declined to return my serve. Sue winked at me—as if to say, *what a character*. Oddly, though I didn't sense any animus between them. She looked mildly amused. I would have wanted to be anywhere but next to that immature jerk.

"You can't talk to Herb if his mind's made up," she agreed.

"He's made millions, and he doesn't really give a damn what some bow-wow of a gumshoe thinks," Archie bellowed. People stared at us again, and young Mr. Gottwaldt made an exaggerated expression of embarrassment. He leaned over toward me in a conspiratorial way, and whispered, "I bet Dad's sitting out in that house all by himself, like he's daring 'em to come and get him."

"Doesn't someone live with him?" I exclaimed. "A caretaker or something?"

"My folks got divorced a long time 'go," Archie slurred, diddling around with his keychain. "Mom got the house in Edina. He built that new one on Lake Minnetonka, not far from the shop." He put his keychain down on the table in a puddle of spilled rum/cola. "I hate it, though. 'S sterile's hell. Metal and glass and ugly wood. None of his girlfriends ever stay there. Dad doesn't like it if they do."

I didn't like it, either—Gottwaldt all by his lonesome in a big house on a huge lake lot. "How's about I get someone out there tonight?" I said. "Keep an eye on him. He doesn't have to know."

"But he'll find out and he'll get *real* pissed," predicted Sue.

"Yeah, he would and he would," Denny agreed.

"Please. What's the address?" I asked.

Shaking his head, Denny wrote it down on a cocktail napkin and handed it to me. Then he took a peek at his Rolex. "Listen, Marta, I gotta get some zzz's. I'm just absolutely dying here."

"And you're driving all alone, after my big spiel?"

"Hey," he grinned, "I'll be careful. Cross my heart."

I slid out of the booth and he after me. He threw on his down vest, and bopped on out of the place, threading his way nimbly through the carousing hoopsters.

I reclaimed my spot, facing Sue and Archie. Sue looked tense as a drumhead, like I do when I sit down in the dentist's chair— an unpleasant task that has to be done. Archie took quite the opposite tack. Loose as a goose, drunk as a skunk.

Excusing myself for a moment, I visited the john and made a call on my Nokia. It was about eleven.

A sleepy voice belonging to my favorite operative, Bruce Prochnik, mumbled an unenthused, nearly unintelligible greeting.

"Jeez, Marta," he whined when he heard my voice, "I was in bed."

"With whom?"

He laughed like a donkey, on the inhalation, braying. "Several dozen gorgeous porno stars."

"Not the ugly ones?"

"Nope. Told 'em to pack it up."

"Just be careful, big boy. Silicon can bruise you pretty badly."

More braying. "Hjelm, you're no fun at all."

"Damn betcha I'm not. Want a little gig tonight?"

"Like *tonight* tonight? Right *now* tonight?"

"Uh-huh. That's what 'tonight' usually means."

"Yeah, guess so. I got alimony payments comin' up."

Bruce and I had known each since we worked for Tookie Peterson. He had way more time in the business than I did, and could have had his own license. But he claimed he never could raise the money he needed for his bond. So he went on working for me and others around town. My theory is that he just didn't want the hassle of running a business. He didn't mind working, but didn't like responsibilities. Thus, two ex-wives and several kids.

I told him to keep an eye on Herb Gottwaldt's digs and gave him the address. He was to note any comings and goings, and tail Gottwaldt if he went anywhere. Until further notice. I described Gottwaldt's cars, a black Mercedes E350 4matic and red Humvee. Bruce could call 911 like any good citizen might, if anything nasty looked imminent. If he wanted to play the hero, he had my permission.

When I came around the bar—an island in the middle of the joint that contained three bustling barkeeps in sports-official zebra stripes, like the waitpeople—I saw that Archie had just gotten another rum/Coke, but one of many. And though he should have been getting the brush-off, he wasn't.

He was leaning toward Sue Hewlett, *on* Sue Hewlett. Before his addled sensory apparatus could grasp it, with a fine sense of spatial relationships, she knocked her Coors Light over and it gushed right onto his lap. He squawked loudly and soft-shoed out of the booth, trying to dust off the brew. He grabbed some napkins from an empty booth and did his best to sop it up.

"Li'l accident," he mumbled, stumbling past me, heading for the head.

"I know what you're thinking," the lady said when I sat down opposite her. She was still a mite steamed, but cooling rapidly. "He's really not so bad. He needed slowing down. He just gets a little pushy when he's had too many rum-colas. "

"No kidding?" I said, trying to imagine how Archie could be less pushy. Rapine and pillage on the table top? "Doesn't he know what your husband used to do for a living?"

"Yeah, but I'm not gonna tell Doug. Doug'd kick the daylights out of him. Then I'd be out of a nice job. Anyway, I can handle Archie. He's really not a bad kid."

"You'd've been in trouble without your beer."

"Nah, it's okay."

"Looks to me like he has the hots for you."

She shook her head and howled. "Archie? And me? Come on, Marta. Even if he weren't too young, he's not my type. So what if he, um, thinks I'm a babe? It's flattering, but it doesn't mean anything."

When she said all that, I had to admit to myself that it did seem like an atrocious mismatch. She was smart and good looking and somewhere over 30. He was a lazy, arrogant kid riding his daddy's coattails.

"Do you think Archie'll get the agency when Herb retires?"

"Jeez, I suppose he'll get a piece of it."

"How about Archie's big sister?"

"That I wouldn't enjoy." She rolled her eyes and shook her head, simultaneously.

"She married?"

"Yeah. Husband's COO of Nelsontek. A couple of kids. She's a rich young housewife, whatever that means."

"When's Herb supposed to retire?"

"You heard about the 800-pound gorilla?"

"Yeah." I'd known a few of them in my life.

"Whenever he feels like it, Marta. Whenever he feels like it."

"Do you have any theories about this, uh, incident? I mean, do you really think it's terrorists?"

"It sure seems wild, doesn't it?" She had a little Coors left in her bottle and she poured it into the recently emptied pilsner. "I'm as stumped as anyone. If it's someone in the agency, why would they want to screw up an entrée to Amfoodco? I mean, the account makes more work for everyone, bigger bonuses."

Archie was taking his sweet time in the men's room, probably passed out on the throne. Which was fine with me. I went over the timing of the rancid-cola incident with Sue, and it sounded identical to the way Meg LaGrange described it. A cola-holic, Sue grabbed one of the two cartons as soon as Meg set them down and poured herself a glass before anyone else. She saw no one mess with it.

When I told her she hadn't been exposed to raw nicotine, even if she had inhaled, she looked relieved. She claimed, though, that she still had the taste of the gunk in her mouth.

"You know, Marta," she said in a low voice, leaning across the table, "I'm still damn spooked. These…*people* could really end up killing someone."

"Is Archie pretty plastered tonight," I asked, "compared to normal?"

"Above average."

"Maybe we'd better lose these for him." I picked up his keychain. He drove a Porsche. Not bad for a kid just out of college.

"Good idea," Sue agreed. "Except how'm I supposed to get home? I rode with him."

"I'll take you, not a problem. Archie can wait until tomorrow. Think his hangover will tone him down a bit?"

"You never know," Sue speculated. "Hope he has cab fare."

"Me too."

We pulled our coats on and went over to the bar. One of the bartenders, a plump, jovial woman with a rosy complexion and granny glasses, kind of jumped to attention when she recognized Sue.

"Hi, Sue, nice to see you," she chirped. "Doug with you tonight?"

Sue smiled and shook her head. "He's at home watching a game."

I handed Archie's keys to the bartender and told her not to find the gentleman's lost item until tomorrow. She winked at me and Sue, and put them in a drawer next to the beer taps. I guess a lot of car keys get lost this way.

Chapter Thirteen

I'd forgotten to replenish my wiper fluid, and the Merc's front window had accumulated a layer of salty, melted road slop over the course of the evening. It was kind of like driving through a filthy slurpee—the equivalent of automotive glaucoma. Even the rear window was a mess. That's why I didn't notice the tail that Sue Hewlett and I had collected. I just plain couldn't see it.

It was about half past eleven. I'd gotten off 494 at the second exit heading east and swung into an all-night gas station. I bought a gallon of bright blue wiper elixir, popped the hood, poured it in the proper receptacle, then squeegeed off the other windows. Sue asked me to get her a Snickers bar.

Our ghost appeared when I drove out of the gas station and headed south, back to the freeway entrance. Looking in the rearview mirror, I noticed a dark green Escort doing a U-turn in the street behind us. It must have tailed us to the gas station. He came down the entrance ramp about five or six car lengths behind, with only one car between us. Had only one headlight.

For the moment I gave the driver my benefit of the doubt. It could be a totally innocent citizen heading somewhere in a green Escort to meet a boyfriend or girlfriend. But anyone we encountered in a green Escort with a single peeper needed to be treated with a modicum of caution.

As we headed east, down the Bloomington/494 strip, I asked Sue how she'd gotten into advertising, how she ended up at Gottwaldt and Ryan.

"I grew up in San Diego," she said, biting off a small corner of her Snickers. The caramel went immediately to the roof of her mouth, and she worked at getting it off. "Went to a junior college there, in journalism. I had visions of putting the screws on corrupt politicians." She took another little bite. "Me and about a million other J-students."

"Your mom and dad still there?"

"My dad ran off right after I was born," she said matter of factly. "Never knew him. Mom raised me alone, she was a secretary. And *very* practical. She thought it was just plain stupid that I'd have to do time at some crummy little rag in the boonies, then go to Peoria or wherever, still get paid crap, and work my fanny off. Finally, if I was lucky, I'd maybe get a slot on a big-city newspaper and still not make *that* much money. Print journalism is a crummy place to be if you want to make a buck."

"At least there were still a few jobs then," I sniffed.

"I guess my mother knew something I didn't. She said if I liked writing and newspapers and stuff, why didn't I switch to marketing or advertising? I checked it out, it looked okay, looked like I could make some dough, so I changed majors. Herb was kind of my mentor. I'd met him first in high school. I'd thought about advertising or marketing back then. But you know how kids change their minds a lot. I also wanted to be a marine biologist. Anyway, Herb and I bumped into each other later on, when I was planning to move into an advertising major. And why deny it—there's always a demand for competent people of color."

"Any other African-Americans at the agency?"

"Yeah, six of us."

We cruised by one of the big Delta hangars out at the airport, and I could see people through the cracks in the huge doors, crawling all over a 757, like ants on a sugar cookie. On the opposite side of the freeway it looked like things had slowed down at the Megamall. Just a few pub-crawlers' cars were creeping in and out of the Brobdingnagian shopping center's ramps.

I peeked in the rear view mirror again, and that's when I knew what I had.

The one-eyed green Escort was still back there, like a sore thumb. Changing lanes when I did, slowing and speeding when I did. Not a pro, definitely not a pro. The best PI would have a tough time pulling off a one-on-one tail. Too many things can happen. Two drivers talking to each other is the way to go, if you can afford it. I wasn't that good at tails myself, but I'd have wiped this character.

But where to burn this guy, and how?

"Think you made the right choice?" I put to my passenger.

"Yeah, I think so," she nodded. "Some of it was just being there at the right time to meet Herb. After college I was lucky to have a job lined up here at his agency. Lots of my friends needed jobs in California, and didn't get them."

And how. I still missed Santa Barbara, for the climate, the sun, the fun. But life is easier and cheaper here in flyoverland, winters notwithstanding. A dollar goes further. The ground under your feet—literal and figurative—seems a lot more solid. You can find a pretty decent double skim lattè, too.

"So I packed my bags in the Toyota, kissed my Mom goodbye and—" She stopped, noticing that I'd swung north by the airport. "You know, you coulda just gone over to 35E. It's quicker."

"Yeah, I know," I said. "It's reflex goin' this way. We'll shoot up to Lake Street. Sorry."

"No problem," she said. "Anyway, I got into traffic at the agency, and loved it. Thought I wanted to be a copywriter, or account exec. But I'm not clever enough, don't have the patience for the ego hits copywriters have to take."

"What's that mean, 'traffic'?"

"Someone's got to keep track of everything, keep everything in line. The copy, the art, the media buys, the production. Are the actual ads finished when they're supposed to be? Do they go to the right media at the right time? Did they run properly? If not, do we get make-goods? All the logistical stuff. Making the trains run on time. Like for Hamburger Shack, right now I have to deal with a dozen different billboard ads in various stages of completion that go out to over thirty billboard companies around the country at specified times."

I asked her when her mother and sister joined her.

"Three, four years ago. I'd been trying to talk Mama into it since I got here, I missed them so much. Anyway, she got a good secretarial job at a bank downtown. She was laid off a little while ago, though. She's working temp now. Michelle's in this really nice prep school over on River Parkway. She's a junior. Mom and I share the tuition costs."

For a moment I held my tongue, and eyed the green Escort a

block or so to the rear.

"Has Michelle gotten over the cola incident?"

"Well, she's a little worried about me. But she's a pretty cool kid."

"How'd she get the intern gig? Isn't that kind of a plum for a kid her age, getting to work in a bigtime ad agency?"

"Pure nepotism," Sue laughed. "I pulled every string I knew how, begged Denny to give her the spot. He knows how special she is."

"Can I meet her sometime?"

"Oh sure. No problem."

"Does Herb still have any connection with San Diego?"

She pondered for a moment as we passed an airport runway. A jet came thundering down out of the low winter clouds and roared over our heads.

"He owns some property out there," Sue said, "a strip mall and some apartment houses. He had another agency, too, before he came back here. He sold that."

"That's when Meg must've worked for him the first time," I said.

"Yeah, exactly."

"De ad biz bin berry, berry good to Herb," I ad-libbed, as we tooled north up Hiawatha Avenue, past the sprawling VA Hospital.

She chortled. "Yup. Berry, *berry* good."

Our tail was still there, hanging back nearly a block, trying to look unobtrusive. Which isn't easy when you're one of the only two vehicles within eyeshot. With a single headlight. Along the way I'd tried to use my arcane skill of reading license plates backwards in the mirror with a nearly complete absence of illumination—with no success. The time was about a quarter to twelve.

We sat silently for a couple of minutes, cruising north up Minnehaha Avenue, beyond the waterfalls that Longfellow immortalized in *The Song of Hiawatha*. I slowed to the speed limit of thirty, a heresy among such a lead-footed breed as Minnesotans. Our little companion companionably slowed to the same speed, to maintain separation.

I asked Sue if she minded my stopping for a can of cola, and she shook her head absent-mindedly.

I just wanted to give our tail one last, prove-me-wrong chance.

We pulled into a convenience store at 39th and Minnehaha. I got out and bought my pop, and, God help me, a Twinkie. The green Escort didn't drive by. He'd pulled over down the block somewhere. When I got back on Minnehaha and turned east on 38th Street, he came along, still about a block back. I decided then to dazzle and bamboozle him (or her).

Between the big wars, builders packed this part of Minneapolis with thousands of little bungalows. Miles and miles of solid, two-bedroom starter houses that working people can still afford. Not a bad area, either, with the Mississippi River Parkway close by and one of the last pristine neighborhood movie houses, the Riverview. Rick and I rented here briefly, four blocks from Ol' Man River, after we became an item.

So I knew my way around. But to outsiders every one of these streets and alleys looks pretty much like any other. It wasn't hard to get lost here, or, I hoped, to lose someone.

"Hold this," I told Sue, handing her my soda. "We got a tail and I'm going to try to burn him."

"Huh?" was all she could get out before I hung a sharp right into an alley. Cola spilled on her lap—a casualty of battle.

I put out my lights and fishtailed through the icy slush, past tiny garages, fast as I could manage. Yard lights with motion detectors came on as we shushed by. Dogs barked, and an ambling cat leapt for dear life. I took a hard left at the end of the alley, crossed the avenue, then another hard left into the next alley to the east. Our tail had come into the first alley just as we had exited, going way too slow. I pulled into a darkened driveway, cut the motor and told Sue to slouch down in the seat.

We sat for about five minutes and the Escort seemed to have disappeared. I tried to call Archie at the bar to warn him, but he'd left about five minutes earlier. Maybe we'd been lucky and drawn the only tail.

We crept down the alley, lights out, then made our way back to Minnehaha Avenue.

"Who was it?" Sue asked, suddenly shaky.

"Probably one of bad guys. I couldn't see his license number."

"Why'd he follow us?" Fear resonated in her voice.

"Maybe he doesn't know where you live."

"Shit," she said, her black eyes wide in the dim light.

"Are you guys in the book?"

"No, Doug doesn't like fans bothering him at home."

And she didn't say much after that, except when I asked how she met Doug. Through Denny, she said, all vivacity drained out of her voice. They'd been friends for years. Good old Denny introduced them at a Vikings game, and apparently the electricity flowed. Go figure.

"You know," she said, "maybe I'd better stay at a hotel downtown. I can call Doug from there."

• • •

The drive home just seemed too much, so I decided to crash on my office sofa.

Apart from a white-haired drunk weaving along in front of the Ace Cafe, cheerily whistling an Everly Brothers tune, nothing was moving on the street in front of the old Amalgamated Manufacturing Building when I arrived. The melting snow and ice glistened under the street lamps, looking way prettier than it had any right to.

The Amalgamated covers half a city block. A hulking, blunt, utilitarian eight-story pile with lots of factory-style windows. The developer who renovated it in the early '90s chopped up the old production and warehouse spaces into dozens of offices, studios, lofts, and light manufacturing spaces. Down on street level were the Ace, a factory temp agency, a drop-in insurance adjustor and an organic bakery. Our little suite was on the third floor, almost directly above the cafe.

A pile of mail had come in through the slot in the door. Bills, a letter requesting certain stock photos that Rick had, computer and photo supply catalogs, a copy of *Photo District News*. I just kicked it all aside. The only thing I wanted to do before sacking out was check my voicemail and my e-mail. There was another message from Terry. He reminded me about the Red Hot Chili Peppers that weekend at Target Center, and he thought I was making a mistake not going with him. The invite was still good. I had to admire his perseverance, but I didn't have any energy left to worry about it right then.

In my e-mail I found a report from Deb Brown. I sat there bleary-eyed: Do I read it now, or wait? Better do it now, I thought, and write Denny's report in the morning. Gotta show the client you're doing something other than sucking up hours and expenses.

Heaving off my coat, I turned on the radio—a David Sanborn retrospective, all smoky and sexy—and sat down at my desk, booting up my old Mac. I rubbed my eyes, then skimmed Deb's e-mail.

Meg LaGrange had several arrests and convictions for trespassing, for damaging property, for simple assault, going back to her college days in Madison. Her first had to do with a sit-in at a Wisconsin plant that manufactured herbicides. She got over-enthusiastic, trashed some files and smashed a PC. She did 100 hours of public service. There were a few other arrests at various pro-environment actions, but only suspended sentences. Within the last few years she'd been active in the Sugarlake Project, a long-term protest against the big coal mining company of the same name—infamous for stripping off mountain tops in the Appalachians. She'd never been busted for that. During her time out west she helped found the Escondido chapter of PAP, People Against Pollution. If memory served, Escondido is just a stone's throw up the road from San Diego.

Very strange that a lady like this would shill cigarettes.

After closing the blinds, I tore off my duds, threw on one of Rick's old T-shirts and tossed my sleeping bag on the sofa. I doused the lights and crawled in.

I don't know how long I'd been snoozing when the cell rang. Miraculously, I managed to find the thing in the darkened office and punch the proper button. "Marta Hjelm," I groaned.

"Marta? This's Bruce." He was talking fast, nearly panicked, on an adrenaline-rush. A rare occurence. "I'm at Gottwaldt's place. An' holyfuckinhell you better get your patootie out here soon's you can. The hit has shit the fan, baby! I just called 911. The house's goin' up like a goddamned bonfire."

Chapter Fourteen

Bruce had sat tight all the livelong night in his rusty, trusty Civic, down by the shore road. He couldn't have done it during the day. Beaters like his parked for long spells out near Lake Minnetonka get noticed. He'd called in the alarm, phoned me, and sat back for the whole movie—in spectacular 3D.

That comprised four fire trucks, a fleet of police and sheriff's squads, an ambulance, several TV news crews. Right ahead of him a pumper truck had punched a two-foot hole in the ice, to suction water out of the lake.

I got there about 6:30 a.m., but had to park a good hike down the road, because of all the gawker traffic and glowering police officers. I tiptoed along, dodging cars, trying to stay safely on the icy shoulder. The instant I hopped in Bruce's Honda he started to yammer about the fire and calling in the alarm and what a fantastic show it had been. Sometimes even professionals get carried away.

I told him to shut up *please*.

"What about Gottwaldt?" I said when he calmed down.

"One of the cops told me both his cars were in the garage," he said as soberly as he was capable of. "The Mercedes, the Humvee. It's separate from the house. So unless he's at a lady friend's or something—" Bruce trailed off, and made a weird, disgusting sizzling sound.

"*Bruuuuce*," I groaned, making a face at him. "The fire?"

"They got it out pretty quick, but I guess the house's in crummy shape. They think it started slow, then it gutted the main floor in the central part of the house. I guess the upstairs mostly has smoke damage and water damage."

"So it might've started a while ago?"

"Yeah, I guess."

I managed to convince the local cop at the bottom of the drive that I worked for Mr. Gottwaldt, and he let us through.

We crept slowly up the winding, black-topped driveway, a few dozen yards, bumping over the serpentine tangle of hoses, until the Civic's front wheels spun uselessly on the frozen overspill. In a matter of hours the temps had turned nasty again, and all things liquid or slushy were hard as steel. Not nasty like two days before, but definitely ice cube territory. Bruce reversed down the hill, fulminating beneath his breath, and parked where we had started.

We hiked back up toward the house, tippy-toeing carefully over hoses and icy patches. Another cop stopped us halfway. She was thirtyish, with an upturned nose, winter-red cheeks and short-cropped blonde hair under a Russkie-style police-issue fake fur cap. The air was brisk enough again that she'd pulled the flaps down over her ears. I did my spiel again, told her we worked for Gottwaldt and Ryan, and showed her my license. She said I'd find Deputy Sheriff Grabowski up with the firefighters. I nodded.

"Okay," I said to Bruce, as we tramped around the driveway side of the unburnt garage. "Before I talk to the people, give me the *Reader's Digest* version one more time."

My best little helper pushed his Buddy Holly-type bifocals back up to the bridge of his nose. He'd taped one fractured bow together with a wad of blue masking tape. It drove me nuts, his pushing his glasses up every ten seconds. Somehow I'd successfully resisted a horrible urge to snatch his specs, stomp on them and put them out of their misery. Some day, though.

"I got here about midnight," he said. He reached into a coat pocket for his matches and Freshaire weeds, the Bertram brand. "Mind if I smoke?"

"We're in the great outdoors, amigo, puff your brains out."

Bruce is shortish, balding, skinny, with an odd little potbelly; like a half basketball under his shirt. But strong and wiry. I'd guess his age in the mid- to late-40s. He won't tell me. He had on burgundy jeans, a green plaid Pendleton shirt and a beat-up Sears trench coat open at the throat. A typical Bruce ensemble from hell. His salt-and-pepper beard and moustache needed a trim. They always did. The first time I saw him I never would have guessed his line of work. "Homeless" maybe? A perfect nebbish. He could clerk in a store with pilferage problems, do a tail, do a surveillance, and be practically invisible. That's why he stayed busy, for me and others. I'd been lucky to find him without a gig.

He pulled a Freshaire out of his shirt pocket and lit it. I wondered if it really "Put a little excitement in your life," as some other ad agency had been asserting for years.

"Anyway," he continued, "I got here about midnight. I saw only two cars go in or out. The first one was a black Porsche Cayenne, the second one an Acura Integra, light blue."

I guessed that Archie had found his keys after all.

"Plates?"

"Too dark."

"Okay. How about the drivers?"

"Couldn't see 'em at all. Coulda been Simon Cowell and Lindsay Lohan, for all I know." He grinned foxily at the mention of Lohan, his improbable *femme ideale*. Apparently he hadn't gotten the memo that Lohan swung the other way. "The Porsche arrived about one, the Acura fifteen minutes later. Porsche didn't stay real long. He or she peeled on out just a few minutes after Acura got here. He musta been like totally snockered, though. He nearly drove into the lake. Wish I'd been a cop.

"Another fifteen, twenty minutes and the Acura came on down," Bruce continued. "Whoever was driving was mad, or scared. He spun his tires up on the driveway. I heard him. They both went back toward Wayzata." Bruce rubbed his peepers with his knuckles, without taking off his chi-chi eyewear. "Man, I'm tired."

"Tell me about it," I commiserated. "So what then?"

"Not a damned thing, until about an hour and a half ago. I was gettin' stiff, an' I had to take a leak. So I thought I'd sneak up the driveway, fertilize a bush and have a look-see. I kinda went around the side of the garage, and peeked over at the house, around the corner. And brother, things'd gone seriously sour. 'Cause flames and smoke were comin' out of the main floor windows."

"No fire alarms, smoke alarms?"

"No, nothing. Not a peep. So I skiied back to the car,

grabbed my mobile and phoned 911. You coulda been here twenty minutes sooner, if you'd left from home." He grinned at me. "Out cattin' around, or what?"

I shook my head, and started to go red in the face. "Sleepin' at the office."

"Rick kick you out?"

I bared my fangs. "None of your frickin' beeswax."

He nodded sagely. "Want to talk about it?"

I looked out at the fire trucks, the squad cars, the scurrying men and women in heavy yellow raincoats with big dayglo letters taped on the back. About half a dozen local cops and sheriff's deputies had clustered around a tall, imposing guy in a gray overcoat, probably Grabowski. And not a smile in the bunch. "Dammit, Bruce," I said, "odds are my client's just croaked, and you want to play Dear Abby. Anyway, you're the last person I'd ask for advice on relationships."

He slapped me on the shoulder and made a sound like a jolly bullfrog. "Hey, who do you know who has so much experience with 'em?"

We went out into the courtyard. It was my first good look at the place.

Gottwaldt had built his manse close to the lake shore, out of sight of the road, at the end of a long S-shaped driveway. The architectural style was modernistic—three levels of glass and stainless steel and cedar units that nestled together to form something greater than the parts. An alluring rustic site, an architect's wet dream. On a good, sunny summer or autumn day the pines and oaks that surrounded it would have made for a beautiful setting. But that morning, in the dismal, overcast winter light, the trees looked like a coven of gnarled old witches caught in the act of admiring their malevolent handiwork—a charred, smoking ruin.

The stench of combustion made my stomach turn. It always did, ever since our house burned down when I was a kid. I wonder why burnt cottages can't smell like logs in a fireplace. Isn't wood *wood?* They always have that acrid, nose-twisting aroma.

We skated over to the tall guy with the cops—out in the

courtyard at the back of the house. He gave us the once-over. He had steely gray eyes that matched his gray parka, and silver hair cropped close in a classic crew cut. Perfect color coordination. His lips were thin and straight, his nose lean and aquiline, his face tan and weathered. Marine retiree, an old leatherneck MP, I bet, about to double-dip. Anyone else his age ought to have been riding a desk.

"You the officer in charge here?" I queried.

He nodded. "Deputy John Grabowski, Hennepin County sheriff's office." His voice was gravelly and tired. "Who are you?"

I told him my name, how I'd been retained by Mr. Gottwaldt and Mr. Ryan, and fished around in my Domke satchel for my license. He peered at it like it was a spent pulltab that hadn't paid a nickel. I waited for him to offer his hand—surprisingly tidy and soft-looking for such a macho guy—and he didn't.

"So why are you here, Ms. Hjelm?"

Chapter Fifteen

"What I've been working on has been confidential up to this point," I said grimly. "But in light of this…" I nodded at the smoldering mansion. "I guess you'd better hear me out."

He nodded as taciturnly as humanly possible, but I saw a spark of interest.

The deal with Denny and Herb, after all, had been: If an additional "terrorist" incident occurred, the authorities would hear about it. All bets were off.

In under five minutes I managed to tell him about the Hemo account, the letters and e-mail, the green Escort, the tainted cola, the sabotaged Lexus, and the second encounter with the Escort. He jotted brief notes on a little tablet he pulled out of an inside parka pocket.

"Do you have a card, Ms. Hjelm?"

I dug down in my satchel and handed him one.

"We'll be in touch soon," he said in a monotone, "and I'd appreciate it if you could come downtown for a longer visit."

I said okay, but could I ask him a question right now. He said fine, though he didn't know if he could answer it.

"Do you know," I said, "if Mr. Gottwaldt was in there?"

He shook his head. "Not for sure." He paused, and looked me over again, and Bruce. "Both his cars are here, and we've called relatives and people from his business, including Mr. Ryan. Nobody's seen him since last night."

I turned to Bruce. "You better tell him what you saw. Especially about the Porsche and and the Acura." Then I peered at Grabowski. "This is my operative Bruce Prochnik. He was on a surveillance here last night."

The cop and the nebbish investigator caucused for a few minutes and the only thing I clearly heard was when the Deputy raised his voice: "Black Porsche Cayenne?" When they finished, I skated over to Grabowski.

"The Porsche probably belongs to Gottwaldt's son Archie," I said. I explained how I had sequestered his keys at the sports bar. "The blue Acura, don't know whose that is."

Grabowski muttered something like "Harummph," and took a few notes.

"Found a cause yet?" I asked, nodding toward the smoldering house.

"We're waiting for the fire to cool down. The firemen—" He blinked as a female firefighter jogged in front of us, carrying an oxygen cylinder back to her truck. "The fire*people* have got to make sure the structure's safe when they go in to look around. The mobile crime lab should get here in a little while."

We stood around stoney and silent, staring at the eddies of smoke still wafting off the charred framing. The house had been L-shaped, with a cobblestoned courtyard/parking area in the crook of the L. The landscape architect had placed a gaggle of young paper birches in the middle of the courtyard, with a gorgeous vine-covered cedar arbor over a marble-topped picnic table. Six black wrought-iron chairs had been chained and padlocked together next to the table, waiting for that first *al fresco* dinner of the season that would never come. I wished I'd seen Gottwaldt's house the day before.

"You think it was arson?" I asked Grabowski.

He didn't answer, but turned to the uniformed county and local cops, all of them shuffling their feet on the ice to keep their little piggies warm. He told a couple of them to nose around the grounds, see if there were any signs of break-in or unusual activity. He instructed the others to go down the driveway and keep gawkers out, but to let in any news crews or people connected with Gottwaldt. He was also expecting someone from the state criminal bureau. Rubbing his hands together, he peered at me, and Bruce. "Sorry, what did you say?"

"Think it was arson?"

"Could be. He should've had a better security system. It might've made a difference."

"How's that?" Bruce said.

"We called his security company," Grabowski answered. "He just had a system that guarded against entries, some motion detectors. Burglar alarm, that's all. No fire alarms except a few battery-operated smoke alarms. You know, the kind you get at

Home Depot. Nothing hooked into a phone line or internet that would've gotten the fire department here quicker."

"Maybe the batteries were shot," Bruce theorized. "He didn't get woken up."

"Maybe," Grabowski answered, waving at somebody behind us. "Listen, I gotta talk with this guy. Stick around if you like. Just don't get in anyone's way." He shuffled back across the icy courtyard and climbed into his unmarked car with a township cop.

Bruce and I stood around for a while, feeling our toes going numb, and watching the media circus. We had a couple of videocams stuck in our faces, but pleaded ignorance, and pointed them at Grabowski. We spent a few minutes back in the Civic, warming up, and split a semi-frozen Salted Nutroll. Finally, about nine, Denny Ryan turned up, with Terry and Gottwaldt's daughter, Jennifer Nelson.

The princess was stick-thin, tallish and strawberry-blonde. Lucky for her, she hadn't inherited her father's predator looks. She had a pale Scandinavian face, with Arctic-blue eyes, button nose, full lips coated in dusty rose lipstick and a gentle splash of freckles. She was wrapped in a double-breasted Burberry coat of gray leather. I'd tried on that identical item a few months before and boy-oh-boy, *was it me*. The three grand price tag, alas, wasn't.

Jennifer's cream-complexioned features, though, sure didn't looked like they were excessively worried that Daddy may just have gone up in smoke.

After introductions that were chilly in more ways than one, we walked back up to the house, with Jennifer and Denny taking the lead.

Terry strolled up beside me, looking concerned about his ex-wife's well-being. He also seemed to be considering putting an arm around her shoulder—perhaps out of old habit—but I glared at him and he thought better of it.

"So you doin' okay, Marty?" he asked.

I didn't have the energy to lecture him about my name. "Yeah."

He sort of hunched over and whispered in my ear, "You think Herb was in there?"

"Don't know, Terry. Is Bertram outta here now?"

He nodded, and kept his tone to a whisper, so Denny wouldn't hear. "*Oh yeah*. We can't be hooked up with this. Don't tell *Denny*, though. I'll do that." He kicked the ice under his boot. "So— Think you can make the Chili Peppers?"

I dug my heels into a patch of frozen soil and scowled at him. "Jee-sus, Terry. There might be a dead man in there and you're trying to score a date with your ex-wife."

"Not a date," he mumbled, with an exaggerated, childish frown. "Just getting together with an old friend. Does that mean no?"

I shook my head, looked heavenward, and walked out ahead of Terry to join Denny. When Jennifer was a bit out of earshot I quietly told him that I'd spilled the beans to Grabowski.

He stopped, shook his head. "Shit. Yeah," he said. "Suppose you had to, huh?"

"I suppose I did," I returned.

Denny's razor-sharp look had sagged again under the pressure. His features seemed more gaunt than yesterday or the day before, the understated jowls responding to gravity. All he needed was a Guinness in one hand, a slouch cap and some baggy tweeds to play the properly morose, down-at-the-heels son of the old sod.

"I don't know what the hell to do, Marta," he said hoarsely, as Terry went by with his poor-hurt-baby look. "I never expected—" He rubbed his stubbled cheeks with both hands, powerfully, as if he wanted to squeeze his face together. "Shit! *Shit!*"

"Does Jennifer know what's been happening?" I whispered to Denny.

He nodded.

"If you want to talk to somebody, that's the guy over there, in the car." I pointed at Grabowski's unmarked Ford. "Deputy Grabowski." I blew out a geyser of condensed air. "Anyone you know drive a blue Acura?"

He blinked, puzzled by the question. "Why do you wanna

know?"

"*Anyone you know drive a blue Acura, Denny?*"

"Well, yeah, Meg does."

"Oh shit!" I moaned. "You better go over and tell Grabowski."

"But why?"

"Archie was here last night, and so was Meg. The cops'll be very interested in them."

Looking shell-shocked, he headed for Grabowski, leaving me to entertain Terry and Gottwaldt's daughter. So Bruce and I went through our schtik again, recounting the story so far.

"I told him not to go after Bertram," Jennifer sighed when we'd finished. Her tone wasn't regretful, just fatalistic. "I told him he was chasing blood money. You're trying to make a profit off of addicted people, kids that don't know what they're getting hooked on. You think Bertram isn't targeting teenagers? C'mon, *vampire cigarettes?*"

Terry grimaced, yet had the sense not to argue.

"But Herb didn't listen to you," I said.

She shook her head. "Dad doesn't listen to anything he doesn't want to hear. Doesn't matter who's saying it." She pushed a strawberry blonde bang off her forehead with a calf-skin-gloved left hand. You could see the substantial lump of what I assumed to be a very large rock, under the glove. "Well, unless you're a client. Nobody else counts." A half-smile warmed up her ice-princess expression. "Mom used to say that some day she was going to start a company and hire Dad, then he'd *have to* pay attention to her." She seemed to want to laugh, but she couldn't quite manage it. "I don't want to sound naive, Marta. But I kind of hoped he'd take me more seriously when I owned stock. No such luck."

"How much do you have?"

"Dad gave me five percent of the agency a few years ago, and five to Archie. But that left him with sixty percent, just like he has now. Five percent doesn't get you much leverage. It's his shop."

"When did he give you those shares," I wondered, "and how

old was the agency at that time?"

She pondered the math a little, double-checked it, staring up at one of the big, witchlike oaks. "He started it twelve, thirteen years ago, when he came back from the coast. I got married eight years ago. It was about then."

"How's the agency been doing?"

"Good enough. But business's been stagnant. We're making a decent profit. No one's going hungry. But we haven't picked up any big new national accounts in a couple of years. Hamburger Shack was the last one. Hamburger Shack and Honeymoon Cruises are really keeping our noses above water. Chippewa Motorcycles is pretty good. Minneapolis Mutual Insurance is important, too. There are maybe a dozen smaller accounts, too, but that's only a few million each in billings."

"Hemo would be a big boost?"

"Yeah, for sure. Blood money, but still green."

Funny, I thought. Doug Hewlett had used a similar turn of phrase. "You plan to stay with the agency for the long run?"

She was giving me some kind of there-but-for-the-grace-of-God-go-I look, and I winced a bit.

"Of course I am. I put the stock in my kids' trusts." She paused, looked from me to Bruce and back. I think she expected us to be impressed with her parental devotion.

"It's not like it's a big deal, of course," she continued. "Duane, my husband, he co-owns Nelsontek with his brother, and he's done awfully well. They have some big contracts, they fabricate circuit boards for major electronics companies and the military. The kids' Gottwaldt and Ryan stock is barely worth two million."

"I can understand that," I said with a perfectly straight face, then I nodded companionably at Bruce. Bruce nodded back sympathetically—*two million, yecch!* Terry hadn't failed to notice my ironic tone. He knew me all too well. He stifled a grin. But Jennifer seemed to have missed my little jest.

That's the trouble with rich people. They have no idea how ridiculous they look to ordinary people. They've been conducting class warfare, reaming out the middle class, making like locusts for decades, but at least we can make jokes at their expense.

Off to our right, thirty or so yards beyond the house, in what passed for Gottwaldt's back forty, I noticed that three police officers had gathered where an old creek bed emerged from a dense, embanked copse of maples and young oaks. They'd discovered something. One of them had squatted down in the snow, another came scurrying back to the courtyard, and grabbed the police photographer and Grabowski. They took long strides, crunching through the crusted snow, like Boy Scouts on a hike. I wanted to go see, too, but I couldn't.

It looked like they'd found themselves something interesting, several items. A uniformed officer picked them up with gloved hand, and dropped them in a plastic evidence bag, one by one. I saw a glint of brass as the sun peeped through a sliver of clear sky. Maybe shell casings.

I cranked myself up for the next question: "Can you think of anyone in the agency who could have anything to do with these incidents?"

Jennifer blinked at me like I was a certifiable Danish crumb-cake. Then a sub-zero cold front blew out from between her dusty rose lips: "I've never heard anything so *absurd* in my whole life, Ms. Hjelm, and I think I'll just forget I ever heard it. Suffice it to say that employees, and the rest of us, thought the world of Daddy and would never have done him any harm. Either by hurting the business or hurting him."

I guess she hurled eye-daggers at me for the amount of time it usually took her to put a sales clerk or waitress in fear for her job. But I just don't frighten easily, try as I might. Too dumb, I guess. So Mrs. Nelson excused herself with a curt nod and skittered back down the driveway in her Uggs—a very sensible, if homely, shoe for a cold day.

She'd barely disappeared around the bend when Grabowski gave me a high sign from over by the house, and I waved at Denny. The three of us hiked over. Terry went with Jennifer and starting doing that which he had always done so well: Chatting up a good-looking lady.

"We found these little goodies out there, by that ski trail that goes through the woods," the Deputy said when we arrived. He held up the plastic bag that contained seven intact 9mm cartridges. "I'm assuming somebody emptied their clip out there. Any chance any of you guys know of someone with connection s to Mr. Gottwaldt who has a 9mm handgun?"

Denny, blinking nervously, assured the Deputy he never had, never even owned a gun.

"How about you, Hjelm?"

"Well, *Grabowski*," I said without much pleasure, "you can make that a big affirmative."

Grabowski's hard gray eyes opened a little bit, but not much. Just like Dirty Harry. "So?"

"I saw a frosted stainless 9mm yesterday. A feminine handgun, a darling little weapon for milady's Bauhaus boudoir—"

He gave me a scowl: *Cut the crap.*

I sighed. "It belongs to Meg LaGrange, Gottwaldt's lead copywriter for Hemo. The cigarette account, in case you're not up to speed."

"Really?" the Deputy purred, oblivious to the stunned, knock-me-over-with-a-feather expression on Denny's face. "The lady with the blue Acura. How'd you—"

Before Grabowski could finish his question, one of the dirty-faced, yellow-slickered firepeople came running/skating/sliding up and said that Grabowski better come along pronto! They'd found something inside the house.

We three rubberneckers followed the Deputy, and I was properly impressed that a guy his age could still clamber up a slippery embankment like a rookie. Bruce—lacking traction from his Hush Puppies—fell on his ass, and slid back down.

The arson investigator was waiting for us with the guy he'd sent inside. My heart came up in my throat. Bruce arrived around the corner of the house in a slow hobble, dusting off snow and ice, bitching about his bad back. I told him to put a lid on it.

Grabowski was even grimmer than before. He said, "We found a body in there, pretty badly burned. Male."

"Was he shot?" I asked.

"Too soon to say. There'll be an autopsy."

"Any spent shells on the floor?"

"Dunno yet."

Denny took a deep gulp. "Do you think it's—"

"Who do you think it is, Denny?" I spat before I could stop myself. "*Santa Claus?*"

Grabowski scowled at me. He was a world-class scowler. "I really don't want to speculate the victim's identity at this point, Mr. Ryan."

Chapter Sixteen

"Oh my God," Denny wheezed. "I— I better go tell Jennifer." He began scampering away and didn't take a tumble only because of divine providence.

Grabowski shot me that terrific scowl one more time.

For my snottiness I grumbled a few words that resembled an apology. It didn't feel good to have a paying client suddenly transformed into, shall we say, a— No, let's not say it. But it definitely wasn't smart to PO the officer in charge.

Grabowski took my mumblings in equally good grace, kicking at a chunk of charred wooden gutter. It scuttered a few yards across the icy ground, twisting to a stop. "Yeah," he said, "I got a similar opinion about who we got here, *probably*. But the medical examiner'll get Gottwaldt's dental x-rays sometime today, and then we'll know."

"Can Bruce and I look around some?" I wondered.

Grabowski nodded curtly. "You know the drill, right? No messing with anything interesting. You spot something, give me or one of the guys a shout."

"C'mon, Bruce," I said, and off we went who knows where, searching for who knows what.

We'd spent about half an hour crunching around in the snow and brush around the house and the lake, shivering as we went, looking for whatever it was that needed finding—ideally a signed confession note tacked to a tree. My toes were getting numb all over again, and I couldn't imagine how Bruce's feet felt inside those flimsy Hush Puppies—which, God knows why, had suddenly become fashionable again. But it was all I could do to assuage a gnawing certainty that I, Marta Hjelm, licensed and bonded screwup, had somehow let one of my clients die. *Again.* The incipient frostbite—whether real or imagined—provided a welcome, contrary discomfort.

Finally I gave in and put a stop to my wintry self-flagellation. "I think I better get to the car, Bruce."

"You okay, Marta?" Bruce asked.

"Okay as I can be."

"Think this gig is over, then?"

"Stick a fork in it, Bruce. Get me your hours and I'll talk with you later."

"You wanta catch some breakfast? There's a Panera up the road a piece."

I just shook my head, reversed course and followed my own footprints back to the path. When I walked by them in the courtyard, Denny and Jennifer were still standing there, looking kind of dazed. No point in bothering them.

Terry was gone.

My feet were totally anesthetized by the time I got to the Merc. I started it and let it idle for a few minutes. I somehow contorted myself, got my boots off and rubbed some warmth back into my toes. They tingled, then came pins and needles, as I stared straight out through the windshield. For a little while I daydreamed myself back into a waiting room at the University Hospital.

A gray, chill January morning a lot like this one, about eight o'clock. The nurse walks up, a perky young Filipina who'd laughed at my Dad's corny jokes and Spoonerisms because she really, truly liked them—and him. I put down the six-month-old copy of *People*. She doesn't look perky. In fact, looks pretty grim.

Ms. Hjelm? she says, her voice a little trembly. I nod, catching my breath. You better come now, ma'am.

He'd hung on through the godawful night and the godawful pain so I could be there in the morning. Donald Roger Hjelm had summoned up everything he had, and he *waited* for me—good soldier that he was. I mean, this was a guy who patched up the wounded kids on Pelelieu during WWII when he was just a kid. He was a Wildcat, from the 81st Division. He knew how to hang in there.

They say fathers teach us how to be adults. Competence, independence, mastery, all that. I suppose it's lots harder to lose a child or a spouse. But you never feel more next-in-line-for-the-big-sleep than when the last parent's place is empty. When the old man goes down—more so than mom, for some reason—then you really become a grown-up.

And I sure as hell was sick of it.

• • •

What I needed most was a few hours of sleep. Wouldn't do anyone any good the way I felt. So I headed back to Prospect Park.

"The Park," as we denizens call it, is really a sort of bedroom neighborhood for the University of Minnesota, embracing a gracious, tree-shrouded promontory a mile or so east of the sprawling main campus. Its roomy, heavily shaded yards tend toward the overgrown, with craggy oaks, dense hedges of lilac and honeysuckle, lawns long since conquered by creeping charley. Lots of old houses look just enough in need of repair to have a certain eccentric charm.

You can wander the tangle-town streets—up and down the hill, again and again—and never quite remember street names. Only landmarks, like the Witch's Hat Tower or the Frank Lloyd Wright house perched just behind the freeway noise wall. I-94 had sliced the neighborhood in half in the mid-'60s, taking dozens of homes with it. Down the hill a little further is the Mississippi River gorge.

I own a slightly shabby duplex in the Park's "low-rent district" on Emerald Street, right on the Minneapolis side of the city line, across from a wholesale lumberyard in St. Paul. Rick and I could only afford living in the Park because we had a tenant upstairs paying in on what remained of my mortgage. My Dad had fronted me a loan for about half the duplex's value.

The minute I opened the door the birds started at it. Manic, whistled greetings from the cockatiels. Earthy "I want to hold your hand's" from Taco the parrot. The aviary inmates needed a bit of quality time with me, but I only had the energy for a "Hi guys," and a slow, desolate trudge into the bedroom.

Don't remember flopping on the bed fully clothed. Don't remember the birds screaming for me. Don't remember the phone ringing. I just remember waking up and needing to go to the bathroom about mid-afternoon. I picked up the phone to check voicemail. Two messages.

"This is Rick, hon, and it's about one. I nabbed a quick lunch with Cal. Put him onto your lead, and got some good stuff back. Call me at work and we can meet somewhere and talk it over. Hope you're okay. Love you."

"Oh, Rick," I said. "Me you too."

I barely listened to the second message. The elderly, housebound woman I delivered library books to just across the river had to change dates. Not so housebound as we let the library believe, the retired professor was going on a five-day cruise with her niece. Wish I could've gone with them.

Rick's voicemail answered when I called the museum, and I suggested we meet at six at Betty's, a Chinese joint on Grand Avenue in St. Paul. He called back a few minutes later, heading out on a quick grip 'n grin somewhere, and said that'd be fine. I didn't tell him what had happened.

I blinked at the mirror. I'd seen bag ladies who looked more with it than I did. My hair—a sort of tired, darkish blonde at the best of times—was tangled, matted, going every which way. The bags under my bloodshot eyes carried luggage of their own. My eyeliner had smudged like little Rorschach blots. My neck looked like a chicken's. The knot in my back still burned like red-hot charcoal. And there was no way to get my mouth out of its pout.

You would not automatically assume that this particular specimen had two guys hot after her.

• • •

I got to Betty's a little before six and grabbed a table in back. My significant other arrived a few minutes later, toting what he called his "light kit"—a black Domke bag containing two Nikon D3 bodies, five lenses, two strobes, umpteen filters, and a future hernia yet to be named. We exchanged a squeeze of the hands and pecks on the cheek, and ordered our usuals—stir-fried crab in sweet bean sauce and a big bowl of corn soup with chicken.

"How'd Cal like the dainty little nothing I provided?" I asked as the perpetually grinning waiter scurried away.

"As you perspicaciously observed, it has a piquant charm," said my old man. "Cal thanks you for the *quid pro quo*." He sort of ground his jaw a bit. "So did anything happen on the case since last night?"

I almost laughed at his totally accidental understatement. Then it all gushed out. It felt good to share the crummy day with him. Looking at his face, I almost thought that this thing might come out okay.

"So what did Cal say?" I asked, grabbing across the table for his left hand.

"What he had is stale, really. But I think it'll help us."

He peered at me for a reaction, and I guess I gave him a kind of Mona Lisa smile. This, despite having not a drop of Italian blood in me.

"Remember my idea, Marty? Can we work a deal? You help me, I help you, we hop in the sack together every night."

"I for sure like that last bit," I said. "But you turned the tables on me. I want to get in *your* business."

"I'm not planning on channeling Sam Spade or anything, but I really would like to help," he replied intently. "Hell, you can bill for my time—when I'm free for a gig—and you don't have to pay me anything. Just like I can bill your time as an assistant when you're doing a shoot with me. Or at a day rate when you're shooting on your own. Why not? After that, we let the chips fall where they may. If you really, *truly* want to get out of investigative work—which I *genuinely* don't believe for a second—you can. I won't stop you. Then we might as well work together."

"And vice versa?" I put to him.

"I'm at least willing to be honest and admit I can't imagine not having a Nikon glued to my eye. But I do the PR schtik at the museum, because the Great Recession sucks, and I don't mind earning a few reliable bucks that way. Why not throw in a little investigating, too?"

"You're beginning to convince me," I admitted, doing my best not to sound grumpy. After all, he had as much right coming into my profession as I did invading his.

"So do we have a deal, Ms. Hjelm?" He grinned that damned, irresistible Tom Sawyer grin at me.

"Yeah, maybe," I said, mugging valiantly. "Let's see how it

goes this time. Then we'll hash it over some more."

"Deal," he said, and stuck his big, calloused hand across the table at me. I grabbed it and we shook.

"So," I said, "what did Cal give you?"

Rick blew on his green tea and lightly sipped it. "Well, Herb Gottwaldt makes the rounds, does the top parties, hangs with the big hitters. He buddies up to the sports stars and show biz types, CEOs and politicians. Politically, big in Democrat circles. He controls the agency, and has real estate investments all around town. He makes it into Cal's column a few times a year."

"Past tense, Rick. Like I said, it's probably past tense."

He frowned and nodded slowly. "He had a DWI a few years ago, and took a swipe at the cop."

"Like father, like son," I chimed in.

"So Cal knows the salient points in Gottwaldt's celebrity profile. What's not well known about him is the California side of his business. Owns property in Escondido and down in San Diego. Apartment buildings, a strip mall, part of a golf course, pieces of condo projects. They say he's as well heeled from his real estate out there as the ad shop here. He had a small agency out there, too. Long since folded, even before he moved back here. That's how he learned the biz.

"He built those businesses up mostly after he came out of the Navy. The ad agency did pretty good at first. Went gangbusters, Cal said. Herb developed his style, began winning awards. But for some reason it just faded. He had some real financial problems with it."

"Did Cal know what happened?"

Rick shook his head. "But that failure's what brought Herb back here."

"And the real estate wasn't affected?"

"Apprently not. He's got a holding company out there runs it all. Three, four people work for him, managing his interests there. Tough times for real estate these days, but apparently Herb's is holding its own."

"He's from California?"

The ridiculously large tureen of corn-and-chicken soup

arrived, and we paused to distribute it into the bowls.

Rick took a tiny sip from his flat-bottomed ceramic soup spoon, puckered, and nodded. "A little hot. Not too bad."

"So?"

"He's from near Albert Lea. Little burg called Conger. Farm boy anxious as hell to get off the farm at the very first opportunity. Joins the Navy out of high school, goes to Vietnam just toward the end, serves on an aircraft carrier. Re-ups once."

"Rising to what rank?"

"Hell if I know."

My stomach was growling madly. I cased my soup with a certain predatory air. After a few slurps I asked, "So what's your point?"

"Gottwaldt still has business ties and friends on the Coast. Some of them he's brought out here to work at his agency."

"Like who?"

"Like Meg LaGrange."

"I knew that."

"But, dear one, did you know that she was one of his California sweeties?"

That caused me to put down my spoon. "Approximately when?"

"They broke it off just before he came home to Minnesota. But they both allowed for water under the bridge. He needed her talent."

"If not her affections."

Rick nodded. "And she wanted to get out of San Diego."

"What in the world for?" I said.

He shrugged. "She's a Cheesehead, Marty. Maybe she missed the gouda."

"Or the beer joints on every corner."

"I would." Rick extended the thumb and little finger of his right hand and mimed imbibing from a beer stein.

"So does Cal think Meg still carries the torch for Herb?" I wondered. "Maybe we got a little green-eyed-monster action here?"

"I asked him that, and he said he doubted it." He took a beat for a sip of corn soup.

"'And why is that?' asked Marta Hjelm. Rick Mueller just happens to have an answer. Drumroll, please." He did a passable job on the table with his chopsticks. Some college kids at another table looked over, spotted the perp, and rolled their eyes. We were almost their parents' age. It embarrassed them to see us having fun. Most unseemly. "Because her current squeeze, Marta dearest, is *none* other than Lee Gorney."

"No shit?"

"No shit. Within spittin' distance of billionaire. AmberGrain heir. She has herself a *major* honeybun. Way outta Herb's league."

Our main dish arrived and two of us went to work on it without saying much.

So what was the rub, if any, between her and Gottwaldt? If those were bullets from her 9mm automatic that Grabowski's people found, why did she bring it when she visited Gottwaldt? She expected to be threatened by her old lover and current boss? She intended to kill him, plain and simple? Or was she just carrying it in self-defense, as any other Hemo team member might reasonably do in the current circumstances? Did *she* even bring the weapon?

All of a sudden my squeeze and I found our plates stacked with the chitinous ruins of formerly splendid crabs, and we set to wiping our faces and hands with the moist towelettes liberally provided by Betty's.

"So what did Cal say about Gottwaldt's current relationships?" I said.

"Well," answered Rick, with the surety of the sharp student who has all the answers, "he's long since divorced from his first wife."

"She still alive?"

He nodded. "Lives in Edina somewhere, winters in Tucson. Likes to be near the two grandkids part of the year. Meg was just one of a series. She lasted longest, though. Three or four years. There was a TV news anchor from here in town."

"How about recently?"

Rick lifted up the teapot so our waiter could see it needed replenishing. Permanent broad grin in place, the waiter dashed over and grabbed it. I took the opportunity to order us two ginger ice creams with almond cookies.

"Cal didn't know about anyone specifically." Rick yawned, stretched, and reached over into a pocket in his camera bag for a little bottle of Excedrin. He washed down three pills. "Camera bag headache. So, one of the people in the case is married to Doug Hewlett?"

"Sue Hewlett. A real attractive, bright woman. African-American. Don't know how she ended up married to Doug, though."

"A pretty fair defenseman," Rich pronounced with the authority of a true-blue hockey fan. "Duluth State. Played a few seasons in the NHL, coached a minor league team. Too bad about the shoulder."

"What do you know about his restaurants?" I wondered. "They doing well, or what?"

"According to Cal he's more than just a front man," my boyfriend said as the tea, ice cream, and cookies arrived. "As I understand it, he tied everything up in the restaurants. He may have some investors, too. Problem is, the bars are in a heavy competitive situation. Big national chains, the Megamall. His places don't have the glitz. You know, a little tatty, shopworn."

"I had the pleasure of meeting him just yesterday," I said in my most facetious tone. "And visiting one of his establishments last night. One visit was enough for me."

"Must've been a thrill meeting him," Rick deadpanned. "I've heard he enjoys the juice of the grape."

"More like the juice of the barley and hops," I said, attacking an almond cookie. "I wonder how those two got together. I mean, got to like each other well enough to get hitched. She's smart, perceptive, a regular pip. He's a, a—"

"A regular poop?"

I nodded and smiled gratefully at this man who could always make me laugh, even when I'd gotten myself in a total funk. It seemed like I was the one who always needing lifting, and he

provided it. "Seems to me that if Denny Ryan keeps me on—
Not a good bet. But if he does, it'd be worthwhile to go west
young lady, go west."

"You mean check out Gottwaldt's background in California?"

"Elementary, my dear Mueller."

"What would you like me to do in the meantime?"

"Google and Bing the hell out of it and see what you can
find out about our cast of characters. Maybe even take a dive
into the newspaper microfilms." I pulled my reporters' notebook out of my satchel, jotted down all the appropriate names,
and tore the sheet out.

"Doesn't Deb Brown usually do this stuff?"

"Yeah, but she's not for free."

He tipped his invisible hat. "And I'm worth every penny," he
chuckled. "Can I ask another question?"

"Shoot."

"Seems to me," he began, "that we haven't said a word about
secret anti-tobacco terrorist groups. What does that mean?"

"What do you think it means?"

"That you think one of the Gottwaldt and Ryan crew is behind all this mayhem."

I shrugged and told him that that was a theory, *only* a theory.
But it was the only thing I was in any position to investigate
anymore. The cops would look out for real or imagined terrorists. We looked at each other for a minute, run out of dialog.
I reached across the table, took his hand, gave it a squeeze. He
returned the favor and raised his eyebrows. No need for him to
say a thing. We aren't an old couple that communicated by ESP.
Just a few years' of living together. Not exactly "holy macaroni,"
as my Dad used to call it, but pretty close.

"I think we better eat this ice cream before it melts," I said.

His smile evaporated and he stared at me with an earnest
intensity that almost caught my breath.

"It'll be okay," I said. "Terry's not a problem."

The only answer he had for my glib reassurance was a moment of saying nothing. I hated the sound of it—that roaring,

clangorous silence.

"I'll get home soon," he said, answering me before I could ask. "I promised Scott I'd watch *Fringe* with him tonight. And tomorrow night he got passes for some Celtic music group. He likes the company, you know. He's alone so much."

"No problem," I said. It was kind of nice, actually, the way Rick looked out for his little brother.

After paying, we stood up and reached for each other. A hug, a light kiss, and we both pulled on our coats and darted out the door. Rick listed to port with the "light" camera bag on his left shoulder. We skittered in opposite directions down the sidewalk. The traffic was heavy, creeping by, like it always did on Grand on a weekday evening.

Back in the Merc I checked my cell and found a message from Denny waiting for me, what I'd expected.

"Hi, Marta." His voice droned, a monotone, washed out and bleached and wrung out a thousand times. A pause, a deep sigh. "It was Herb. Shit—" Another pause. "They shot him in the chest, twice. I can't believe this, Marta— They say the bullets may be from Meg's gun, and she's in custody for questioning."

There was another long sigh, then a reaching for air to propel the words out of his mouth.

"The fire looks accidental. No sign of gas or accelerants being used, at least at first blush. There was maybe some kind of struggle or something and a cigarette got knocked in a trash basket. He was a pretty fit guy. I hope he gave a little of his own back. I guess I'm in charge of the agency until we know what Herb has in his will. We're all meeting at Jennifer's house on the St. Croix. Nine o'clock tomorrow morning. And I'd like you to be there."

He told me how to get to the Nelson house in St. Francis Point on the St. Croix River.

Terry had called to say he was sorry he behaved so insensitively out at Gottwaldt's house.

Finally came a message from Deputy Grabowski, requesting the pleasure of my company late Friday afternoon.

Marta Hjelm was one popular gal.

Chapter Seventeen

First thing the next morning I called Rick with the news about Gottwaldt and Meg LaGrange. He observed that the game had just leapt well out of my particular little league. What reason did Denny have to keep a certain detective rattling around to the tune of $75 an hour?

I couldn't disagree. Then I asked him what he'd found out.

Turns out he didn't spend the evening guzzling beer and watching *Fringe* with Scott. Little Bro had gotten himself an actual blind date—with another Star Trek fanatic whom he'd met in an online chat room. So Rick did a spot of Googling and Binging and decided to head out to the big library in Edina.

"Just reading up about some of the people in the case, hitting the microfilms, like you said." He gave a vast, baroque yawn and excused himself. "I got a bunch of printouts for you."

"Just leave 'em on my desk at home. Anything else?"

There wasn't and we said goodbye.

• • •

Gottwaldt's daughter lived in St. Francis Point on the St. Croix River just across from Wisconsin.

The irony of the town's name hasn't been lost on social critics. I doubt if any resident of the place ever took a vow of voluntary poverty and gave up all his goodies, like their namesake saint. Long, woodsy driveways, impressive river frontages, sprawling homes with tennis courts and pools and guest houses don't put one in the mood for acts of contrition and self-imposed poverty—the actual saint's approach to life.

At least St. Franciscans deserved brownie points for not having the gates and high-security setups that rich folks had in other places. You could literally walk up to a demi-billionaire's front door and ask if he'd loan you a cup of sugar. It's a Minnesota conceit: "Aw shucks— I may be worth more than you'd earn in 500 lifetimes, little lady, but I'm really just an ordinary guy."

Not that Jennifer's husband played in that league. But half interest in an electronics manufacturer will still get you a pretty nice spread. And hers was—a two-story Tudor with wings going hither and yon, pool to the left, double courts to the right, private beach and boathouse in back. She answered the door herself that Friday morning. She had on crisp, fine-wale gray corduroy trousers, a red cashmere sweater, and some kind of pricey silk designer scarf around her neck.

"You're the first to get here," she said rather mournfully, without so much as a hello. Her eyes were bloodshot, ringed red. But the hair was perfect—swept back rich-lady style, held with a couple of turquoise-and-silver combs. "Come in."

"Beautiful house," I observed, as we passed through a hallway and a room chockablock with country antiques and American primitive paintings. They looked like the authentic articles, too. Our feet clattered on the knotty pine flooring and the air danced with cinnamon and apple scents. A little too much of them, actually, like falling into a large, redolent pie.

She just nodded, deaf to small talk, and led me into a white sun room filled with white wicker chairs that looked out on the white, icy beach and white, icy river. It was a dazzling, sunny morning, and I regretted leaving my shades in the Merc.

"Coffee? Can I make you an espresso or *au lait?*"

She seemed almost eager to undertake building me a java. Something to occupy the hands, for a moment or two. I understood. I had repainted the whole lower duplex after my Dad died. I wouldn't let Rick help me. Then I did it again.

"Au lait please, with one sugar," I said.

She nodded, and disappeared into her warren of exquisitely furnished rooms.

Denny and Archie Gottwaldt arrived about the same time as my caffeine, and before long they had theirs, too. Jennifer brewed it deep and rich and full of kick. She didn't have any herself. Instead, she sipped from a crystal tumbler of cranberry juice. Sue Hewlett arrived late, with her husband in tow. She said hi and gave me this pained look, as if to say: You poor thing, thrown in with this bunch.

We sat in a semi-circle facing the river. Denny peered around at us, drawing sustenance from his espresso. He finally had the look of someone who'd gotten a decent night's sleep. He told the assembled throng that Herb's personal attorney had confirmed that he, the legal eagle, was executor of the estate, as per the late ad man's will. Denny assumed that the will would eventually put Jennifer and Archie in control of the shop.

Hemo was history. As was Amfoodco.

"Terry woke me up at six," Denny said stoically. "With Herb dead, and the attendant publicity about the murder and the extortion, Bertram has no other option but to go with their backup choice, Harrison Bledsoe out of Chicago."

The reaction was fatalistic. Denny seemed grim, seeing the opportunity slip away. So did Sue. Doug Hewlett was unreadable—phlegmatic and distant. Jennifer merely nodded, but Archie looked a little anxious. It heartened me some to note that at least the son seemed a tad broken up about losing the account. Maybe some of that old Gottwaldt-ian tenaciousness would come out and redeem him, now that he didn't have his dad's long shadow looming.

Herb's daughter then announced that the wake would take place the following week, at Nicollet Island Inn in Minneapolis. No one in the family was even slightly religious, she explained—no funeral, no memorial service, no speeches. That brought the conversation to a dead halt—pardon the turn of phrase. Jennifer stood up slowly, as if rising through heavy water, looking for air. She took a few deep draws of breath. "Can I get anyone some more coffee?"

I allowed that another au lait would be nice, and handed her my cup. No one else did. The silence was heavy when she left the room, but sometimes I like that. I briefly had a Chinese roommate in college, and she taught me the value of not saying things at the right time. She even managed to do it when she later on served a few years as a political prisoner—she never did snitch on her friends, never did say where she got the "treasonous propaganda" they found in the heels of her sandals. In her little-girl voice she declared: "Never be shy about using silence."

So when Jennifer returned with my java, people were ready to talk about Meg and Herb.

"Do you think she did it?" I asked, gazing around the room.

Jennifer, something of a robot until this point, reared up in her wicker seat and glared at me.

"Not a snowball's chance in hell that Meg killed Daddy," she said, frustration roiling in her voice. "Those two had a history, sure. A long history. Not always a happy history. But Meg's weapons are words. When she's finished with you, you feel about this high." She held up a thumb and index finger an inch apart. "I've seen her chew Daddy to shreds."

"Then she could provoke someone," I suggested, "make someone mad enough to come at her. She shoots in self-defense."

"Maybe someone else," Jennifer said. "Not Daddy. Daddy hurt people with his choices, his business dealings. Daddy could be an SOB. But I don't think he ever hurt anyone physically."

"She coulda gone off the deep end," Doug theorized. "He finally did something she couldn't take, and pow!"

"That's bullshit, Doug, and you know it," Denny snapped. "Herb rode all of us hard. Jennifer's right, Herb was a tough old bastard. If any of us acted out what we felt sometimes, he would've gotten murdered a hundred times. But no one did. Why would Meg do it now? Okay, she went out there and got in an argument with him. But there's just no way I can believe she shot the guy."

The only person there who might have had an answer was sitting silently, staring into his au lait, diddling with his teaspoon, perhaps pondering his own fate in the advertising game.

Archie had been at his father's place when Meg LaGrange arrived. For a few minutes only, according to Bruce. I asked the apple-cheeked lad to tell us what transpired, and he squirmed like an earthworm in a frying pan.

Couldn't do it, he said. Grabowski said to keep his trap shut. All he'd say was that he told the cop everything he could remember. He had been a weensy bit snockered, after all.

I assured Archie right back that we all wanted the same thing—the truth about what went bad and why. It could only help if I knew what happened. "Just tell me what Meg was like, how she acted," I coaxed.

"You're sure this'll be okay with Grabowski," he said.

"He won't even know."

"Okay then." He exhaled through his nostrils, loud and long, to underline the weightiness of the moment. "She was steamed. I mean really flipped out. Red in the face, practically snarling. She has a key to the place. Most of us do. She let herself in and just marched in on Dad and me. I mean, she slammed the door behind her."

"Did she say why she was so PO'd?"

Everybody was at attention now. Sue's eyes were wide open, and Doug leaned forward in his chair. Denny chewed on one of his manicured fingernails and stared at Archie. And Jennifer meshed and unmeshed her long, fine fingers, like an inmate in an asylum.

Archie shook his head. "She told Dad that she was ready to talk with him, alone. When I said I wasn't done, she told me to get the hell outta there."

"My God," Jennifer whispered. "What'd Daddy say?"

Archie smiled the flaccid, twitchy smile of losers everywhere—saddened, mortified, bemused all at once.

"What'd he say, Arch?" Jennifer repeated.

"He told me to scram."

I sure didn't think much of Archie. People born with the breaks make me feel judgmental, as if they couldn't possibly achieve much on their own. I'd worked my tail off, climbed out of a couple of deep, deep holes, and it felt good looking down on someone like him. It's a character flaw I have, that prejudice. Just then, though, I could have wept for him.

The kid looked around at all of us and steeled himself to say what he had to.

"Last time I see him alive and he says, 'Archie, go home.' Not 'Archie, go home, I'm okay.' Not, 'Archie, that's enough for tonight, drive careful.' Just 'Archie, go home.' Like I'm a lost fucking dog, or something." He locked his eyes on mine.

I looked down, embarrassed to hear him, embarrassed to be there. Then I made eye contact with him again. "Did you hear any of the conversation he and Meg had?"

He shook his head. "Would you want to stay? Even if you could?"

"Why'd you go out there, Archie? You shouldn't've been driving at all."

"Yeah, I know," he answered. "I lost my key but I had a spare in my jacket. Otherwise I wouldn't have even been there." He shook his head angrily. "I just wanted to get him outta that stupid, ugly house. He shouldn't have been there all alone. I tried to get him to come to my place."

"You never would have gotten through to him, Arch," Jennifer said. "Never."

Archie stood up, with a kind of cornered-animal look on his face. "I'm sorry, but I really can't do this anymore."

"Archie!" I yelped, as he dashed out of the room. I jumped up and went after him. "One more question."

He stopped out by a colonial chest of drawers underneath an ancient portrait of some early 19th century gentleman, who looked as grim and Puritanical as damnation itself. When he turned to face me he put a hand on the top of the chest. It was shaking and tears were starting to come. He wasn't faking it.

"Fine," he said, half-swallowing the word. "What's the question?"

"You think Meg could have killed Herb?"

"Who knows for sure?" He blinked at me, trying to pretend he wasn't weeping. "Only Meg. Maybe she did."

I started to ask a follow-up. If she did, why? But he waved me off and clumped off toward the front door. I went back into the sunroom just as the distant door slam reverberated through those thousands of square feet of American colonial.

"Okay," I said, sitting back down, squinting in the bright light, like some petty crook in a police lineup. "We have Meg leading two-one. Jennifer and Denny think she wouldn't pull the trigger, Archie thinks maybe. Sue?"

The handsome black woman squirmed a bit and blinked at her husband, who looked as uncomfortable being there as I felt. It puzzled me why she'd bring him. Moral support, I suppose. I just noticed she had a wrist done up in an ace bandage. She must have sprained it somehow, I assumed. Maybe she had carpal tunnel.

"I'm with Denny and Jennifer," she stated quietly. "Obviously she had some reason to get mad at him. But I don't think she'd hurt a flea."

"Then why," I put to her, "did she have a gun? This hot-shot environmental activist? Doesn't seem right."

Denny looked surprised that I knew that about Meg. So did Jennifer.

"Self-defense, Marta," Doug spat. "Jeez. The lady got mugged, coulda got killed. Then there's the last few days. Why shouldn't she have it?"

I shrugged. But people who would never hurt people sometimes hurt people, particularly when they have stainless-steel 9mm automatics in their purses.

"Do you know Meg well enough to vote, Doug?" I smiled at the ex-hockey star. "A minute ago it sounded like you thought she could have done Herb."

"I don't know," he vacillated. "But from what I hear, she's some kinda liberal. And I don't see liberals having the balls—" He blinked suddenly at Jennifer, who scowled at him. "To, um, do something like that."

"I've heard," I said, "that they were an item out in San Diego for a few years, before Herb came home."

Jennifer nodded, then shook her head-two answers to one query. Yes, and too bad. "I kinda hoped they'd get married. I liked her a lot, I still do."

"Why'd you want them to get hitched?" I asked.

Jennifer pondered for a moment. "'Cause she's not a ditz. She's not even very good looking. Which meant Daddy liked her for her. She's got a brain, like Mom, and a great sense of humor. Talent, too. Maybe she was hot stuff in the sack. I don't know. I just think Daddy screwed up not grabbing her. She would have been good for him. After Meg it was just a parade of babes. Getting younger every year. Kinda sad, really."

"How'd they get along?" I said. "Was it the can't-live-with, can't-live-without kind of thing?

Denny heaved a sigh and took another drag on his coffee, now cold as the stale air in the sunroom. "I heard they had their blowups, I mean real roof rattlers. Two big egos bumping up against each other. But they handled it okay. Even after they weren't lovers anymore they were friends, and he really counted on her. Honest to God."

"I was just a kid in college," said Jennifer, "and I remember some scraps they had. But they always patched it up."

"Scraps about what?" I asked.

"Don't know, Dad wouldn't say. And I didn't see Meg too often."

"Who broke it up, then?"

Denny and Jennifer looked at each other. Who would say it? Finally, Jennifer took the ball.

"Meg did. It caught Daddy right between the eyes."

"Herb did unto others, you know," Denny said. "He'd dropped Jennifer's mother and God knows how many girl-friends over the years. He'd never known what it was like to be done unto himself. And man, it shocked him. He told me so."

I was already halfway down on my new brew, but had more than enough caffeine zinging around in me. "Why'd she leave?"

"You know," Denny said, "Herb never said, and I never had the guts to ask. I tried to get it out of Meg one time, but she told me—real nicely—to forget about it."

I looked at the remaining heir. "Do you know?"

"Not for sure," Jennifer said, "but I think Meg got bored with Daddy. He's a— He was a brilliant man in his field. But his interests were so narrow. His work. Big-money poker. He won half a million in Vegas once. Honest to God. Tennis, golf, sports cards, the Vikings, the girlfriends."

"So Herb was too shallow for her."

Jennifer nodded.

"But they remained good friends, as well as colleagues?"

"Yeah," Denny answered. "Absolutely. In a way, she was his creative conscience these last few years. I don't think I'm speaking out of turn by saying she's the reason Gottwaldt and

Ryan is still a force to be reckoned with. She's our brain trust."

• • •

That was about it for my sojourn in millionaire-land, but for one thing.

Sue and Doug had taken off, and Jennifer stood off to the side, looking like the snow princess incarnate. The pupil-contracting light had moderated, with some hazy clouds rolling in. Looked like we could get a little snow—some fluffy stuff.

"I think now that the police have both cases," Denny told me, pulling on his overcoat, "we won't need your services anymore. Of course, I'll cover all the hours you've done and the bonus for the accident, plus any more medical expenses resulting from it."

I blinked at him, surprised to be angry that he'd sacked me a second time. I mean, I'd expected it. Still, I hissed: "Then may I ask why you hauled my ass all the way out here on a cold morning?"

He shrugged and pointed a finger at Jennifer. "It was her idea."

Of course, it might have been better for everyone if I'd stayed sacked.

Chapter Eighteen

Jennifer and I watched Denny march out, and she came over to me.

"I'm sorry," she said. "I knew he was going to terminate you. But it wasn't my place to say anything. Not until we know what's in Daddy's will."

"That's okay," I said, almost cracking a smile, picturing a younger Arnold Schwarzenegger swooping down on me, naked on a Harley. What a way to go!

"I expected it. Hell, why not? That's the second time he's fired me."

I hadn't figured Jennifer for a new pal, but she asked me to stay a few minutes. She had some questions. Seeing as how I was suddenly at liberty, I thought, why not?

Like an obedient puppy, I followed her into the kitchen. It was bigger than my living room, with sapele mahogany cabinets and engraved glass all around. Her stove was one of those tank-like, commercial gas jobs, and they'd built the fridge into the wall behind a pair of sapele doors. She perched on a tall stool next to her espresso machine, a big red Gaggia—the kind you'd see in a coffee cafe.

"I have a favor to ask," she said, so softly I could barely hear her. There was no inflection in her voice

"If I can help, Jennifer, I will."

She tapped her fingers rapidly on the fancy tile counter. "If you honestly feel you have more to give to this matter—" She stopped tapping. "What I'm saying, Marta, is—" She stared at me intently, and decided. "I'd like to hire you to continue this inquiry."

"I'm flattered," I said. "But the sheriff's office'll handle the murder investigation and look into the alleged terrorist plot. Doesn't seem much more for me to do."

"Probably so. But I know I'd feel lots better if I knew I had someone working directly for me." She climbed down off the stool, went over to one of the sinks and closed the stopper. She started the water, squirted in some detergent, and began washing dirty wine goblets.

"Hope you don't mind," she said, glancing over her shoulder at me. "I have that dish washer unit there, but this kind of calms me down. Sort of like meditation, I've always thought."

I trotted over, grabbed a cream-colored linen dish towel, and started drying for her. I set the dried items on the marble counter one by one, off to the side.

"So," I said after a long silence, "you'd like me to keep on just as if I were working for Denny."

"Right. Do what you think needs doing, let me know how it's going. Keep track of hours and expenses. Quit when you feel like it, or when I tell you to."

"Fair enough."

"What's your rate?"

"Seventy-five an hour."

"Sounds good." She rinsed the last goblet and handed it to me. "So what'll you do next?"

"I'd like to interview more people locally. Like Harry Litzky, who I really haven't visited with yet. Then I want to get someone in San Diego to look into your dad's associations there. I mean, he spent just as much of his adult life on the Coast as here."

"Good idea," she said. "He had some tough times with his agency out there, and he never would talk about it afterwards. Maybe that's a good place to start."

• • •

Harry Litzky, the art director, had holed up about one hour south of St. Paul, near Northfield. The drive gave me time to unwind and empty out the noggin, to just go totally on cruise control, like the Merc. I popped in a CD—good old Stevie Ray Vaughan and Double Trouble—and all the way down admired the glittery magic of a sunlit snow flurry. Pixie dust glinting everywhere. For lunch I indulged myself at the Hefty Steer truck stop just west of the Northfield exit. A jumbo burger, onion rings, a malted, and a quivering slice of coconut cream pie.

I got to Litzky's hobby farm about 1:30. It sat in a ravine a few miles east of town, down a windy dirt track. A real farmer wouldn't have touched it, or even thought about raising anything there but goats and shinsplints.

The tableau that greeted me came straight out of a Ralph Lauren catalog.

The big log house had a huge, covered front porch with sturdy pine rockers and kerosene lamps hanging from the rafters. Hickory-tinged smoke wafted up from a massive red brick chimney. Old, rusticated farm implements were meticulously scattered about, for maximum effect. Muscovy ducks—so ugly they were cute—pecked for cracked corn in the snow up by the barn. A pair of Irish Setters bounded up to meet the Merc, all slobbering anticipation—ready to French-kiss the first sucker who came along.

But when the cabin's front door cracked open, I saw the double barrel of a shotgun emerge, followed by Harry Litzky in a Hudson Bay Co. blanket jacket. With a querulous expression he peered down at the Merc as I rolled down the window.

"It's me, Harry," I shouted. "Marta Hjelm. Call off the hounds, I surrender."

He laughed like a bell ringing and his ruddy moon face did a jolly Santa Claus turn. Much to my relief, he cracked the shotgun open, draped it over his left arm, and resumed the persona of a mild-mannered and very tasteful art director. He hopped down the stairs and skittered the ice-walker's shuffling walk over to the Merc.

"I'm really sorry," he said. "Just gotta be careful, I guess." He wagged a free finger at the pair of mutts. "You two fellas, back off!"

"What do you call them?"

"Zeus and Apollo."

I laughed hard. "The dobermans on *Magnum P.I.* Seriously?"

He laughed back. "Yup, seriously."

"I had a huge crush on Tom Selleck when I was a kid."

Harry sighed a nostalgic sigh. "Me too, Marta, me too."

I opened my door and climbed out, slamming it behind me. I stood a few inches taller than Litzky. The setters snuffled at me, hoping at least for something interesting in the food department. "Got no chow on me, guys," I said, leaning down to pet them. They looked disappointed and wandered off.

"Those two, they're always begging," Litzky said, ushering me up the steps onto the porch. "I feed 'em the best dog food, and they're always trying to cadge a potato chip or hunk of a candy bar."

"C'mon, which would you rather have?" I laughed as he swung open the big oak front door.

He chuckled again, and patted his not insubstantial belly. "Yeah, why should my babies be any different?"

Litzky's great room surprised me. It was capacious by any standard, but handsomely spare: A massive stone fireplace, some Mission-style furniture, Indian rugs and blankets for color, luminous male-nude photos on the pine-paneled walls. A picture window looked out on Litzky's private, snow-covered stream. The oak floor glowed. The only major indulgence seemed to be a deluxe audio system—a slim, stylish Bang & Olufsen setup—with a big Sony flatscreen between the speakers.

"Ms. Hjelm—"

"Marta."

"Marta— Please make yourself at home and I'll be right back. I was finishing up chopping wood out behind the barn just before you came. Gotta do it while I have a head of steam. Just give me five or ten."

He grabbed a tweedy Irish hat off a side chair and scurried back outside. I took my coat off and plopped down on the Mission-style sofa, which was comely but not comfy. The wooden back dug into my shoulder blades. Like Meg LaGrange, Litzky didn't seem to have a single book in his living room. It cried for lavishly illustrated coffee table tomes opened to breathtaking photo layouts of Tuscan picnics or Big Sur vistas. Or, failing that, stacks of artsy volumes on tables and floor. Meaning I had nothing to look at but the great outdoors. Scent-wise the place reeked of cigarettes.

I didn't even hear anyone pad up behind me until he said, "Ms. Hjelm?"

My heart went *booom* and I nearly gave myself whiplash trying to spin around. Somehow I managed to scramble to my feet, and as I did the young man who'd snuck up on me back-pedalled a step or two.

"I am *so* sorry," he said, looking mortified with himself. "I didn't mean to frighten you."

He reminded me of the character in that movie who everybody thought was a gorgeous girl until it became suddenly rather obvious that he wasn't. Only this fellow wasn't mulatto. Maybe of Mediteranean extraction. He had curly, jet-dark hair, brown eyes like your proverbial limpid pools, a perfect oval face, olive complexion, and a lean, athletic figure. He wore a red Champion sweatshirt over black jeans. He was in stocking feet. Thus the sneak attack.

I peered at him a bit. "As they say, you have me at a disadvantage."

His face lit up with amusement. "I'm sorry! I'm Harry's partner, Keith. Keith Langosis. This is my place, too."

He stuck a finely manicured hand at me over the back of the couch and I shook it. Obviously, he did not chop wood himself. "Good to meet you, Keith. I just didn't know anyone else was around."

"Well, how could you?" He came around and took my arm as gently as Rick's maiden aunt would have. "I'll tell you one thing."

I waited.

"I'm awfully glad you're here, because Harry's just *exhausted* with worry. I've never seen him so nervous."

"It's understandable," I said. "What a mess."

"*Indeed*, 'What a mess.' All I can say is that whoever's doing this shit is one *real* sickie." He pursed his lips and shook his head with disgust—also as Rick's aunt would have done as she pondered the world's incivilities.

"In the meantime, Marta— May I call you Marta? Let's go in the kitchen and rustle up some drinks for us and Harry. How about hot cocoa with peppermint schnapps?"

• • •

Harry, like Bruce, smoked Freshaire. Incessantly. As we chatted around an oval oak table in the kitchen, I had to ask if he'd mind dousing the weeds for a bit. I pulled out my old line about being mildly allergic to smoke. Even though I'm not. Much more polite than: "*That stench makes me sick!*"

"They calm me down," he said apologetically.

"If you must have one while Marta's here," Keith lectured, sipping his cocoa, "you can go out in the living room for a few minutes."

Harry fatalistically nodded and stubbed out his cancer stick in a saucer already full of butts.

I happened to make eye contact with Keith, and he winked at me. As in, *good for you.*

First, I filled in Litzky and his partner on what I knew about Gottwaldt's murder and Meg LaGrange's detention. Then that I was working for Jennifer now, not the agency. They listened intently, and it seemed obvious that Litzky had something to say. He squirmed, and I don't think it was just because he couldn't have a smoke.

"I would've called somebody with this, but—" Litzky trailed off.

"We had an ice storm a few nights ago," Keith hastened to put in. "The phone line went down for a while. And guess *who*—" He glared at his boyfriend. "—Forgot to bring his cell phone? He's scared to tell anyone, anyway. I think even if the phone hadn't been off, he'd've waited for someone to ask."

"So?" I said.

"You hate to think about a friend this way, Marta," said Litzky, "but Meg had what amounted to a pretty damned good reason."

"To kill Herb, you mean?" I asked.

Litzky blinked at me, then Keith. Keith nodded at him: Be a big boy, say what needs saying.

"Meg called me the night Herb died," Litzky pronounced grimly. "Middle of the bloody night. Three, four a.m. First decent night's sleep I'd had going in a week, and she wakes me up."

"Why?"

"'Cause Herb dismissed her."

If I'd been a Bugs Bunny cartoon, my jaw would have plummeted to the floor and gone "*Clank!*"

"He *what?*"

"He sent her an e-mail, Marta. 'You're sacked, old girl,' or some such. 'Come on out and we can discuss it.' She blew a gasket, then ran out to Lake Minnetonka to pummel him about the head and shoulders. At least figuratively."

"And he told her the reason?"

"No, actually. He said that he'd been considering changes in staffing for some months, and was finally getting around to making decisions. Which sounded like pure bull manure to Meg. And she told him so. To his face! He said, too bad, and asked her to leave."

"Have you told this to anyone else?"

"Like the police?" He shook his head and shrugged. "Well, we had the phone problem, then— Keith's right, I was scared to tell anyone. You're the first to know." He squinted at me, then at his partner, who had his radar on. Keith could see that his honey needed something. Just like I could with Rick.

"Yeah, Harry?"

"Keith, get me a couple of red Excedrins, will you? I think I got a bruiser of a headache coming on. Shouldn't've chopped the wood, I guess."

"Sure, hon," Keith said, and scurried off.

I told Litzky that I wouldn't be a lot longer, but I had a few more questions. He tiredly agreed and washed down his pills as soon as Keith popped them in his hand.

"Tell me about the dynamic between Herb and Meg." I said.

"You've heard about Herb's ego by now," Litzky said.

I nodded.

"Well, Meg's not unendowed in that area. I think if you're talking raw intelligence—IQ ratings, memory, stuff like that— there is no one in the whole office smarter than Meg. And she knows it."

"So?"

"Even though the two of them were lovers a while ago, and colleagues, they were also, um, rivals."

"I don't get that," Keith said. "It was Herb's business. She's just an employee."

Litzky strummed his fingers on the glossy oak. "True. But I worked closer with them on Hemo than anyone. And before that on Hamburger Shack and the motorcycle campaign. That's three or four years now. I've seen 'em work on things a hundred times. I've seen 'em hash out hardcore issues. And I'll tell you this. Whoever lost didn't like it. You could see it in their eyes. Didn't matter that they'd made nookie for three, four years back in San Diego. Didn't matter that they both wanted to make the greatest ads in the world. Those two just hated losing.

"You shoulda seen them playing tennis. Herb usually beat her. He was just stronger, quicker. But she scrapped like a damned little terrier. She'd hit Herb garbage shots, she'd hand-cuff him, give him impossible lobs, zap shots at his head. She'd come to the net whenever she could, she'd go on the deck after a shot. Anything to win. She's still that way. I mean, this is a woman on the downhill side of 40."

I almost said *ouch*, but kept my trap shut.

"I hate to say it," Litzky said in measured meter, "but I think Meg's fully capable of getting steamed to the point of hurting someone."

• • •

When I was heading back up Interstate 35 at about four in the p.m. I got on the cell to Bruce. Would he be available for a bit of work out of town? Alimony payments do wonderful things for a guy's motivation, and he allowed that he would. I told him what I wanted him to do, and he said a trip to San Diego sounded "spiffy." He actually uses that word in ordinary conversation.

I desperately wanted to head home for a stiff, stiff martini and the new Susan Tedeschi CD I'd picked up. But Grabowski had said five sharp, Friday, and I made it downtown. Just barely.

The crew-cutted cop had hunkered down in his cubicle in the Sheriff's offices in the county courthouse. His plaid sports jacket was folded next to his computer, and he had on short sleeves and a plain blue necktie loosened at the collar. I'd been pretty close about his background. He'd tacked snapshots of himself on the fabric-covered walls, in Army dress uniform and in M.P. mufti—looking less leathery than now, but not that much different. He had on Captain's bars. And there was a "United States Military Academy" bumper sticker slapped on the side of his desk.

Grabowski suggested, "Why don't you tell me what you've come up with."

"Why don't you ask me some questions?" I replied, sitting on a folding chair.

He nodded, and asked away.

I unloaded the beans and he took notes. The accident with the Lexus. What I knew about the principals in the case. The meeting at Jennifer's that morning. I mentioned that Denny sacked me and Jennifer picked up my option. All he gave me were "Uh-huh"'s and nods. I also fished my little Canon out of the satchel and he copied the relevant shots off the SD card. He thanked me for providing them.

"Can I ask a thing or two, Deputy?"

"Doesn't hurt to try," he said.

"Have any more e-mails come in since Herb got killed?"

He shook his head. "The one received after the Lexus incident was the last."

"Have you found anything on the dark green Escort?"

"Nope. We're looking. Any Escort that was stolen and reported in the U. S. in the last month wasn't dark green. An old Escort was stolen over in Wisconsin a few weeks ago, blue in color. Of course they could've painted it."

"Is the FBI going to come in?"

"They and Homeland Security are interested in the terrorism aspect of the case. But nothing official yet."

"When does the media get in on it?"

"They have a juicy murder case to chew on. I don't think the extortion thing's important right now. Unless someone in the prosecutors' office decides to go after it. We think it's something coincidental."

"Do you have physical evidence that ties anyone other than Meg LaGrange to the killing?"

"I really can't say, Ms. Hjelm."

"Do you plan on charging her?"

The Deputy shook his head. "We have plenty of probable cause. She was very mad at the victim. She has motive."

"Because he fired her?"

His deadpan twitched a mite—an eeny-teeny chink in the the armor. I wasn't supposed to know that. "How'd you find out?"

I told him about Harry Litzky, and he allowed that he ought to spin down to Northfield for a chat. He'd already debriefed Bruce about the nocturnal doings out at Gottwaldt's place.

"At any rate," he continued, "she was there with him at the right time. Her 9mm's gone missing, so she can't prove that it didn't kill him."

"Well, it's all plenty logical," I agreed, getting ready to go, "but you can't prove that it did. It's all circumstantial. And besides, maybe the gun was stolen. Maybe it was someone else's 9. How many thousands of 9mm's are circulating around the Twin Cities?"

He offered me a genial smile and a shrug.

Chapter Nineteen

After my little *tête à tête* with Grabowski, I grabbed some Thai noodles in spicy tomato sauce over by the University's West Bank campus. It was one of my favorite hole-in-the-wall joints, in Seven Corners, the Emerald Thai. Windows steamed over, air redolent with zippy Asian spices, walls papered with Thai Airways posters gone blue from too much sunlight.

Two long-in-the-tooth grad students—boyfriend and girlfriend, perhaps, I couldn't tell—tilted over some obscure sociohistorical theorem at the table next to mine. She was a Marxist, I gathered, and sprinkled her part of the chat with the term "dialectic." Whatever that meant. He handled her with kid gloves—any member of a nearly extinct species deserves a gentle touch. Or perhaps he had hopes for a spot of nooky later in the evening. The traffic rolled by slowly out on Washington Avenue, a kind of abstract, red-and-white animation luminescing from behind the windows' heavy condensation.

With every hot-flash bite I cogitated about Grabowski and gulped ice water. He was right, of course. They had enough on Meg LaGrange to make an assistant DA feel all warm and fuzzy. Why hadn't they arrested her yet?

Apparently, it was just a case of the slowly grinding wheels of justice.

Jennifer Nelson called Saturday morning with news that Meg was being held on a charge of murder, and would appear in court first thing Monday morning. Grabowski had given her a preview. I told her I was sending an operative out to San Diego and she agreed. She said how much she liked the notion of someone making inquiries for her.

"I want to keep a hand in the game," she said. "Besides, Denny just about begged me to fire you." She chuckled. "Said I was wasting my money, a damn fool. Now I couldn't let you go if I wanted to. If he wants you gone, I want you to stay. *Jerk.*" It sounded like she wanted to say a word that began with "a" and ended with "e," but was too proper to do so.

It was time to be honest. "But he might be right. Might be a waste of money."

"So what?" she said. "I can afford it."

As for Meg pulling the trigger, Jennifer still didn't believe the charges.

"Harry's right about Meg's temper," she allowed, when I recounted his comments. "But murder? Even if she's totally— No. Doesn't sell me. She went out there to chew him out, find out what he was pulling, not to kill him."

Regarding a jaunt to San Diego, I had a chum from Tookie Peterson days who'd moved to L.A. to become a screenwriter. When that didn't work out—as it usually doesn't in L.A.—she went to work and got a California license. I could have used her to check out Herb's San Diego history. But I wanted someone doing it whom I knew like a book, and who knew me likewise.

Bruce met me at a coffeehouse on Hennepin Avenue later in the morning, and he nearly yodeled with delight when I confirmed his gig. Technically, he'd be working for my L.A. friend, Betty Wisocki, who had an agency in Pomona. But *she* would be working for Jennifer Nelson through me. If Bruce needed help, Betty could provide it—herself or some other PI.

"I'd like you to talk to Herb's advertising buddies," I told Bruce, "the people who work in his property management firm there, old friends, his tennis and golf buddies, check out any organizations he belonged to, whatever. Just drop Jennifer Nelson's name." I handed him a sheet with names, numbers and addresses.

"But what am I looking for?" he asked, folding up the paper and slipping it in a coat pocket.

"Damned if I know." I peered warily at my cappuccino, put it down, and decided that I shouldn't take another sip of java that day, even at three bucks a cup. My mouth tasted like the inside of an ancient percolator. "But as they say about pornography, you will know it when you see it."

He tapped a finger on his temple. "Ol' eagle eye here, when it comes to porno."

I rolled my eyes. "I've told you every bloody thing I've heard about the guy, Bruce. If I haven't covered it, then that's the stuff

I want. You have the names and numbers."

"Okey-dokey, *mon capitan*." He gave me a smart salute. "How about my flight and car?"

"I'll book 'em tonight online and e-mail you the info. You've still got the Visa card I gave you, right?"

"Sure do," he said.

"Keep it frugal if you can, Brucie."

"Aboslutely. Anything else?"

I squinted at my friend and colleague, and decided there was. With hand quickness that might have done a hockey goalie credit, I grabbed Bruce's taped, dilapidated spectacles right off his nose and wagged them at him.

"Before you leave," I growled at my gape-mouthed operative, "preferably yet this afternoon, you are to visit a one-hour optical store of your choice and get new glasses. This should cover it." I snatched my pocketbook out of my satchel and pulled out two $100 bills.

"If I ever see you wearing these miserable things again," I said, waggling the the funky specs, "I'll bust 'em in two. While you're still wearing 'em. Got it?"

"Got it," he said, grinning, and reached across the table to give me a brotherly squeeze on the arm.

After that I needed a breather.

Rick had an out of town assignment—a bed-and-breakfast shoot down in Dubuque for a travel magazine. If I hadn't had the case I might have driven south with him to set up the lighting and chat up the locals while he got his shots.

I could have spent the rest of the weekend with Terry, who called again about the Chili Peppers. But I hid behind my voice-mail and didn't return any of his messages.

Instead, I drove home and booked Bruce's flight and car. Then I packed up my own Nikon, a D200, and headed out to the big zoo in Apple Valley to shoot stock Saturday afternoon. And all day Sunday at the Como Zoo in St. Paul. Mostly kids watching the animals.

For the shots to be of any use, you have to approach the parents and ask them to sign a model release. Usually, they're flattered that you think their rug rats are cute. The kids can be stiff at first, but soon forget about the silly lady with the big camera around her neck. If parents want a picture of sweetums, I e-mail them a JPEG. After all, a released photo can sell for commercial purposes—ads, promotions, marketing. Sometimes for hundreds of dollars. And you can resell it again and again.

The money's not nearly as good as it used to be—before cheap and free digital images. But you can still make a few bucks.

• • •

Of the two people in town who knew anything about Herb Gottwaldt's San Diego days, one sat in jail. I heard on the radio Monday a.m. that the judge set Meg LaGange's bail at half a million.

The other hadn't gone into work at Gottwaldt and Ryan that morning, nor had she stayed at home on Grand Avenue. I tracked down Doug Hewlett at one of his sports bars, and he told me his wife had gone to her mother's place in Prospect Park, not six blocks from my duplex. Her kid sister had broken a leg skiing the day before, and Sue was trying to help her mother get the teenager settled.

Rick and I had walked by Emmaline Norton's place dozens of times on our frequent rambles through the Park. It was a hulking two-storey blue stucco, with white trim, a tiny lawn, a broad front porch and a new cedar shake roof. Two mature Dutch elms—survivors of the elm plague—made a gothic arch over the front yard, sidewalk and street. I would have walked over that bright, sunny morning, but icy sidewalks made a stroll up hill and down dale fraught with peril.

Sue Hewlett answered the door in stocking feet as rap music bubbled out from some distant room, thrumming like a migraine in search of a head. Sorry, I'm a blues and classic rock gal. Always have been.

She had on bleached jeans and a turquoise UCLA sweatshirt, and a beautiful mother-of-pearl necklace. I caught a subtle whiff of Obsession on her. Just enough to interest anyone interested in beautiful women. I could also catch a hint of a headier perfume in the house—frying bacon. But dark hemispheres quivered beneath her bright black eyes. Her hair looked frazzled, as if she hadn't had the energy to take care of it that morning. Who could blame her, with the wringer she'd gone through in the last week? She was still nursing a banged-up wrist, and also had an irregular bruise on her left cheek.

"Hi Marta," she stuttered. "What are you, uh—"

"Doug told me I could find you here," I said.

"Susan," came a contralto voice from the shadows behind her, "who's there?" There followed a clomping of wooden sandals and Emmaline Norton came striding into view. She was nearly as tall as her daughter, but a bit overweight. She also had a magisterial presence—the look and posture of someone used to getting her way.

"Who's your friend?" she asked Sue, peering at me through gold-rimmed bifocals. Not displeased, but definitely neutral.

"This is the lady I told you about, Mama, that Denny hired," Sue said. "She was looking into the problems the agency was having."

"And doesn't she have a name?"

I could almost see Sue blush. "Yeah, Mama, she does." She took a long, deep breath. This was not a new experience, being instructed by mother. "Mama, this is Marta Hjelm, a private investigator. Marta, this is my Mama, Emmaline Norton."

"Well, Marta Hjelm, private investigator," said Emmaline. Norton, "why don't y'all come on into the kitchen? I just got some nice scones, or I can whip you up some scrambled eggs."

"Mama," Sue interjected, "I'm sure Marta's had her breakfast."

"That sounds awful good, Mrs. Norton," I allowed. "I'd love some eggs."

"It's *Mizz* Norton, Marta," she said, leading Sue and me back through the plainly furnished living room and hallway bedecked with posters by Picasso, Matisse, and Kandinsky. "I was a missus once, but that was a long time ago."

Kind of like me, I thought.

The kitchen was a large, square room in the back of the

house, with a blue porcelain sink, Formica counter, and oak cabinets on one side, fridge and newish stove on the other. A capacious blue-painted trestle table sat dead center, with four blue chairs on roller wheels arranged around it.

Dozens of snapshots adorned just about every vertical surface. Most of them showed Emmaline's teenaged daughter mugging happily at school events, slumber parties, skating and swimming get-togethers. The apple of every eye. Her National Honor Society certificate occupied a place of honor front and center on the fridge.

One of the pictures—which I stopped to peer at—showed the girl posed proudly at Gottwaldt and Ryan with Sue, Meg, and Herb Gottwaldt. She stood in between the boss and the sister on either side. The girl resembled Sue, but seemed taller, even prettier. Her features sharper and finer. Emmaline turned up in a few shots, and so did Sue and Doug Hewlett. Doug didn't look all that happy. Like Terry when I brought him home to Minnesota. Rick, by some miracle of fate, never has minded my relatives. Perhaps because he's not related to them and doesn't plan to be.

"You sit yourself down there, Marta," Emmaline directed, pointing at a specific blue chair.

I figured I better not disobey. Emmaline ruled here, and I sensed that her older daughter didn't really enjoy her mother's authority.

"Tea or coffee?"

"Tea, please. Black if you have it."

"Irish Breakfast okay?"

"Sure is."

"Now tell me what you're doing about this awful thing that happened to Mr. Gottwaldt," she said, flipping on the burner beneath a stainless steel teapot. Then she pulled a carton of eggs out of the fridge and set about cracking three of them—the organic brown-shelled kind—into a Pyrex bowl.

"I was working for Denny Ryan until a few days ago, Mizz Norton—"

"Emmaline. You just call me Emmaline." She whipped the

eggs into a froth as she added milk and cracked pepper.

I nodded. "Certainly, Emmaline. Anyway, Jennifer Nelson—Herb's daughter."

"I know who she is," she observed, and not with pleasure.

"She hired me to look into the circumstances of the murder."

Sue had sat down across the table from me. She furrowed her brow. "Jennifer hired you?"

"Uh-huh."

"I thought the police are handling everything now."

"They'll probably come up with some answers," I said. "But anyone can hire an investigator to look after their interests. Jennifer particularly agreed with me that Herb's California connections needed checking out. It could be weeks before the police get to it."

Emmaline nodded. "And you're here to talk with Susan and me about San Diego days."

I nodded. "Did you know Herb?"

"Well, I sure did." She turned on the fire under a frying pan that she'd melted some butter in and dumped in the egg mixture, mixing it slowly with a wooden spatula. "I worked as a receptionist in his real estate office about the time Susan was in college."

"Great. Then I can ask both of you questions."

"I don't see why not. Right Susan?"

"Right, Mama," said the advertising lady.

While Emmaline supervised the eggs, I reached across the table and touched Sue's bruised cheek. "What happened?"

She giggled nervously. "Middle of the night two nights ago. Doug was having a hockey dream. I zigged when I should have zagged. He caught me with an elbow."

"Dangerous sleeping with a defenseman, huh?" I said.

"Yeah, sometimes."

But my bullshit detector went on. The wrist, the bruise on the cheek. A husband who'd been in a violent business. I began to wonder.

The teapot whistled and Emmaline poured a mug of hot water. She stuck a Irish Breakfast tea bag in it, then handed it to me. Next she slid the scrambled eggs onto a plate and garnished it with two thick slices of bacon she'd had sitting on a paper towel on the counter.

Such sacrifices I make to put my subjects at their ease.

"I've already sent someone out to San Diego to conduct interviews," I said between bites. "We're just curious to know if Herb had any ongoing business relationships out there that had gone sour. Or even personal relationships. Maybe he shafted someone in a deal."

"In other words," said Emmaline, "did someone from there carry a grudge back here?"

I nodded with a mouthful of eggs and bacon, chewed a bit, then swallowed. Emmaline knew how to make eggs. "You know, the odds don't favor it, unless it relates to something recent."

"Why would anyone wait such a long time to kill him?" asked Sue, intent as a judge.

Emmaline laughed again, and it looked like Sue almost cringed. This was one mother-daughter relationship that reeked of friction—two strong-willed women toe to toe. Seemed to me like Sue was stuck between a rock called Emmaline and a hard place called Doug. Despite her looks and smarts, I didn't envy her. Now she even had me wondering about Doug.

"So what do you want to know, Marta?" Emmaline said.

Neither of them could think of anyone who hated Herb so much that they'd want him dead. Sure, they remembered people who came out on the short end of deals, as well as competitors who resented Herb's successes. I took down names and said I'd forward them to my guy in San Diego. Emmaline recounted what happened at Herb's real estate firm while she worked there—what she could recall so many years later. Major sales and acquisitions. Hires, fires, and resignations. Partners. Charitable projects Herb participated in, such as fund raising for the hospital that had cured his wife's cancer. I scribbled it all down in my reporter's notebook.

"So you can't think of anyone who really hated Herb?" I

said.

"Like people were saying out at Jennifer's, he could be difficult," Sue said. "You caught a whiff of envy sometimes. But kill
him? No, no."

Emmaline laughed softly. "A good looking man like him
with a handsome family? Making really good money like there
was nothing to it? Susan's right that folks envied him"

"I'm not quite clear how you and your daughter met Herb." I
popped the last bit of bacon in my mouth and washed it down
with the last of the tea.

"Well, Susan's the one who met him. She was still in high
school. Right honey?"

"Right, Mama."

"Well, tell Marta the story."

Herb had come to speak to a business club meeting at her
high school. She visited with him at his agency and told him
how she wanted to get into advertising. He told her about the
best ad/marketing programs at colleges around San Diego. But
she was seduced by journalism. They ran into each other again
when she was a sophomore in college, and having second
thoughts about journalism's rotten career prospects. She moved
into ad/marketing. When she got her B.A., he hired her east to
Minneapolis.

"So how'd *you* get hooked up with Herb, Emmaline?"

"Nothing like this Facebook or LinkedIn nonsense that they
have going now, I can tell you that." And she laughed a hearty
one. "Just old-fashioned networking. I needed a job with real
benefits, after I had Michelle, and Susan thought I ought to call
Mr. Gottwaldt. He had an opening for a receptionist in his real
estate office. Simple as that. Later on Michelle and I followed
Susie east."

"Well," I said, "it must be nice for the whole family to be
together out here."

"Sure is," Emmaline said. She looked at her older daughter
expectantly.

"One big happy," Sue pronounced in response, not too
convincingly.

"Must make you feel great to have such a successful daughter and son-in-law," I essayed.

Emmaline's smile narrowed and Sue's shoulders tightened. "I am *very* proud of my girl."

Her less than comprehensive encomium hung forebodingly in the air, and was mercifully put out of its misery by the rubbery clatter of a pair of crutches advancing down the hall.

Michelle Norton appeared in the doorway, her mouth scrunched up in a distillation of adolescent frustration. Her lower right leg was bound up in some kind of high-tech plastic cast in bright red, encircled with strips of blue-green Velcro. A Calvin Klein sock protruded from the bottom. Her jeans were cut from the knee down, and she had on a maroon sweatshirt from her prep school.

"I *hate* this thing," she said, shifting her weight on the crutches. "I am going to *die* if I have to keep wearing it for *six* weeks!"

"Listen, girl," Sue said with big-sister steeliness, "you're just darned lucky it wasn't a compound fracture. With your bones stickin' every which way outta your hide."

"Don't say that," whined Michelle, "it's gross."

"It could've happened, punkin," Emmaline said authoritatively. "You're lucky."

"I still hate this cast," Michelle whispered. Then she finally noticed me, and Sue made our introductions—explaining that I lived in the neighborhood and was a private investigator, working on behalf of Herb's daughter.

As adults often do, I asked the girl about what she was studying and what her college plans might be—always good small talk when a teenager needs to be engaged. As it turned out, she was on the school paper, played drums in the jazz band, acted in school plays, competed in volleyball, liked English but hated math and wanted to be an actress. She *was* a gorgeous kid—tall, athletic, eyes as bright and keen as her sister's.

"So you're a real PI, like on cable, huh?" she asked.

"Well, I don't know if it's like on TV, but, yeah, I'm a PI."

"It's gotta be pretty exciting."

"Well, it's mostly long stretches of utter boredom punctuated by moments of sheer terror."

She, her mother and sister all laughed.

"No, really," the girl said, "what's it actually like?"

So I told her.

Chapter Twenty

I caught lunch at a Greek restaurant in Golden Valley, alternating between noshing on a plate of shrimp in tomato/wine/feta cheese sauce, and dictating my first report for Jennifer Nelson. I still hadn't written a final report for Denny, and at the moment I didn't give a damn. He'd get it eventually.

I spent the rest of Monday visiting people who knew Herb Gottwaldt back in the day. His personal attorney. His best friend, the marketing VP of Minneapolis Mutual Insurance. Also, I chatted with Herb's ex-wife in Tucson. Not a skeleton could be heard rattling anywhere.

It was after dark, around seven, and I was driving home through Stadium Village—named after the old, demolished Memorial Stadium, lately replaced by a towering new football-viewing excrescence named after a bank—home to the dreadful University of Minnesota football program. The cell phone beeped at me.

I told it to do something anatomically impossible for a person, let alone a piece of electronics. Why I picked it up, I don't know. It felt like the starch had gone out of me about the time I left Minneapolis Mutual, and only my exo-skeleton of winter clothes kept me upright. Which would make me something Kafkaesque, like a large crustacean or insect.

"Large insect" seemed about right, considering my mood and the state of things.

It was Jennifer Nelson, sounding every bit as unstarchy. She said that Meg had made bail and she'd called Jennifer's house, fortunately connecting with Mr. Nelson instead of the bereaved daughter. Meg wanted to talk to my client, but my client—despite believing the accused murderess innocent—couldn't hack it.

"I don't have it in me, Marta," she sighed. "I just can't talk to her yet. Could you go over and see what she wants? She's at Lee Gorney's place on Lake of the Isles, 1444 Grant Avenue. And tell her when this mess is cleared up, I want her back at work, okay?"

"Okay, fine," I said with minimal enthusiasm, hanging the

first of the three rights that would get me headed in the direction of that upscale neighborhood south of downtown.

• • •

For someone worth however many hundreds of millions, Lee Gorney lived fairly modestly. His four- or five-bedroom colonial didn't even sit on Lake of the Isles, and had only a partial view of the water and the myriad bicyclists and 'bladers that teemed its paths in the summertime. I knew which house from the news trucks parked in front.

A grandfather and great-uncle of Gorney's had created a grain elevator company that became a huge agribusiness conglomerate, AmberGrain. Gorney, his two brothers, and a clutch of cousins still owned most of it, and kept it private. Not as massive as Cargill or ADM, but with gross sales approaching $30 billion, it trafficked in everything from grain milling and transport to food manufacturing to banking and derivatives. Nowadays Lee Gorney just sat on the AmberGrain board, and underwrote liberal and green causes.

At the foot of his sidewalk two reporters were doing stand-ups for the ten o'clock news, looking like they knew big time what was what. They seldom do, of course. The term "TV journalist" is usually an oxymoron. Still, I hoped one of these well-coiffed simpletons would ask me something when I went up the sidewalk so I could glibly pronounce, "No comment." No such luck. They ignored me.

I punched the door chimes. A very tall and comely man answered, all chiseled features and immaculate brown hair coifed in a sort of JFK style. Possibly a rug, but a good enough one to make me wonder. In blue blazer, pink shirt open at the neck, and crisp tan trousers, the gent looked like he had an answer or three, and didn't want to share them with me. If superficial, short-term, steamy relationships had appealed to me—which they don't—I might have batted my eyelashes at him.

"Sorry, she's not giving any interviews," he growled.

"Good for her," I said. "I'm Marta Hjelm, the investigator. Jennifer Nelson asked me to come over."

He showed a glimmer of recognition, nodded tiredly and

swung the door wide open. I popped in.

"Lee Gorney," he said, offering his tidy but well calloused paw. "I just assumed you were media."

I took his hand and pumped it. "No problem. Good to meet you, Mr. Gorney. I understand Meg wanted to relay some information to Jennifer Nelson."

He nodded, his mouth all scrunched up. "She's watching TV. Come on."

I followed him upstairs, rubbernecking all the way. It's fun to try to gauge people by how they live, where they live, what they own. But Gorney's place, through inadvertence or guile, didn't have anything to say. The house could have belonged to some garden-variety doctor or lawyer without any specific taste— ordinary beige carpeting, ordinary white walls with some middling-quality contemporary prints on them, no personal touches. Gorney probably just used this as an in-town *pied-à-terre*. Certainly he had to have residences grander than this.

Meg LaGrange was curled up in a tan leather recliner in a bedroom, staring at a big flat screen up on the wall. Somebody in an ER was trying to save someone's life while an hysterical relative made the patient's survival that much less likely but more dramatically interesting. The recent guest of the Hennepin County sheriff took a couple of winks to notice that we'd arrived.

No looker to start with, she wore the demeanor of refried hell itself—bloodshot eyes, ashen complexion, unkempt hair, hunched shoulders, no spark whatever in those formerly penetrating peepers. I expect she hadn't slept in a couple of days or more.

"Hello again, Marta," she said with the intonation of stale wash water.

"I'm sorry we have to meet like this," I said.

She nodded tiredly. "Me too." She yawned a good long one. "Take a load off." She gestured at the edge of the bed.

"Either of you girls want a drink?" Gorney asked. He was staring at Meg like he really did care. He wasn't faking it.

"Just an orange juice, hon," she said. "Put in a tiny drop of vodka. Enough to give it some character."

"Stoly? Ketel One?"

"Don't care."

He nodded and looked at me.

"When Jennifer called I was heading home for a Bombay martini—"

He cocked his head. "Plymouth alright?"

Twist my arm! But for purposes of professional decorum I answered simply in the affirmative.

"Straight up or rocks?"

"Rocks."

"Olives?"

"Two, please." I decided to push my luck. "Anchovy-stuffed?"

"Blue cheese-stuffed okay?"

"Fine with me."

He nodded and vanished. I divested myself of overcoat and down vest, and plopped down on the corner of the king-sized bed, facing Meg.

"First, Jennifer wants you know that as soon as all this shit gets cleared up, she'd like you back at the agency."

She smiled wanly and nodded. "Sounds good."

"So why'd you phone her, Meg?" I asked. "What do you want me to tell her?"

She unfolded herself and extended her long legs out in front of her. "I didn't kill Herb. I wanted her to hear me say it, and to tell everyone else in the family."

"But a 9mm like yours," I said, "killed Herb Gottwaldt. You were there at about the right time. You had opportunity, and it sounds like you had motive."

"Don't think I don't know it, Marta," she said. "But I hadn't seen the gun since Wednesday, early afternoon, after I talked to you. I took it to the office with me, in my purse."

"Who knew you had it?"

"Ever since I was mugged I carry it sometimes." She shrugged, not exactly happy about it. "Everyone knows I have a carry permit. So someone might've guessed. Pretty stupid, huh?"

"Who else from Hemo was there?"

"Denny. Herb. Sue came in to get some stuff. Doug was with her. Archie was around for a little while. I got a glimpse of your ex. The whole gang. Everyone except Harry."

"Why'd you go into work?" I wondered.

"Thing is I had papers in the office that I had to get. It was some stuff for the Hemo test market. It would have knocked their socks off. When I went off to my meeting that afternoon—"

"What time?"

"About three. When I was ready to go, I looked in my purse and the gun was gone."

"So just about anyone could have taken it, including anyone else on Hemo."

"'Fraid so."

"Do you know if Grabowski's people found out if anyone saw someone going through the purse?"

"I suppose they asked around," she sighed. "He's not saying much to me or my attorney."

"Did you tell anybody about the 9mm after it disappeared?"

"I was in a hurry to get out of there. I thought maybe I left the damned thing at home. I should have said something." She gave a hollow sort of laugh. "Man, that's an understatement."

"Yup," I said. "So tell me what happened that night after Herb contacted you. Everything."

Gorney arrived just then with the drinks, and I greedily accepted my Plymouth martini, which sloshed the rim of a large tumbler bedecked with waterfowl of various sorts. I call this a Daddy-sized cocktail, after my old man, who taught me how to mix a killer "martoony," as he liked to call it.

Meg accepted her screwdriver from Gorney, took a sip and set it on the side table. She looked up at him questioningly. "Should I tell her?" she asked quietly. "Jim says I should keep my trap shut."

"That's the advice we pay an attorney for," he said, moving behind her and affectionately rubbing her shoulders. "But it's up to you, hon." He leaned down to her left ear, whispered a few words. She barely moved, just a slight nod when he whispered. Then he ambled out of the room.

"What do you think, Meg?" I said.

"Oh shit!" she replied, rubbing her eyes with the heels of her hands. "*Shit, shit, shit!*"

"If it makes any difference," I said, "I don't think you did it. If you'd wanted to kill Herb, you'd have done it smarter. Even if you'd gone nuts, you'd have done it smarter. You got set up, Meg."

"No kidding," she answered tiredly, putting down her drink on the carpeting and rising to her feet for a cat-like stretch, a yoga move that looked very comfy. She eased herself back down. "I just don't know if I can trust you. You're working for Jennifer, and she wouldn't even talk to me when I called her this evening."

I shrugged and took the first sip of my martini, savoring the chill fire of it in my mouth and throat. My hands were clam-cold from clasping the big tumbler full of ice, vermouth, gin and blue cheese-stuffed olives, but I barely noticed.

"Do you blame her?"

"Not really," she answered.

"So?"

"What the hell," she said, reaching for her drink. She sipped on it for a moment, almost meditatively, then returned it to the side table.

"Got home about ten that night," she said. "I have a little office in the spare bedroom. I was working in there, a while later. My Mac's set up to beep at me when something comes into my Gmail account. For some reason, getting something at that hour didn't seem right. That's my most private e-mail account. Only stuff from friends, work colleagues comes in there. So it couldn't be spam. Sounds crazy, like some stupid feminine-intuition thing. But it just felt *very* wrong."

She actually looked shook up even talking about it, and I let her take her time. Finally she seemed ready to continue.

"I waited a while, then I opened it. Herb was firing me. He said I should come out and talk with him. *I. Could. Not. Believe.*

It."

She shut her eyes and shook her head—bad dream time. "I spent ten minutes trying to figure out his game. Made no sense at all. So I called him, but all I got was his voice mail."

Herb's timing struck me as peculiar. Why at this juncture, when the agency is about to clinch the Hemo test market? Why sack the lead copywriter? Why not just wait until the project succeeded or failed? Or until the account was well established. Then no one would much care.

"So you drove out there," I said. "Archie had already arrived."

"I was pretty pissed anyway," she said. "I guess I lit into Herb, and screw Archie."

"He did tell Archie to scram."

"Yeah, that he did. Then he said that—" She cleared her throat, like a growl. "He said that he had good reasons to fire me, but it'd be best to talk about it later. I screamed at him. That was pure bullshit." She gave a pro forma chuckle, a gallows laugh. "He was kind of tut-tutting me, and trying to calm me down, like he used to do when we were—" She trailed off.

I let her take a minute to ponder the good old days, then she continued.

"I shouted at him some more, he got steamed. He always did this kind of slow burn. Then, kind of quietly, he said, 'That's all.' Like I'm the fucking upstairs maid. 'I'm not taking any more of this *shit* from you,' he said."

"Any more of what shit?" I asked. "Did he explain himself?"

"Just what I said. He didn't answer me."

"I understand you have a temper, Meg."

"So I've heard." Her voice turned chilly. She peered down at her knees. "So do a lot of people. So did Herb."

"All right. What happened then?"

She pursed her lips strenuously and looked from side to side—a kind of somebody-wake-me-up look. She peered at me straight in the eye and said, "*Kaboom!*"

I pointed an index finger and shot it like a pistol.

She chuckled. "Don't be an idiot, Marta. I *really* blew up. We shouted at each other for a while and I stormed outta there. Just like I used to in the bad good old days. But I didn't touch him, he didn't touch me."

The award-winning copywriter stood up again, rubbing the back of her neck.

"I'll tell you, I'm so damned, *fucking* tired," she said, wilting visibly out of her ramrod posture. "I'm not trying to stonewall you or anything. I just don't know how much more I can do tonight. I gotta get some sleep." She peered out the open door. "Lee?"

I had a feeling I wasn't going to finish my Plymouth martini. Very sad. "Listen, Meg, I'm sorry," I said. "If you don't want to talk anymore, I understand. I wouldn't either. But I think Jennifer deserves to know a few things."

"Of course she does."

"Just talk to me a few more minutes, Meg, then I'll go. I can come back when you're feeling up to it. Okay?"

Gorney came into the bedroom in a rush and looked at his lady, then me, like I'd just molested her.

"I'm sorry, babe, false alarm." She laser-beamed a grin at him, and I was glad she loved somebody that much. She'd be needing him for more than just her bail money. If it came to that.

After he vanished again, I asked Meg how Herb had seemed early that morning.

"He didn't seem upset or anything. Kind of calm, actually."

Had she appealed to him on the basis of their past relationship?

She nodded.

And it made no difference?

Another nod.

How long did she did stay with Gottwaldt?

"Fifteen, twenty minutes, tops. I was just so sad driving home, like someone real important to me had died. Before I left— One time we were on a vacation in Micronesia, Marta. On Palau. We had this cottage right on a beach, like out of a dream. Most beautiful place I've ever stayed in my life. Herb promised me no matter how pissed we ever got, we should never hurt each other. I asked him if he remembered that. He said he did, and it didn't matter anymore."

A deep, rattling sigh escaped her. And her chin dipped down to her chest. I could see her mouth trying to form a determined shape, but collapsing into a quiver.

"Maybe it's bedtime, huh?" I said.

She looked up at me wanly. "You got it straight, Marta."

Gorney showed me out and I told him to take good care of the lady. He said I could count on it.

On my way back to the Merc, a TV reporter rushed up with his camera gal and blaring lights, and asked if I'd seen Meg LaGrange and if so what had she revealed.

My five seconds of fame had arrived.

"No comment," I snapped as I brushed past the nattily-attired news hound.

Chapter Twenty-One

First thing Tuesday morning I phoned Jennifer from the duplex and filled her in. Then I tracked down Denny Ryan at the ad agency. He didn't seem too tickled to hear about Herb giving Meg the sack.

"That's c-c-crazy!" he stuttered, trying to get his mind around some rationale for eighty-sixing Meg. "Totally nuts! Herb didn't say a peep about anything like that, and I talked with him that evening, after I left you guys at the sports bar. He never said a damned thing about Meg being a problem."

"Assuming a real firing offense, what could it have taken?"

He snorted. "Marta, I really don't think I should be talking with you about this matter."

My turn to huff imperiously. "Denny, I work for one of your new bosses. She's asked me to keep going."

The line went uncomfortably silent for ten or twenty seconds. I liked the thought of Denny twisting in the breeze.

"You're assuming she'll inherit a big piece of G&R."

"I think it's a safe assumption, don't you?"

I could have sworn he said something about me under his breath that rhymed with "rich." But I don't like to assume the worst about upstanding business people.

"Okay," he said. "Nothing I can think of would have justified Herb canning Meg." He coughed and cleared his throat. "Do you think she did it, Marta?"

"No, I don't," I said, leaving it at that. "I have a guy out in San Diego doing interviews. Do you remember Herb ever talking about people out there who he had trouble with? Anyone with grudges?"

"He had that tough spell with his own agency," he said. "Business reverses. Could happen to anyone."

The rest of the day I spent dropping in on various players in the Twin Cities ad industry, from the local correspondent of *Ad World* weekly to yet more former Gottwaldt associates and competitors. If any picture was forming, I couldn't see it.

On the way home, in the stop-and-go on 494, I picked up

the first of two voicemails, from Rick, back from his Iowa shoot. He said he had articles for me to read. He'd see me about nine that evening. And by the way, he thought he'd come home tonight for good. I smiled broadly.

But the smile didn't last long. The second voicemail conveyed the mellow and amorous tones of my ex-husband, who planned to drop by, oh, about nine that evening.

I issued a steamy expletive into the chilly confines of the Merc, and blinked at the digital time on the CD player: 9:45.

• • •

Terry had perched on the front porch swing, going lazily back and forth, with a bottle of Laurent Perrier champagne clasped in his arms. He was rather over-bundled for the purpose, in a puffy green parka—a common failing among warm-weather types cut loose in a Minnesota winter. A bit younger than me and about my height, he still had the bemused air of a wandering philosopher.

"I'm glad you're late," he purred. He held up the bubbly—our favorite back in Santa Barbara—and flashed me his perfect pearly whites. "I just got here a little while ago. Got a ride from the garage."

"What do you mean?" I blurted.

"Got in a fender bender with the rental car and I didn't want to mess with another car."

"Then you'll have to take a taxi back to the hotel," I said.

He looked a little disappointed. "I was hoping to visit with you a little while."

"Were you now, Mr. Rosen?"

He shot me yet another of those little-boy-hurt looks, then a sly smile. "Rick dropped by a few minutes before you got here."

My heart did an instant rumba. I felt like Mike Tyson had landed a right hook in my gut. *Fan-fucking-tastic!*

"He left you this." Terry held up a big white envelope with a Mueller Images mailing label on it. "I said I'd give it to you."

I wanted to ask what Rick had said, but bad idea. It didn't take much imagination to figure out what Rick was thinking when he discovered Terry camped out on our front porch.

I began rummaging in my satchel, but I was too damned frazzled to even find my keys. Terry set down the envelope and champagne on the floor beneath the swing and came over. He laid an arm around my shoulder and gently bussed me on the cheek.

For some reason the advice of my old high school choir director—a big, beefy man with a gray goatee and a Prussian manner—came surging back to me. When you're frightened, panicked before a concert, he lectured us occasional soloists (I was his favorite alto), remember to breathe deeply and slowly from the diaphragm. As many times as it takes.

Standing there next to my first and only ex-husband, I sucked in the icy January air one deep, slow breath at a time. Again and again and again. Then I dug in my satchel again and extracted the errant keys.

"Terry, we've got to talk."

He nodded and said "Absolutely." Then he grabbed the envelope and the bottle of Laurent Perrier.

• • •

I hadn't had a decent glass of champagne since Terry and I were back in Santa Barbara. We were very much in love then, both working at the same small chain of record stores. I'm pretty sure he hadn't started chasing women at that point. It was still a time when bricks-and-mortar music sales was a business worth being in. Just barely. He managed the advertising, and bought print space, air time and online ads for stores up and down the central coast. I parlayed my knowledge of blues and classic rock into an assistant store manager gig.

It didn't seem right, him sitting in Rick's chair in the living room. So I suggested we go back to the kitchen and I'd nuke some red beans and rice in the microwave. I got it zapping at a slow speed—I don't like to overheat stuff—and pulled out my parents' old Waterford goblets. Terry popped the cork, poured and took one side of the breakfast nook. I took the other. There we sat with full glasses, and I'd seldom felt sadder.

He lifted his glass and peered at me with bogus cheerfulness—trying to prove he didn't know what I was about to say.

"To the old wife and husband routine," he whispered.

"To the old husband and wife," I repeated, and clinked the rim of my goblet to the rim of his.

We drank, memories and champagne both, and sat without a word. I had Paul Desmond's dry-martini alto sax playing in the distance, without Brubeck.

Of course, Laurent Perrier ain't Dom Pérignon. But it's awfully good, in my humble opinion. The fizzy beverage danced and sang in the mouth—liquid joy. It could give you the most wonderful evening of repartee and rumpy-bumpy, and the most awful hangover the next morning. Kind of like my life with Terry.

"I made a horrible mistake," he finally said, staring down into his empty goblet. I looked him square in the face and my old self came rushing back—a kid in her twenties, crazy in love. "After I had my, ah—"

"Flings?"

"A polite way to put it, thanks. Incredibly stupid. Didn't matter that they kind of threw themselves at me. I think if you'd gotten really, *really* mad at me. Hit me. Called me a mother-fucker, a son of a bitch— I'd have felt like we had something to work from. But you were so—" He reached for the right word.

"Stolid?" I said, catching the aroma of sausage and fennel seed seeping from the microwave.

He nodded. "Yeah, good word. Like nothing could get through that thick Norwegian skin of yours. I don't know if I ever even saw you cry over it."

I couldn't answer him, because he might have been right. He'd begged me to patch it up. But I felt like I couldn't let him get through to me like that. I wasn't about to let him turn Marta Hjelm into a character in a soap opera. Hurt me, yes. But leave my dignity the hell alone.

In my family you were polite, you bottled it up, you were a good little soldier. Even if you'd just gotten shot between the eyes. Someone betrays me bigtime, however, and they're out of my life. Gone, defunct, kaput. That's why my reaction to Terry's reappearance—to prevaricate for days, and leave Rick dangling and worried—left me totally confused.

Why did I take the case? Why hadn't I definitively kicked Terry's sorry ass out of my life for the last time?

I could only conclude I wasn't as tough a cookie as I'd fancied. I know I didn't love him. But maybe I was prepared to forgive.

I'd emptied my goblet and had the thought of pouring myself another.

"We all react the way we're programmed to, Terry," I finally responded. "You hurt me so damned bad I decided that I couldn't let you know how bad."

Chin on chest, he nodded. "Yeah, I knew that. But it made it impossible to fix things."

"Do you think I wanted to fix things after what you did?"

"You know," he said, "after I got here and called you, I almost felt like maybe you did." Across the table he grabbed my right hand. "I didn't realize till you were gone how damned much I love you. I thought about you every day. I—"

He sidled to his left, stood and drew me off the bench, to my feet. I was shocked at myself: *I let him do it! I said nothing!*

I hate to say it, but I liked the way he put his arms around me, the way his lips merged with mine, the pressure of his pelvis against mine. Pheromones started bouncing off the walls and all that old, memorable lust reared up out of some dusty corner of my brain. We began groping each other.

He felt and smelled and sounded so damned good!

Just like the old Terry, that velvet-voiced charmer.

And then, just as his fingers were touching the top buttons on my blouse—

The microwave blared.

It was like a slap across my face: *What in hell are you doing girl?*

I batted his hands away and back-pedaled, exclaiming: *"NO! NO! NO!"*

He looked truly shocked. He thought he was getting somewhere. "What's the—?" he said, and came at me, grabbing at my shoulders again.

My reaction was pure reflex.

I snatched his right hand with both my hands—his index and middle fingers in my right hand, the other fingers in my left—and jammed his wrist back toward him. He skittered to the rear, eyes wide with shock. And suddenly he was down on his knees howling in pain.

"*Marta*," he wailed, "*you're breaking my hand!*"

The whole thing couldn't have taken more than six or eight seconds. I didn't let go, but backed off. "Terry," I panted, "we can't go there. It's off the table. I'm not gonna let you mess me up again. I can't trust you. *Do you understand?*"

He just stared up at me and I almost started to pressurize his hand again—but restrained myself. That would have been wrong. I let go. He remained on his knees, but looked up at me with the recognition that his old Marta was history. I reached down to help him up, but he flinched back.

"I'm sorry about that," I said. "It's my fault, too. I didn't mean to hurt you, but I couldn't let anything happen. I shoulda said 'No' sooner."

He hauled himself to his feet, gently rubbing his right paw. He was still looking at me kind of wide-eyed. "Where'd you learn that shit, Marta?"

"My old street-fighting instructor, a former SAS guy and briefly my boyfriend. We're still mates, as he he puts it."

"Well, it certainly kills the buzz, doesn't it?"

"That's the idea."

"You know, I'm sorry, too. It was outta line, way outta line. I deserved the, um, hand thingy. But I really thought that there's something—"

I shook my head emphatically. "Nope. No. If there was, I just dug and deep, deep hole and I'm throwing it in there and burying it. I'm your ex, you're my ex. That's all there is to it. Finis. The end. Got it?"

At that I headed for the red beans and rice. They were steamy hot and roiling with kitchen-filling scents of Bourbon Street and bayou. We ate without talking. Between sips of Perrier, the bottle almost dead.

I guess somewhere along the line I'd stopped hating him, that was clear now. But he'd done the deed, actually multiple deeds. He'd stuck that knife in my back again and again. I'd moved on, explored a couple of careers, and found someone who was ten times what Terry had ever been. Now all I could feel for my ex-husband was pity. For a few short years he had been the biggest thing in my life.

"Why didn't you ever remarry?" I asked, sloshing the very last champagne around in the goblet, watching the bubbles well up.

He sighed and he blinked at me. "I did. Only lasted a year and half. She was just too young, had other ideas about things."

He peered around the room, marking time, then made eye contact again. "I don't know. I just kept thinking about you, missing the times we had together, wondering if maybe you'd give me another chance." He sat down again.

Excusing myself, I wavered down the hall to the bedroom, threw on some sweats, and called Rick. His brother's voicemail answered again. I started to speak, and a sort of wheeze came out.

Clearing my throat, I blurted, "I'm sorry about what happened, hon. I didn't know he'd be here. *Really* I didn't. I'll talk to you in the morning. Sleep tight, okay?"

Back in the kitchen Terry hadn't moved a muscle, with hands folded in his lap, staring straight ahead. He even didn't glance up at me when I walked in. His fading tan had vanished completely, leaving him ashen, almost as if he were nauseous. Maybe it was too much champagne. Maybe we were just too beat and beat up. We both looked like hell.

I busied myself with fixing some coffee in the French press. The two of us could use it. I felt him following me with his eyes.

"So, Terry, you still stay in touch with Clarice and Chuck, huh? I call her every Christmas season."

He brightened a few watts—still the rejected little lad, but taking it like a grown-up. "Yeah, sure do. My ex-girlfriend and I went camping with them last spring. I guess they didn't tell you. You still camp?"

• • •

We talked until 2:30. Me catching up on old mutual friends whom I hadn't stayed connected with. Him on how in hell I ended up with a detective's license in Minnesota. He wanted to know about my Dad's cancer. Then he told me that his dad—a real sweetie—had just had a quadruple bypass and wasn't doing well. It made me sad, because I'd liked that man a lot, and he liked me. Abe had taken me out to lunch after the divorce, and almost cried. He said he thought of me like the daughter he'd never had, and he hoped I'd write him or call him. Obviously, I hadn't. There's some guilt to chew on when I run short. I got the old man's e-mail address and promised myself I'd drop him a note.

Try as I might, I just didn't have the heart to send Terry on a long cab ride home in the cold and dark. I said I'd give him a ride to the hotel first thing in the morning.

Rick would have to trust me on this one.

I covered up the birds and got my ex settled on the living room sofa with a down quilt and a pillow. The second I jumped in my bed I zonked, totally and absolutely.

The next thing I knew it was six-thirty, still pretty dark out. I laid there on my back, trying futilely to pick out the cracks in the ceiling.

Just as I shut my eyes again, I heard Terry's hand on the knob of the bedroom door, opening it very gently. The hinges squeaked ever so slightly and I could feel him staring at me. He must have stood there for ten minutes. Maybe it seemed like ten minutes, and it was actually two or three. He didn't say a thing, just breathed very evenly. I pretended to doze, turning once from one side to the other, scrunching up the pillow in my arms, locking my eyelids like deadbolts.

I wanted to get up, scratch my thigh, do a few stretches. Whatever happened, I didn't want him to know I knew he was there.

Finally, the door shut. He shuffled down to the bathroom and turned on the water. I quickly threw on my robe and padded into the kitchen to wash the French press. He came in, said hi, asked how I slept, nothing more. He looked a hell of a lot brighter and happier than he had a few hours before. We both pretended that our little incident hadn't happened.

After a breakfast of omelets, OJ, and pumpernickel toast, I grabbed a quick shower, dried my hair, and threw on one of my serviceable business outfits. A gray wool skirt, oxford-cloth blouse, and a blue silk sweater. After I dropped Terry off at his hotel in Plymouth, I could go straight to work—more jaw wags with Herb Gottwaldt's old compadres.

The thermometer didn't look too bad—up in the high 20s. So I decided to protect myself from the winter elements with the old Burberry trenchcoat that Dad bought me back when I worked for Denny Ryan the first time. It wore like steel and had a really warm lining.

For once I had the time to indulge in a nice, toasty vehicle. So I decided to use the remote car starter my Dad installed in the Merc. I rummaged around the vestibule junk drawer and found the thing.

Terry was walking up the hallway toward the living room and I told him to come double-quick if he wanted to see a little Minnesota ingenuity at work. We stood in the front window, looking out over the porch onto Emerald Street. The Merc had gotten a coating of powdery snow overnight, and the white stuff glittered jovially on all the bare branches of the young boulevard trees. It was about 8:30.

"Take a gander," I said. "This is how we clever inhabitants of northern climes avoid freezing our patooties off when we climb into a chilly car. I will press the magic button and in ten minutes the inside of my ol' land yacht will be as cozy and warm as a hot toddie."

"Fire it up, oh great Norwegian one," Terry laughed, peering out through the chinks in the living room mini-blinds.

"Regard," I said haughtily.

With a flourish I held up the remote—a brown, clunky thing that looked like a steam-powered Bulgarian garage door opener—and punched the round white button. A little green bulb on the control winked on and we heard the first resonant

160

grind of the Merc's starter, as the engine roused itself from the cold. I began to turn my head to say something to Terry, another wisecrack.

But before I could, my eyes—not my brain—began to percieve a dazzling nimbus of light that flared out from the Merc.

It gave me no time to think. No time to react. No time to do a damned thing.

Just—for the minutest fraction of a second—to sense subliminally that something was horribly wrong.

The car bomb blossomed like a huge, incandescent flower.

Shockwave and thunder and debris slammed into us.

Chapter Twenty-Two

We were lucky as hell that we didn't hit our heads on any furniture when we went down.

Mostly, though, luck smiled on the fact that my mini-blinds filtered out all but a bit of the shattered window glass. If I had pulled them up or tilted them too far open, the two of us would have gotten chewed up like so much puréed veal.

Of course, if the remote hadn't worked, and I'd started the Merc from the driver's seat, it would have meant *Götterdämerung* for a certain fortyish divorced couple.

Nonetheless, we bounced hard off the floor. Terry was dazed. I walloped my right shoulder pretty good—the one I'd dislocated a couple of years before. It began hurting like a son-ofabitch almost immediately. Somehow I managed to check out Terry. He nodded groggily at me—okay, old girl.

The birds were screaming off their pointy little heads and flapping around inside their cages. Nothing I could do for them, right then. Both oriental fans had leapt off the walls, but Rick's Cartier-Bresson photo merely tilted on its picture hook, sending the River Marne flowing uphill. Some knick-knacks and family pictures and pillows had flung themselves onto the Persian. And shattered glass covered the floor underneath the windows. The winter air was beginning to surge into my living room.

I staggered into the hallway, down to the kitchen, and punched in 9-1-1 on the wall phone. With a voice shakier than I liked, I told some woman on the other end what had happened, the address, and said to notify Deputy Grabowski at Hennepin County, too. She assured me that squads and a paramedic unit would be there pronto. "Anyone hurt?" she asked.

Something dripped into my left eye. I rubbed it and came up with a fingertip covered with blood. I touched my forehead and felt a gash. Some of the glass had gotten through. "Could be," I told her, hanging up.

Next, I lucked out and got Rick at the museum, and did my level best not to scare the sap out of him. I didn't do a good job.

First to arrive on the scene didn't come in an ambulance or

squad. It was our upstairs tenant, Grace Corelli—all six feet and 300 pounds of her. She fussed over us like a big Italian Mamma and muttered "Holy Mother of God" more times than I could count. I think she would have lifted me up and cradled me to her substantial bosom, if I'd let her. The first thing I had her do was haul the birds upstairs.

Four or five squads zoomed up, lights coruscating strobe-red against the fresh, white snow. Paramedics followed, then a couple of unmarked cars. Emerald Street got blocked off. Finally, the media descended. Though I didn't see much of the street action from inside the kitchen.

For an hour it was a noisy blur. Cops. Paramedics dabbing at me and asking the usual questions, trying to talk me into taking another ambulance ride. Terry looking stunned. Grace babbling, hovering and begging to stay. When Rick arrived in a breathless rush we had a good, long hug, and he had the sense to not deliver the lecture I expected: *You're-going-get-yourself-killed-and-why-didn't-I-tell-him-this-case-was-so-fucking-dangerous?*

Rick, Terry, and I trudged out to Rick's Explorer—parked a block away, because the cops wouldn't let him through. We went right past the mangled wreck of my Dad's Merc. The sedan's front end had been torn apart, like some abstract-expressionist sculpture, and burnt. Most of the flying metal whanged across the street into the lumberyard wall, in St. Paul. My first floor windows would all have to be replaced.

"That was a good car," I blubbered into Rick's ear, as we shuffled along the snowy sidewalk. "A *very* good car. Daddy picked it right off the lot."

"I know, Marty," he whispered back.

We drove down to Hennepin County Medical Center in silence, Terry in the back seat. He stared out the window. But once in a while I caught him peeking at Rick and me. I earnestly hoped he was thinking: *Boy, did I screw up a good thing.*

After the ER docs gave both Terry and me the once-over, and stitched up my forehead, we three caught a cab to Minneapolis police headquarters a few blocks away. It was about one o'clock,

Terry was questioned first, since he'd booked a flight out early that evening. He wanted some time back at his hotel for a long, hot shower. And Bertram headquarters needed to consult with him about the godawful publicity coming out of Minneapolis.

"I'm incredibly sorry I pulled you into this mess, Marty," he sighed, when he emerged from the conference room where Grabowski and company debriefed him. "I thought it'd be a good gig for you. Hell, may as well say it. I was curious to see you again. I thought maybe, umm—" Terry trailed off as he looked at Rick, who somehow didn't scowl. In fact, he managed to waft a forced smile at my ex. "Try to get her off the case, huh, Rick? If you can," Terry told his brief and former rival. "Neither of us want this kid to get hurt, do we?"

He gave me a quick hug, a peck on the cheek, and whispered in my ear: "Sorry about last night." He shook Rick's hand, and trucked on out of my new life as quickly as he had come into it. I almost felt sorry for him, but I was glad *that* was over.

A uniformed female officer led me into the conference room. Grabowski hopped off a gray, two-drawer file cabinet he'd been perched on and offered me his hand, giving me a dose of those cool, x-ray eyes of his. "Glad you're okay. Coulda been lots worse, I guess."

"Yeah, coulda," I replied.

"Introductions, first," he said. "This is Special Agent Jackie Broder of the local FBI office."

The surprisingly young agent didn't get up, but reached over the dark-stained maple conference table to shake hands. She had a round face, close-cropped straw blonde hair, intense brown eyes, and a pugnacious tilt to her jaw line. Her clothes were strictly dress-for-success. A blue silk blouse, a flouncy woman's bow-tie, gray flannel slacks and suit coat with an American flag pin in the lapel. I caught the faint bulge of a weapon underneath her left arm.

Grabowski's colleague from the Minneapolis P.D. was called Sergeant Jim Hobbes, and he looked like a serious runner—lean, hard, gaunt. A bag of pork rinds would take one look at him and flee from the room, oinking wildly.

Hobbes' St. Paul colleague had no such problems, being a regular at the Ace Cafe downstairs from our office. I'd never worked with Lieutenant Billy Wolf, but I'd seen him consuming vast quantities of cakes and hash while guardedly ogling the slightly over-ripe Ace waitresses. His impressive gut overhung his belt and threatened to pop the buttons on his polyester-cotton shirt. But I liked his face a lot. A real face—big, round nose, Santa-like grin, twinkling eyes, all perched above several hemispherical chins that wiggled when he spoke.

At first, I wondered why he was here. Then—head slap moment—I remembered that the bomb exploded right across the city line into St. Paul.

"Ms. Hjelm," Grabowski began, "why don't you sit down." He gestured at a secretary's chair that had been rolled in for the occasion. "I know what you've been up to. Maybe you could reprise it for us, from the top. Then my colleagues can ask a few questions."

I did just that, in under an hour. They asked me a few things along the way, but mainly let me bloviate. After a coffee break, agent Broder led off.

"Clearly," she said in a kind of androgynous tenor, "you've managed to put some fear on the killer or killers of Herb Gottwaldt. Would you agree?"

"Well, that wasn't my alternator that blew up."

Billy Wolf chuckled, and Broder glared at him. Grabowski allowed himself a fleeting smile that only I could see. Hobbes was expressionless.

"So the answer is 'Yes'?"

"Not entirely."

"What do you mean?"

"*Who* was the bomber trying to blow up? Me or my ex-husband?"

Billy Wolf nodded. "If the former, then yes, Marta's putting pressure on someone in Herb's circle. If the latter, we got your terrorist conspiracy."

"So why should there be a terrorist conspiracy anymore?"

said Hobbes in a monotone, his first peep since he said hello to me. All he'd done was scratch notes on a yellow legal pad. "Even if there was one. Gottwaldt's dead, the cigarette account's going to Chicago, the e-mails have stopped. In fact, the last one came after the Lexus crashed. Game, set, match to the terrorists."

"But Mr. Rosen still works for Bertram Tobacco, still's a potential target," suggested Billy Wolf.

"True enough," said Hobbes, "but the threats clearly targeted Gottwaldt and Ryan, not Bertram. I think the target was Ms. Hjelm."

"I think Ms. Hjelm knows something, like Agent Broder said," Grabowski contended.

I put up an index finger. "Ms. Hjelm *may* know something, but she doesn't have a bloody clue what it is. If she *did*, she'd spill it pronto and help you guys stick someone in jail."

"I'm sure you would, Ms. Hjelm," said Broder. She looked almost like a ventriloquist, her straight lips barely moving. "But you know how it goes. Sometimes investigations take weeks or months to sort out, especially something of this complexity. Sometimes never. Mr. Gottwaldt's sphere of influence was large, the potential for hidden issues significant. Your experience helps us because of its proximity to potential perpetrators."

Wolf fidgeted with a rolled up newspaper. Maybe he needed a jelly donut, known in these parts as a bismarck. "She doesn't necessarily know anything, Jackie."

"Really?" the FBI agent said. I don't think she liked someone calling her "Jackie."

"If Marta's the target, all that the perp needs is threat," Wolf said. "I.e, that Marta *may* know something. That Marta *may* have undertaken some action or line of inquiry that seems to point in the perp's direction."

"Playing it safe, blowing me up," I said. "*In case* I know. Even though I may not."

"Yeah, exactly." Wolf slapped his thigh with the paper. "Preemptive strike."

Grabowski tilted his head, then caught my eye. "What intrigues me, Ms. Hjelm, is your interest in California."

"Yeah, I wondered about that too," said Hobbes.

"Do you have anything you'd like to share with us?" Broder put to me.

"Nothing yet," I answered. "All I know is Deputy Grabowski has a murder investigation going, with some help from the state crime bureau. How many people you have on it?"

Grabowski did a little mental tallying. "I've got eight right now. Between the four of us here we may put together fifteen more. At least for a while. Right Agent Broder?"

The special agent said, yes, more or less.

"How many in San Diego?" I asked.

"Not a one."

"And no plans for any?"

Grabowski shook his head and ran a hand over his gray buzzcut. "With our budget these days, I don't see sending someone out. Agent Broder can contact the FBI office out there. But not until lines of inquiry here go dry and we check out Mr. Gottwaldt's poker connections in Vegas and Atlantic City."

"He played with the big boys, Ms. Hjelm, pots in the hundreds of thousands, sometimes a million plus," Broder explained. "In the casino business they call guys like him 'whales.' Casinos fly them in free, put them up in luxury suites, wine and dine them, just so they'll play poker. We're trying to find out if Mr. Gottwaldt got on someone's bad side."

"Well, for my part," I said, "I sent my operative as a way to make myself useful to Jennifer Nelson. Just trying to complement you guys. The theory being that some history jumped up and bit him. Now is it okay if I ask a few questions?" I was trying hard to strike a balance between assertive and respectful. My four friends here knew lots more about this kind of investigation than I ever would, and if they could help me help Jennifer Nelson, all the better.

Grabowski blinked at Broder. Hobbes and Wolf acted like they hadn't heard me.

"I can't promise answers," Broder said cagily, "but give it a try."

Grabowski nodded.

"Okay," I began. "Have you seen the will?"

"Uh-huh," Grabowski replied. "We got a court order to examine it."

"What's in it?"

"His controlling interest in the agency is divided between his two children," he said. "Forty-five percent of existing agency stock goes to his daughter, twenty percent to his son. My understanding is that the daughter and grandkids already have about ten percent, giving her control of the business. I guess sonny boy wasn't entirely the apple of the old man's eye. His real estate interests here and in California also go to his kids, evenly divided this time. He left a nice sum to his ex-wife. And he altered the will recently to leave several million to some hospital in San Diego, to endow a cancer research and treatment center. He also designated several million to set up a San Diego trust fund to provide scholarships to minority students going into advertising or marketing."

"He hadn't donated that money in the prior will?" I queried. "But he did in that last will?"

"That's right."

"Any idea why?"

Grabowski shrugged and stifled a yawn. He had the candle-burnt-at-both-ends look, despite his ramrod posture. "His attorney didn't know. His daughter's theory is that he'd always liked the hospital because that's where they successfully treated Mrs. Gottwaldt when she had leukemia. He'd been on the board there back in the late '80s, helped raise serious dollars for them in the past."

"And the scholarships?"

"That wasn't entirely out of the blue," Grabowski said. "Mrs. Nelson pointed out that her father always went out of his way to hire people of color early in their careers."

Frankly, I was beginning to wilt. It had been seven hours since the bomb. Call it post-traumatic stress, delayed reaction, shock. My hands quivered, I felt overheated, light-headed. If I'd had much food in my stomach, I think it would've come right back up.

My only hope was getting to a coffee cup full of two-thirds espresso, one-third milk, and foam on top. With an almond biscotti dipped in chocolate. That I could keep down.

Thinking a little extra oxygen would help, I heaved a deep breath into my lungs. It sounded like the next worst thing to a death rattle. Grabowski leaned toward me, eyes glittering.

"You okay?"

"Yeah, I'm okay. Still a little shaky is all."

"You know," Broder said, seeming concerned herself, "we don't need anything more from you for now. Why don't you go book a couple of nights in a hotel, relax, decompress. Somewhere the perp can't find you. He, she might try again. Just let John know where you are."

I managed a skeptical grunt.

"I'm not kidding. Someone tried to make you and/or your ex-husband dead, Ms. Hjelm, and they're still on the loose. If you like, Sergeant Hobbes can spare someone to keep an eye on you. For a few days, anyway."

Hobbes nodded. "Good idea."

My reply should have been, *"Youdamnbetcha."* It might have saved me a certain amount of unpleasantness in coming days. But *no*, I had to make proud and dumb.

"Thanks, but no thanks," I said. "I'll do fine."

"Whatever," Broder said. "You could do us a favor by not speaking to any press for a while."

I agreed.

Broder stood up and loaded up some papers she'd been scribbling on in her briefcase. She was taller than she looked, almost as tall as me—lanky and more muscular. I'd have bet a hundred bucks she played varsity volleyball in college.

She thanked me again on her way out, and cautioned me to take good care. Grabowski did the same. Hobbes brushed by without a word, light on his feet. And Billy Wolf sat regarding me like a cynical old Bhudda, calculating the chances of my survival.

"Could I ask you something, Billy?" I said.

169

He pulled a toothpick out of his inside jacket pocket and masticated on it a bit. "They don't let you smoke in lotsa places now, so I gnaw on these things when I can't light up. Like a human squirrel or something."

"Better than puffing away out in front of the hospital in the cold with your IV on a stand."

He cackled and shook his head. "Amazing what the damned weed does to you. Fucking up your dignity like that. You'd freeze your damned wrinkled ass off for a smoke, and let everyone have a peek at it through the back of your hospital gown."

It was my turn to laugh. "Just what you need to see, an invalid's saggy, sorry kiester."

"Not an appealing thought is it?" the St. Paul detective laughed. "So what do you want to know, Marta?"

"Do you have any domestic complaints against Doug Hewlett, Sue Hewlett's husband?"

"Off the record?"

"Won't tell a soul," I purred.

"If you do I'll deny I said anything."

"Fair's fair."

He extracted the demolished toothpick from his jaws and lofted it cleanly into the gray metal wastebasket in a far corner. Swish! Three-pointer!

"We've had four calls up to his house since last spring. Neighbors phoned them in, never Mrs. Hewlett. Twice it looked to the officers like she'd taken a licking. Efforts were made to get her out of the house and connected with the agencies that deal with this kind of thing, counseling and whatnot. They also encouraged her to file complaints against her husband. She refused both times. End of story."

"Nothing before that?"

"Nope. But rumors on the street have it that Hewlett's sports bars are skating on thin ice. The big chains are eating his lunch, so to speak. Money's a big issue in lotsa domestic abuse cases."

He got up, a shirttail hanging out in front. With absolutely no self-consciousness, he tucked it back in, hiked up his trousers, and dug in a pocket for the weeds he'd light up as soon as he went out in the cold.

"See you at the Ace," he said, padding out of the room. "Be careful now."

Chapter Twenty-Three

It's unfair, really, how easy it is to read Rick.

"Open book" doesn't begin to describe him when he's scheming. I know his destination, approximately how he plans to get there, and how yours truly figures into the deal. You can almost hear the wheels grinding and the not-uncommon male mantra: "How can I get this woman to do what I want her to?" Unlike Herb Gottwaldt, my lover and best pal would make an absolutely wretched poker player.

He knows it. I know it. And he just keeps trying. *How can you not love a guy like that?*

We'd bustled out through the lobby and fended off the media types laying in wait. One of them I'd seen at Lee Gorney's place the night before. Today I felt considerably less interested in playing footsy on the flat screen. When she stuck a mike in my face I very nearly inserted it back up her left nostril. Just not in the mood, I guess.

Rick levitated me away from utter embarrassment on the five o'clock news. We staggered out into the cold, across the busy street, and trotted the several blocks back to the hospital parking ramp. With a relieved sigh I heaved myself into the passenger position.

I can't say how exquisite it felt sitting in my usual perch in Rick's Explorer. Not home, exactly, but getting there. I winced a little when he turned the key in the ignition. But the engine growled and caught and purred as it warmed itself up. Maybe things were finally getting back to normal.

"Well," Rick said, elegantly bringing up the subject, "I talked to Jennifer Nelson this afternoon while the cops had you."

I brightened. "She sack me?"

Rick chuckled politely and polished the steering wheel with one of his brown suede gloves. Instead of saying, "I wish," like he wanted to, he said: "Not exactly. She's concerned about you, of course. But she said if you wanted to keep on with the case, it's okay by her."

"That's great," I lied. "What do you think?"

Naturally he didn't tell me what he wanted—that I quit risking my damn fool neck and hang the case up. He unveiled his clever strategy: *Dazzle her with reverse psychology.* You see, if he insists that I do something, generally I'll endeavor to do the opposite. On principle. It's one of my worst traits. Unless, of course, it's something like: *I must insist you don't jump off that cliff!*

"Well, hell," he said finally. "Better you go after them than they go after you!"

"You really think so?"

I caught him off guard, and his eyes wavered a bit. Did I mean it or was it a set-up? He'd leap at the opening I'd given him, and then I'd ambush him. He tried to stall by polishing the wheel some more.

"At least you'll be setting the agenda," he said. "But you're a big girl, you've got to decide."

"Yeah, I do. But you know something, Mr. Mueller?"

"No, what, Ms. Hjelm?"

"I'm too damned tired to decide."

Okay, so I offered him a draw. It was the best he could expect.

"Then decide tomorrow," he said with transparent relief. "Or the next day. Take a breather."

I fleetingly fantasized about sitting in my office at home, letting Jeff Beck and Bonnie Raitt light up the room, with a double Martini in my hot little hand and Rick in the kitchen whipping up a gumbo. Then I remembered that the front windows had been blown out. Right now our place resembled nothing so much as a giant walk-in refrigerator.

"So I don't suppose we want to go home," I essayed.

Backing his 4x4 out of its slot, Rick shook his head. "Not for a bit anyway. Damage wasn't too bad. There's glass inside and out, some things got knocked off shelves. We lost some plants. Grace got the windows covered with plastic and she recruited a couple of her undergrads to clean up inside. We'll pay 'em, of course. I got a contractor to come tonight to put up plywood and measure for new windows."

All of a sudden I panicked as I thought about pipes freezing and bursting. I blurted it out to Rick, and he said that he'd also called a plumber friend to make the house safe.

"The birds?" I asked anxiously.

"Mad as hell to get moved," Rick chuckled, "but basically okay. Grace has them upstairs in that empty bedroom. She shuts the door and they scream bloody murder and flap their wings. She's a little hard of hearing anyway."

"Insurance'll pay for all this?" I wondered.

"Uh-huh. Could be four or five grand, though. And the new windows will take a couple of weeks."

I laughed riotously.

Rick touched the brake and peered at me querulously in that parking-ramp heart-of-darkness. Did the old girl get a few gears shaken loose in the explosion?

I cleared my throat and shook my head. "I'm showing signs of mirth at a contractor promising something for two weeks. Which of course means four weeks, minimum. Probably eight. You know better than to believe a contractor!"

"How," he asked grandiloquently, "have I managed this last week without you?"

"I can't conceive," I chuckled.

Rick cleared his throat. "I'm thinking you're gonna be front-page news for a bit. You ought to at least call Patty and let her know you're okay. She can put it out on the Hjelm grapevine."

I scowled. A chat with big sister was certain to devolve into a lecture on my dissolute, nonconformist lifestyle. But Rick was right. I pulled out my cell and punched in Patty's number. No one was home, so I left a weirdly disjointed message.

• • •

Rick knew a log lodge over in Wisconsin, across the St. Croix River not half an hour from Jennifer Nelson's place. Some turn-of-the-20th-century farm-equipment magnate had built it for a summer cottage on 400 acres of woodland, next to a babbling private trout stream. The current owners stayed open all winter for small business meetings and retreats, as well as the occasional romantic couple. And they offered gourmet meals. Folks could do the things you do while retreating—I never have understood what—and spend their spare moments out in the woods skiing and snowshoeing. There's good ice fishing nearby, too, and lots of the beer-and-burger taverns that line Wisconsin's country roads. Hard to throw a rock in the Badger state without hitting a pub.

We lucked out and had the place virtually to ourselves for three nights. The Presidential Suite, no less. Back in the '20s Silent Cal himself—President Calvin Coolidge, hero of the Teabaggers—vacationed here for a week and tried to catch a few trout. "The fish," reported an ancient newspaper clipping in a frame by the bar, "apparently Democrats, avoided the President's well handled dry flies."

Rick and I kept to ourselves, taking continental breakfasts that arrived at our door at eight each morning. Then we headed out into the woods to shoot stock pictures of ourselves skiing, snowshoeing, bird watching, and photographing. We concocted a fake winter camping scene, too. For some shots, Rick set up one of his cameras on a tripod with a radio control, so he could get both of us in the scene. We'd stand there, leaning on our ski poles, earnestly communing with nature, and that lovely Nikon D3 would be whirring away—the radio shutter release hidden in his hand.

I only took one work call—from Bruce, now rattling around San Diego in a Chevy Cruze. He'd arrived on Monday, but hadn't found anything interesting yet. He'd put the details in an e-mail.

We splurged the first night and ate at the lodge, in the old oak paneled dining room—with its landscape paintings and stuffed animal heads. Only one other party was there, a cute old couple celebrating their 40th anniversary. It was some kind of meal, though.

Pastry turnovers with blue cheese. *Provençal* vegetable soup with garlic, basil, and herbs. Casserole-roasted duck with turnips. A rum and macaroon soufflé. A nice white burgundy to start, and a dense, rich cabernet to finish. By the glass, I hasten to add—not by the bottle. And last but not least, tumblers of Maker's Mark bourbon in the bar room. We bellied up to the marble-topped bar, with an antique oil lamp burning merrily between us.

For some reason the whiskey gave me a little, artificial shot of energy. Weird, since I'd expected the opposite. And even though I'd promised myself I wouldn't think or talk about the case "on holiday," I couldn't stop myself. So we went over the ground again, point by point—as if that might clarify something.

"Terrorist group—" I began.

"Or individual," Rick put in.

"—Wants to stop ad agency from taking cigarette account. They attempt to extort that outcome with letters and e-mails from untraceable accounts on Hotmail and Yahoo. They stage a fake poisoning, with some evil brew they concocted. Next, they manage to get into the agency and dink with a car's brakes."

Again, I conveniently forgot to tell Rick who was driving it.

"Another e-mail comes in promising worse, if said agency head doesn't bail out."

Rick sipped from his tumbler. "Some kind of grudge thing, maybe?"

"Maybe," I answered, not really believing it. "Then agency head buys the big one with bullets in the chest. House burns. What happens then?"

"No more threatening e-mails that we know about," said Rick. "Agency loses account on account of horrible publicity."

"Finally, gifted investigator's very excellent Mercury Marquis goes ka-boom. Investigator is majorly bummed. This indicates?"

Rick essayed a smile, but couldn't get it going. He gave me a protective look, and kind of shuddered. "It means, of course, that gifted investigator either knows something she doesn't know she knows, or the bad guys think she knows it. To protect themselves, they need to—" He looked a little shook, finishing the sentence in his head.

"Yeah, I know," I said quickly. "Let's not get emotional, huh?"

He nodded.

"What about Meg LaGrange? Did she do it? Was the murder a coincidence?"

"Grabowski's right, Marty. She had a motive, the timing was perfect. She can't prove she didn't. Not yet, anyway. But I somehow can't picture her crawling under your Merc with a car bomb."

"Or did someone else set up the whole terrorism thing to cover up the murder?"

Rick blinked slowly at me—part fatigue, part Maker's Mark, part surprise. "Jeez, do you think so?"

"Could be."

"Who?"

"Who stands to gain by Herb shuffling off this mortal coil?"

He shrugged. "His daughter and his son, for sure. They'll get tens of millions. The agency. Real estate in California and at home."

"Yeah, you've gotta look at them. I can't see Denny or Sue or Litzky getting anything at all out of the deal. Denny loses his mentor, so does Sue. They and Litzky get a new boss into the deal—Jennifer. New bosses mean changes, usually. Changes are scary, usually."

"So if it's anyone, it's Jennifer or Archie?"

"All I'm saying is they get the sweetest deal with Herb dead. But I've got to say that Jennifer—"

I wanted to describe to Rick how much she seemed like I felt after my Dad died. Usually I despise the notion of intuition. Like you've got antennae picking up stuff out of the ether. It's pure laziness. But I'd swear that she wouldn't hurt a hair on her old man's head. In fact, I'd allow that she was probably the closest thing to a chip off the old Gottwaldt block.

"I don't think she did anything, Rick. I just can't see it."

"Archie, then."

"Maybe. He's enough of a fuck-up to do something that stupid."

"What about Sue Hewlett?" Rick asked.

"What about her?"

"Other than Herb's kids and Meg she seems to be every-where he was in the past 15 years. She's connected with every-one else. The way you describe her, she's almost too solid."

I wanted to ask him: Now who's getting paranoid? After all, he hadn't even met her. And I hadn't told him that Doug was probably abusing her.

"Yeah," I agreed, not wanting a debate, "I suppose we've got to look at her angle, too."

"How about any other ideas?"

"The only other thing I can think of is something coming out of Herb's past. And how the hell am I supposed to figure that angle? Rent a time machine from Hertz?"

Of course, we fell asleep promptly that night in Silent Cal's bed, and dreamt bourbony, high-cholesterol dreams. The next night, though, after burgers and beers at the nearest tavern, we made love for the first time in weeks. For a few minutes Rick held me like I was made out of Belleek porcelain—as if I might break. I told him he could squeeze me as hard as he wanted.

Afterwards, I was nearly dozing, deliciously exhausted—floating, feeling warm, giddy, exalted. Rick rolled over, put his arm over my chest, then rubbed my stomach for a few minutes.

"Where do we go from here, hon?" he muttered sotte voce. "What do we do?"

"Wha—"

"With the Gottwaldt case."

I gently pushed him onto his back and gave *his* tummy a slow, gentle rub. He almost purred. "Tomorrow," I said, "we'll figure it out tomorrow. And, ummm—"

"Yeah, babe?"

"I'm sorry about Terry."

"Water under the bridge. Water under—" The tempo of his breathing slowed, his body relaxed even more, and he was asleep.

• • •

We headed back toward Minneapolis Sunday morning, through Stillwater—an old Minnesota river town that's a summer and autumn hot spot for tourists with a taste for antiquing. Try to drive through the burg on a June weekend, and you can take half an hour to go eight blocks. Making your way up and down the sidewalks can prove equally as laborious. But cruise into Stillwater in the middle of February, and you see the town as it might have looked on a midwinter morn half a century before—chill, lonely, vacant. A small town with more shops and galleries than it could possibly use. We postponed reality for one more night, staying at a "charming" old hotel—their description, not mine.

Monday morning, we were sitting at a red light on the main drag, listening to some teenager butcher the 10 o'clock news on a public schools FM station. A wiry little old lady bucked a head wind as she crossed the street in front of us. She hadn't braved the morning to go out for antiques. She lugged a transparent plastic bag containing a four pack of toilet paper and a liter of brandy tucked in against it. The essentials of life, I guess.

"So what happens now with the case?" Rick said, suddenly polishing the steering wheel again.

I filed his little body-language quirk away in my mind for future reference, and pursed my lips. "Take it as far as it goes, I guess."

"You don't have misgivings?" The light turned green and he gently gave the Explorer gas. We crept past the ranks of empty shops and slipped south out of historic Stillwater without so much as an antique print or an artsy-crafty thingamajig.

"Sure I do. I think me getting killed could put a serious crimp in our relationship. Don't you?"

"Not funny," he sighed, "not funny at all."

"I'm not trying to be, Rick. Jennifer gives me the old heave-ho tomorrow, fine. I'm not going to sputter out, though. I figure I at least have to hold on until Bruce gets back."

We hit a pothole that just about rung our chimes, and Rick swore under his breath about the damned winter roads. Not that I blamed him, but this is a rugged outdoor photographer with a stout, low-mileage four-by-four.

"Can I ask you something, Rick?"

"When have you ever been shy about asking me anything?" he zinged back at me.

"Not very often," I allowed. "But I need you to help me figure out if I'm in a position to do something about something.

Or if I ought to just mind my own beeswax."

"I figure you'll do what you want to do anyway," he chuckled, "but shoot."

I'd been holding back what I'd heard about Doug and Sue, mostly because it too closely resembled the case that Rick and I had argued about. It seemed too raw to deal with. But I had to tell him that Doug Hewlett was beating up his wife, and why I was telling him—namely, that I might intervene. The wrist, the bruise, Sue's nervousness, the rumors about problems with the sports bars. Off-the-record confirmation of domestic problems from one of St. Paul's finest.

Rick listened intently, swinging the Explorer right, up the entrance ramp onto west Highway 52. He slowed down for a semi, then nipped on, pushing it up to 65. "That's a shitty situation," he agreed. "But you shouldn't let what happened last summer influence how you handle it."

He'd touched a nerve there, so I clammed up. I didn't want to talk about *that*.

Rick drove behind the semi for a couple of miles, through ever-denser suburban sprawl, then passed it. The side of the trailer was emblazoned with the big orange logo and slogan of Gunderson Windows, which has a huge plant on the river a town or two south of Stillwater: "You're Home with Gunderson."

"Want to hear a theory?" Rick finally said, over the hum of the road noise.

"No, not particularly," I replied, my mouth going into a pout.

"Well, you're gonna hear it anyway." He gave the windshield a shot of window juice and flipped the wipers. They went back and forth three times, and the grimy film on the glass vanished. "I am well aware that you feel responsible for that woman who died."

"Was murdered," I said under my breath.

"How many times do I have to say it, Marty? I think you did *everything* you could have. You got the evidence of abuse that that woman's parents asked you to get. You helped them confront her and her husband."

"Who both denied anything was going on," I muttered, gritting my teeth. "Suzy Homemaker, husband a midlevel manager at a good company, handsome kids, stalwarts of the church. *All so much bullshit!* She was scared shitless, the kids, too. Like living under Stalin."

"I know," Rick said. "Then you and her folks tried to get the her off the dime."

"And she just wouldn't budge."

Rick stole a glimpse at me. I saw his blue eyes glint out of the corner of mine.

"So here you are," he said, "on the one hand wanting to move out of the business, 'cause of your supposed failure. And on the other, itching to save another woman with an abusive husband. Which is it going to be?"

I chewed on that for a moment. "Can always quit some other time, I suppose."

"Yeah, that's an option."

"I'm pretty sure I can walk and chew gum at the same time."

"A useful talent."

"So maybe we'll just take it as it comes. Keep two balls in the air. Float like a butterfly, sting like a bee."

"You and Muhammad Ali. Peas in a pod."

"Okay then," I proclaimed. "I'm going to talk to Sue, possibly talk to her mom."

"Meaning?"

"Recruit her mother. Get Sue to acknowledge the problem. She and Doug get counseling. She moves out. She files a complaint. Whatever. *Something.* 'Cause it ain't gonna get any better for her."

"You of all people gotta understand," my honey said, "that it doesn't always work out great. You know what I'm talking about. That doesn't mean you screwed up that case. You tried your best."

"Easy enough to say now. But what if I didn't try hard enough?"

My honeybun groaned, but had the good sense not to launch

another rebuttal.

When we got back to Prospect Park about ten, the duplex didn't look quite as bad as I'd figured it might have. Some of the steel siding in front was beaten up from flying metal and the plywood over the windows definitely didn't look too classy. ("Early Ghetto Riot," I called our new architectural style.) The swing had gotten knocked down. Inside, the place felt different—dark and cold in the front rooms and smelling like a lumberyard. We rustled up peanut butter sandwiches for lunch and I checked out the voicemail on my landline. Lots of calls to reply to.

From my big sister in Duluth, Bruce in California, an aunt in the west burbs, several reporters, and a few others concerned about the status of my scrawny neck. After all, I'd been quite the news item a few days before. Before I phoned anyone back, though, I had Rick take me over to a rent-a-car place down University Avenue, deep into St. Paul. I picked a red Corolla to use until the insurance check arrived. It was a decent car, sure. But I was sure going to miss the Merc—my Dad's last land yacht. That's what I told Rick at the rental office counter, as I was filling out some form or other.

He put a big arm around my shoulder, pulled me close. "You know," he said in a whisper, as if someone were eavesdropping, "your old man saved your bacon."

"Huh?"

He pivoted me around by the shoulders so we faced each other squarely. Like he always does when he's serious, he kind of cocked one side of his mouth, a sort of half smile. Then he levitated his eyebrows. I started to ask again what he meant, and he gestured, "Shush."

"Donald R. Hjelm," he said, "had a boat of a Mercury Marquis that he left to his younger daughter. Being a whimsical fellow and a lover of impractical doo-dads, he hung a pair of corny bumper stickers on it and he put in an ah-oo-gah horn. He also installed a remote control starter, without which said younger daughter, along with ex-husband, would've ended up as two servings of corned beef hash."

"Got a tissue?" I burbled, nodding.

Rick went off to catch a few hours work at the museum, and I started returning my calls.

Most everyone wasn't home. I got Doug Hewlett, not Sue. He seemed pretty concerned about me, and asked if he could help. He knew a couple of guys who'd keep an eye on me, but I told him I was okay, and I'd try to get Sue later. About the only person I caught was my big sister Patty. She seemed relieved that I'd survived, and annoyed that I'd worried her as much as I did. "You were like the third item on the news that night," she whined. "How do you get into a mess like this? For heaven's sake, Marta, why can't you be like a normal person? A husband, kids, a dull, boring, *safe* job? What's so bad about that, huh?"

She had a point, but why would you take a dull, boring, *safe* job when you didn't have to?

Rick and I agreed that it would be smart if we didn't hang around the duplex or office. Much as I detested Rick's brother's one-bedroom walk-up in Bloomington—but a few blocks from consumer heaven at the Megamall—the odds of anyone finding me there were comfortingly slim.

Scott Mueller was overweight, over-bearded, a bit of a slob, and, sad to say, generally a walking-talking form of chick repellent. But he was truly a nice, sweet guy. I mean, he didn't have to give up his bedroom while he got the couch. But he did—tickled to have a couple of roomies, for however long.

Scott was an assistant produce department manager in a supermarket. Though he ate as little of the stuff as he possibly could—pizza, burgers and beer were his main food groups. He devoted the rest of his waking hours to reading and writing science fiction, attending sci-fi conventions, doing Civil War reenactments, and cruising chat rooms and Facebook. He had a closet full of outfits from *Star Trek* and a Civil War uniform. Rick told me that Scott did a great Klingon—guttural language, knarly forehead and all.

Gottwaldt's memorial service was at nine Friday. I had to get up early to wash my hair and get presentable. I was brushing my teeth just before hitting the rack Thursday evening, when Rick told me I had a call on my cell.

"Hi," I mumbled.

"Hi there, Marta," Bruce bubbled from California. "Understand you've had an interesting life lately."

"Could say that, Brucie."

"You okay there, pal?"

"Uh-huh. What have you got for me?"

"One fact and one rumor."

"What's the fact?"

"I just tracked it down this morning. The folks at St. Luke's Hospital—"

"The place Herb raised money for?"

"Yeah, right. I dropped Jennifer Nelson's name around the joint. They called her and confirmed I'm legit, then e-mailed her a release form. Which she printed, signed and faxed back."

"What for? What kind of release?"

"A patient confidentiality release that only a close family member can sign, in the event of the patient being dead. Lets them share medical information."

The little hairs on the back of my neck started to tingle. "So what did you find out, Bruce?"

"Mr. G. had the Big C."

Chapter Twenty-Four

I flapped my jaw for a few thumping heartbeats. "Cancer?"

"Lung cancer. Pretty tough shit."

"He was going to die? Anyway?"

"You of all people oughta know *that*, Marta. Lung cancer, for Christ sake!" I could hear Bruce sipping on a libation. "The oncologist I talked with said sometime later this spring, most likely. Gottwaldt didn't have a chance. Disease too advanced. There were metastases. They didn't catch it soon enough."

"When did they diagnose him, Bruce?"

"A couple months ago. I can pin it down if you want. The oncologist said everyone in the department was bummed about it. Gottwaldt had done a lot of good stuff for them, raised a whole lotta bucks. They were trying to get him into an experimental program out at NIH."

I could hear the distant tinkle of a lounge piano and the clinky-clanky sounds of a bartender working. I guess my operative had placed the call from his native habitat.

"Why the hell," I asked, "did Herb get it diagnosed out there and no one here knows diddly? I haven't read the coroner's report, but nothing's going around about cancer. Neither of his kids said a thing about him being sick. You'd think he'd tell them! You'd think the docs would have said something by now."

"Herb had asked that the disease and his treatment be kept quiet, Marta. Easy to do when the clinic was so far from home. The docs were waiting for someone to ask them, who had the right to know. *No one had, until I turned up, until they contacted Jennifer.* Maybe the kids never knew 'cause he never did say anything."

Rick was leaning on the door frame, frowning, crossing and uncrossing his arms. I was pacing back and forth in Scott's peach-colored bathroom, tripping over a pile of rank towels and shoving sodden dust balls out of the way with my slippers.

"So what's the rumor, amigo?"

"It's like the lung cancer," he said, slurping another sip of his drink. "I don't know if it means anything."

"Let me decide that, Bruce."

"Okay. The general opinion among Herb's pals here is that sometime in the mid-'90s he had a problem with someone. This was before he got it on with Meg LaGrange,"

"What in hell is that supposed to mean, Bruce?" I grumbled. "People have problems with people. It's called life."

"This problem was *special*, Marta. The buzz was that some-one was blackmailing the guy. To the tune of several hundred grand a year. Two years running he reneged on his commit-ments to the hospital."

"Maybe it wasn't blackmail. So he had bad years. Businesses lose money. Doesn't prove a thing."

Bruce must have put his hand over the phone, but not completely. I heard him mumble something, and a muffled re-sponse from a woman's voice. Maybe he'd found himself a little friend in San Diego.

"Sorry 'bout that," he said. "I'd agree with you, except for one thing. I talked with a guy who knew Gottwaldt's old tennis pro at a local country club. A short while after Gottwaldt got his divorce eight, nine years ago, he and said pro put on a bender one night at a tennis camp up in the Sierras at some glitzy hotel. Much crying into beers, or whatever.

"Gottwaldt told the pro that shit was hitting fans. The new agency in Minneapolis was in tough straits, lost some important accounts. The tenancy rates at the strip mall and the apartment buildings in San Diego were down. He lost a lot when the Dot.com bubble burst. He owed his wife mucho big alimony and payments on joint property. Worst of all, he was throwing a substantial amount of money down a rathole that he dug for his own self."

I could see that Scott had taken up position behind his brother, staring just as intensely at me. Big excitement, appar-ently, for a nerd. "So what did the tennis pro say? Did Gott-waldt elaborate?"

"That's the 'Oh, fuck!' in the deal, Marta," Bruce sighed. "The pro keeled over from a heart attack three months ago.

Fifty-two-year-old guy, skinny as a rail, strong as an ox. *Kowabunga!* Over he goes on the base line one morning. I only have the story second hand from an ad guy who knew Gottwaldt who belongs to the same club."

"He got out of the California agency when?"

"His partners bought him out in the late '90s."

"And he founded Gottwaldt and Ryan when?"

"Well, it was the Gottwaldt Agency to start with and that was the autumn of Bush vs. Gore."

"The year 2000, then. So why couldn't it be a sour business deal, Bruce? He provided someone with venture capital he shouldn't have, things didn't work out."

"I know what you're saying, Marta," Bruce replied. "But it lacks consistency with the way Gottwaldt operated. Out of character, you might say. The ad guy who tells the story says Herb never got embarrassed about business reverses. Mad, maybe. Bummed, for sure. But he told people. Only one thing made sense to the ad guy. Gottwaldt had done something personally shameful or something illegal, and got blackmailed over it."

"Out there, or out here?"

"Don't have a clue. Could be either, I guess."

"Drugs? Embezzlement? Murder? Pedophilia? What?"

"Geez, excuse me, Marta, I don't have the script."

"Anyone else say the same stuff?" I growled, knowing I deserved Bruce's put-down. It was the headache talking.

"Not as explicitly as the ad guy," Bruce answered, growling a little himself. "But a couple of folks told me that they'd always wondered. Gottwaldt dropped a few hints—kind of a perverse type boast thing—about someone having him tightly by the balls. And he didn't mean a can of Wilsons."

I asked Bruce to work that thread. When I wished him and his companion a pleasant evening—and urged him to make no whoopy without proper security measures—he giggled almost like a teenaged girl. As for my nosy boyfriend and his equally nosy brother, I told them I'd give them all the gory details first thing in the morning.

Finally—as I brushed and flossed my teeth—I thought I

could see some light. Very much like the bulb going on over Mickey Mouse's head, a tiny epiphany burst forth inside my own noggin. I think I had an idea of just what had happened at Gottwaldt and Ryan over the last few weeks. Then I sloshed down my Tylenol PM, doused the lights, jumped in Scott's bed, and—wonder of wonders—fell promptly and deeply asleep. Rick didn't even wake me up when he climbed in the sack a little while later.

• • •

My notion of my own memorial service goes like this:

A classic wood-paneled barroom with scurrying waitpeople and bartenders, all in those crisp white jackets. Dozens of friends trading risqué Marta Hjelm yarns, and laughing good and loud. Free-flowing ale, pinot grigio, martinis and other spirits. Buffet table piled with good chow. No speeches. No pastors, priests, imams, or rabbis allowed. And Rick sobbing quietly in a corner—showing no interest whatever in the good-looking women lining up to nab him.

Herb Gottwaldt's was pretty close:

The restaurant and bar at the Nicollet Island Inn, with the Mississippi flowing by just a stone's throw away. Scores of advertising and media types—and a smattering of business moguls, a few well-known pols and a couple of Vikings players—mingling. Bloody Marys and cappuccinos flowing freely. No speeches, it turned out. No religious personage. And Jennifer and Archie at the center of things, accepting condolences, but not sobbing. Harry Litzky, looking a bit drawn and bummed out, was there with his boyfriend Keith. I could understand why Meg wouldn't attend. But much to my befuddlement, I didn't see Denny or Sue.

"I don't know why they're not here," Keith whispered in my ear. "You'd think they would be. Harry just doesn't have it in him to ask Jennifer or Archie."

So I basically stood by a window for an hour—sipping steadily on two successive bloody marys, nibbling on *hors d'oeuvres*—and peered out at the icy river and the gray, ugly day. It was somewhere around freezing outside, and the late-morning atmosphere couldn't decide if it wanted to spit sleet or snow. A tossup. Toward eleven I finally was able to pull Jennifer and Archie to a table in the bar. I told them their father had had lung cancer, and probably would have died by summer.

"I expect you would have found out soon enough," I said. "My operative just got to the information first."

"The bastard," Archie muttered, blinking at his big sister. "*Why in hell didn't he tell us?*"

Jennifer shushed her brother, then stared at me with those startling blue eyes. "We noticed he'd slowed down, and he didn't feel good lately. We thought it was his back, from a handball injury. And he was getting up toward 70 anyway. But I guess I'm not surprised. I just didn't put two and two together."

I don't know why I didn't, either. My Dad went through about the same thing—getting weaker and skinnier over a year or so. The bush-league doctor in Duluth said he had diabetes. We wasted half a year on the diet and pills. It took a trip to the Mayo Clinic to figure it out. Then, as for Herb, it was too late.

Also, I told them about the tennis pro's tale, and asked if either of them remembered anything like that. Archie didn't, he wasn't even ten at the time. But Jennifer did.

"Dad pulled me out of Stanford for a year," she said, "and Archie out of a prep school. To save money. For a couple of years his businesses went into the red. He nearly folded the ad agency. I wondered why, and he never would say."

Before I took off I mentioned that I understood why Meg hadn't come, with the indictment hanging over her head. But where were Sue and Denny?

Jennifer was almost able to not smile. Archie didn't look happy.

"I discharged Sue and Denny resigned," she said. "We shut down their network access. They're cleaning out their offices today. And I have somebody keeping an eye on them."

Would surprises ever cease? "Umm, why'd you do that to Sue?"

Now the almost-smile was gone entirely. "I'm sorry, Marta, I can't say. Her severance agreement doesn't allow me to speak about anything other than the dates of her service and her duties. The stock Dad left me, plus my original stock and my kids' stock, gives Duane and me control of the agency."

"Why did Denny resign?"

"I'd suggest you ask Denny that question."

"She's canning me too, Marta," Archie added with surprising equanimity. "She's buying out my 20 percent. A ten year contract."

"He won't have to work a lick for a decade," Jennifer noted, with a sisterly tone of disapproval.

The brother smirked at her. "Well, advertising wasn't my deal anyway, Jen."

"You'll just blow it all."

"Who knows? Maybe I'll shock you."

Chapter Twenty-Five

Sue and Doug were in the process of loading books and pictures from office shelves into boxes. Rubber-banding what I took to be personal files in manila folders. Mating a stack of loose music CDs to their cases. Somebody I didn't know—a dumpy, silver-haired woman in gray corduroy trousers and a heavy black wool sweater—was standing the corner, arms crossed, eyeballing their every move. No doubt making sure they didn't take anything that didn't belong to them.

Doug noticed me first, and smiled sheepishly. "Hey, Marta," he said, hefting a box onto a table and catching Sue's attention, "what's up?"

Sue made eye contact with me, and it was obvious she'd done some crying. We weren't exactly best pals, but she walked over without a word and gave me a long, hard hug.

"I'm so glad you're okay," she burbled. "You had us worried there for a while."

She hadn't seen me since before the car bomb. "Hey, I'm one tough hombrette. Is that a word?"

"It ought to be," she laughed, disengaging, rubbing knuckles to eyes. She briefly glared at their minder, then looked back at me. Good ol' Doug continued to load books into a box.

"Too bad about your job," I said. "Really sorry."

"Jennifer's one bigtime asshole," Doug sighed. "Just like her old man."

Sue flinched at the sound of Doug's profanity. "Doug, honey," she said with a hint of tremulousness in her voice, "why don't you start taking the stuff out now? We've only got till one." She looked at the dumpy, silver-haired woman again. "Okay with you?" She got a nod back.

With a snort Doug threw on his St. Louis Blues fleece-lined jock jacket, hoisted a box full of college marketing texts and back issues of *Advertising Age*, and headed out.

Sue started to say something, and I put up an index finger to shush her. She looked puzzled.

I peeked out the door to make sure he'd gone, then swiveled

around to fix her with my meaningful gaze. She peered at me, quite amused.

"What is it, Marta? My fly open?"

"Oh man, Sue," I replied intently. I wasn't going to let levity get in the way of helping her. "Can we talk, out in the hallway? We don't have much time—"

"Time for what?"

"To talk about Doug." I took her arm and gently led her outside, so the other woman wouldn't overhear us.

You could see the thought in Sue's head: *Is this a joke?*

She scrunched up her eyes and lips. "What...about Doug?"

Maybe she wouldn't make it easy. Lots of abused women get into denial. Lots are in dreadful dependent relationships. I knew all about that, lots more than I ever wanted to know. But I had to do something. I sucked in a deep breath, and forged headlong into the fray.

"I know about how Doug's abusing you," I whispered, "about the calls to the St. Paul police."

Suddenly, her demeanor tightened, darkened. "I don't understand."

"You've been having serious fights, lately he's taken to hitting you. Don't tell me you got that shiner on your cheek from walking into the bathroom door."

She tried to toss it off, but her chuckle just didn't fly. It wavered in the air, and crashed.

"You know," I said as gently and quietly as I could, "you have a lot of options."

"Okay, we had a couple of huge fights, lately," she said, ignoring my amateur social-worker routine. "Too many drinks, too many issues, I guess. The neighbors are jerks, and they called the police. But Dougie doesn't mean to hurt me, really. He drinks a little too much, I say something dumb—"

I'd written down some phone numbers and addresses, and took them out of my satchel. "Here," I said, "when you're ready, give one of these a call. You owe it to yourself."

She took it, folded it, and turned around to stuff it in a pocket in her briefcase. "You're very sweet to be concerned about me," she said. "I'm going to try to do something about my problems. And believe me, I've got plenty of them right now. But I'll be okay, you can count on it."

When she said those words, I felt like beams of renaissance sunshine had just popped out through some black, scudding clouds. She hadn't exactly admitted anything, but she seemed to acknowledge *something*.

"Just promise me one thing, Sue," I said.

"If I can, Marta." She smiled a thousand-watt smile at me.

"If you need any help, if things get bad, *call me*. Okay? Anytime!"

She nodded. "You got a deal."

"Before I go," I said, "a couple of quick questions?"

"Not about Doug, I hope."

I shook my head. "I have an operative in San Diego who tells me that there was some rumor going around that Herb Gottwaldt had been the subject of blackmail. Did you ever hear anything like that?"

She looked more astonished than when I accused her husband of abusing her. "No, never! Where'd your guy get hold of a fairy tale like that?"

"Okay," I said. "Now what about getting the sack from Jennifer. What'd she say?"

"Jennifer has *never* liked me, Marta, and I've never liked her. Oil and water. That's all you need to know. Besides, if I blab to you, or anyone, I screw a year's severance pay. I'm keeping my mouth shut. I'm going to need that money."

• • •

Denny Ryan had already left the agency for the last time. After a few beeps, though, he picked up my call as I tooled east on 394 and snappishly told me if I wanted to ask him "any more fucking questions," I'd have to meet him downtown. No, he wouldn't talk over the airwaves. Then he informed me I should consider myself lucky beyond words to get this final audience, "'Cause I don't ever want to see you again!"

"Sounds great to me," I grumbled back.

Not that it didn't raise my hackles plenty to rendezvous at

Babes, in downtown Minneapolis—where young, flexible, well-endowed women charge hefty fees to leave virtually nothing to the male imagination. I would have preferred getting him in a nice restaurant or a coffee house in the Warehouse District, near the new Twins ballpark. But where would the degradation have been in that?

Much to my surprise, "sleazy" didn't begin to describe the place. The word that comes to mind is "resplendent." Of course, I don't know what the inside of a fleshpot ought to have looked like, before I stepped into Babes and paid my $10 cover.

There were mirrors all over the place, couches not unlike the kind Denny and Herb had had in their offices. Much black leather trim. Gray and black tile floors. Lighting that wouldn't have been foreign to a Hollywood set. Throbbing soft-jazz music. The tinkle of bartenders hard at work. And lots of youngish females va-va-va-vooming around in nothing but high-high heels and teeny, tiny satin bikini panties, bosoms a-jiggle. I know I should have been outraged. But my first reaction, on seeing all that female flesh waggling itself at middle-aged men in suits, was: *Can this be hygienic?*

Guess I'm just an old buzz kill.

Most of the customers were sitting around at oval glass tables in the big central room, sipping on outrageously overpriced drinks. The women—buxom, slender, tall, short, black, white, and Oriental—made the circuit of the tables and provided a few minutes of intellectual discourse for a mere $30 a pop. A whole seminar would have proved very costly, indeed. But as far as I could see, no touchy, no feely with regard to any naughty bits.

Denny, though, had ensconced himself in one of the nooks around the periphery of the main room, on a leather sofa specifically built for two. I hesitate to call it a "love seat"—that gives too much credit to the proprietors and customers. "Lust seat" fits better. The terminology for this particular skin-club activity—courtesy of Rick, who swore up and down he'd only heard about it secondhand—is "couch dance."

Well, I saw a couch, but I didn't see any dancing.

A young woman with shagged blonde hair, and a slim but

curvaceous figure—attired as described above—had plastered herself on Denny's lap, with an arm around his shoulder. She whispered earnestly in his ear, and he nodded as he sipped on a Manhattan. She tried hard to look inadvertent as she pressed a breast to his chest. He looked uncheered by her efforts, yet determined to exorcise his gloom. Given Denny's new career path, I figured it might take him a while to run through enough booze and boobs to make a difference.

She saw me first, and her expression translated into something like: What are *you* doing here?

Denny noticed me then, but before we had a chance to say how much we missed each other, yet another young woman in high heels and panties came mincing up to me, jiggling all the way. "What can I get you to drink, *ma'am?*"

"Thanks, but I don't want a drink."

"You'll have to buy a drink, *ma'am.*"

"I-don't-want-a-drink," I said evenly, edging dangerously close to my "strangle-a-waitperson" persona. "I just came in to talk to Mr. Ryan here. I paid my cover, anyway."

"I'm sorry, *ma'am,*" she insisted, "club policy. You have to buy a drink every hour you're here. Or leave."

Denny looked mildly uplifted by my troubles with the raven-haired, topless bureaucrat. It seemed my struggle might actually get a smile out of him.

"Okay, *ma'am,*" I replied.

Her pert, metallic-pink-glossed lips pouted instantaneously, and I think she would have invited me outside if it weren't the middle of February and she had on about three cents' worth of fabric.

After two bloody marys, I didn't need any more alcohol. "Get me a glass of cranberry juice. On the rocks."

She turned on her high heels, marched away, and it made me feel warm and fuzzy to know that someone that young could develop cellulite. I managed to button my lip just before I said something snarky.

"Sit down, Marta," Denny said with a wan grin. He whispered a few words in the blonde's ear and she hopped up and away.

I threw my quilted coat on the black leather and sat down. "You come here often?"

"Sometimes. After a real bad day. Yesterday was a real bad day. Today continues the tradition."

I started to nod sympathetically, but then thought, screw it. No more Ms. Nice Guy. "You didn't have to dig yourself such a deep hole."

"What do you mean?"

"You think I don't get it? You think I'm stupid?"

He tilted his slightly inebriated head to one side—suddenly the toothless barracuda. He'd had a good head start before he got here.

"Jennifer fires you and Sue and Archie, and makes a deal to buy out Archie. Why the hell would she do that with her dad gone? It's a bad time to sack the number two guy, who knows it all, who happens to own a decent bit of equity. Whatever you three did had to have been, uh, serious."

He feigned bemusement, but I didn't believe him for a minute.

"Here's what happened, Denny."

I scanned the room for other women like myself—pushing middle age, wearing plaid wool skirts, blue blazers, and stern expressions. Hmm, no one but me.

"Herb is losing it, and we know why now. He's dying. Has been for a few months at least."

"What do you mean?"

"Herb had lung cancer. Only a few months to live."

The expression on Denny's face said it: He hadn't known.

"Shit," was all he could say.

"So chasing after Bertram doesn't matter that much to him. But it does to you, because my dear ex-husband put you onto the scent of a potentially huge client. But if Herb isn't involved, no Bertram, no Amfoodco. So Herb's gotta be convinced, gotta be emotionally invested in the project."

Denny had sobered up in a hurry, and I could see his hands shaking. "She told you, *the bitch*. Jennifer told you."

"Actually, no," I said. "She refused to say why you were let go."

He drew a deep breath, but didn't say anything.

"What better way to nudge Herb toward Bertram than by threatening him, extorting him? Given his style, he won't cave. He can't. Even if he's sick. Even if he's dying. He has to push back. He has to fight it out, show these terrorist yahoos he still has some backbone."

Denny nodded so slightly I could barely see his chin wag.

"So— Extortionistic letters, e-mails. Tainted cola that Sue knows to drink in a big hurry and spit out, so Harry or her little sister doesn't have to taste it or, worse, swallow the stuff. Who injected it in the cola cartons?"

Denny shook his head.

"Doug?"

Denny sat still. "I'd rather not say."

"You or Archie got to the Lexus and messed with the brakes and airbags. One of you guys, or Sue, was gonna drive the thing into a snow bank and go running back to Herb. Only Margie Polish-name screws up and gives yours truly the keys. And I nearly kill myself."

"*Nobody was supposed to get hurt,*" Denny said in a rush of whispered words. "We knew we needed to push Herb's buttons a little more. That's why the cola, the brakes, you."

"What? The token detective who was too dim to figure anything out?"

He looked at me like I was an idiot. "Well, *duh*. Why else would I hire you? I hadn't thought of you in years, when Terry brought your name up. A weird cooincidence, him being your ex. But useful. I mean, how good could you be? A smalltime private dick? I didn't think much of you back at the *Bugle*. Why should it be any different now? But—" He was grabbing for some words that were hard for him. "But, you're sharper than I thought you'd be."

Well, even a back-handed compliment is better than none at all. "So Jennifer didn't know anything."

"Until Archie blabbed a couple days ago." He took a long, slow hit on his drink. "She would have spilled the beans to

Herb. She didn't want Bertram, thought it would be bad for the agency."

"Maybe she was right."

Since I sat down he hadn't made eye contact with me, and I gathered he didn't plan to. His stare followed the pantily-clad girls as they high-heeled by, but not with much joy. He didn't even need to be here, except to make me squirm. My drink finally came, and it was the tastiest $10 glass of cranberry juice that I ever had. I planned not to leave a tip.

"So who shot Herb?" I hissed. "Who tried to blow me up?"

He put his hands up in the air, palms forward. "Honest to God, Marta. I don't know. But it wasn't me, wasn't Sue, wasn't Archie. See what's happened without Herb? Bertram's screwed. We're all screwed. None of us gain a thing with him dead. It had nothing to do with our plan."

"No one's talked to the cops yet?"

He shook his head tiredly. "Jennifer said the conversations with Archie and me never happened. But I had to agree to resign and eventually sell my stake to her."

"Small price, after what you did," I said. "But I think you and Sue and Archie better chat with your attorneys, and come clean. Because Grabowski *will* figure it out."

"You're not going to tell him what I said?"

I shook my head. "I always thought you were an asshole, Denny. Through all those shit-eating smiles I had to put on, listening to your bad jokes, half of them dirty— Through all that fucking interference with my writers, making sure they didn't offend anyone. But I don't want to be responsible for landing you in the hoosgow. My life's complicated enough."

Denny handed his drained tumbler to the jiggly, raven-haired hostess and ordered another. He focused a jaundiced eye on me. "Is that all?"

"No," I said. "We have an operative in San Diego who interviewed someone who claimed that Herb had been blackmailed back there. Did he ever speak about something like that?"

Denny thought over blowing me off. I could tell from his look. But instead he shook his head. "No, not as such."

"What do you mean, 'as such'?"

"Herb never alluded to anything along those lines, and I spent nearly ten years with him."

"There's something else, though?"

"It might not mean a damned thing—"

I shrugged. "Might not. But try me."

He peered hither and yon in hopes of the imminent arrival of his libation. No luck yet.

"After I'd been with the agency for a couple of years," Denny said, "Herb asked me to supervise the controller and the accounting firm. I got to know our finances really well. Now this ain't Watergate or slush funds or anything like that. But almost every year Herb would pay out a special bonus to himself. Whether or not we had a good year. Usually a bit north of a hundred fifty grand."

"He could do that?" I said.

He looked at me like I was a four-year-old. "*Of course he could, Marta.* It was his money. He could pay himself any damned thing he wanted."

I noticed that I'd almost drained my pricey cranberry brew, and I still felt a little thirsty. But not $10 thirsty.

"The first time he took that bonus that I knew about was seven, eight years ago, and I mentioned that he must be planning a trip out to Vegas or something. You know, like he had one of those big-stakes poker games of his."

Denny stared into his drink for a few seconds.

"And what happened?" I asked.

"He almost snapped my head off, Marta. Said it was none of my fucking business what he did with his bonus."

"So he was feeling touchy about something," I said.

"Yeah, I would say so. And you notice something else?"

I wracked my brain for a minute, like he'd posed a simple but devilish riddle. I confessed that I didn't.

"Assuming you were in the top bracket a few years ago— Forty percent or whatever. What would you have gotten after you pay taxes on— It was like $166,500 or $165,300 or some funky figure like that. Not a round number."

Never in my life have I even approached gross income in six figures. I didn't have the neurons for this kind of calculation. "Okay, I give up," I said. "What do you pay?"

He finally twisted around and peered into my eyes. His were beginning to waver, and the whiskey on his breath wafted toward me like a mirage on the desert.

"You get a nice, round figure of a hundred grand. Understand?"

He was absolutely right. Blackmailers don't ask for $53,898 and 97 cents. Or for $82,443 and two bits. They ask for fifty grand. Or one-hundred grand. *A nice, round figure.*

Precisely the amount Herb's tennis pro pal put out into the rumor mill.

"I know it sounds awful circumstantial," said Denny. "But I always wondered about it. Maybe it could have something to do with Herb getting whacked like that."

That wasn't much to hang anything on. But it did place possible blackmail activity smack dab in the heart of Herb's Minneapolis days.

I lifted myself off the black leather "lust seat" and grabbed my coat. "You ought to call Grabowski. It'll make it a lot easier."

He nodded. "I'll think about it."

He blinked up at me, a little goggle-eyed, and I almost thought I saw a glimmering of— "Affection" wasn't even close. "Friendship" didn't cover it either, because we didn't share any. Maybe it was "experience." Denny and I had gone through some times together, like grunts in the trenches or kids stuck with each other at some crummy school.

Hemming and hawing, he asked me if he could buy me a martini or something at the Cuban restaurant next door. He said he wouldn't mind reminiscing about our *Bugle* days. No bullshit allowed—for a change.

I said, what the hell.

• • •

I cruised back to Scott Mueller's Bloomington apartment in my "I-really-shouldn't-be-driving-but-I-have-to" mode—a lot under the speed limit, creeping like a geezer-mobile south and east down city streets. People zipped by, giving me the finger and honking. I waved companionably at them, aglow with gin and vermouth. It was rush hour for them, but not for me.

Rick and Scott were sprawled in front of the flatscreen watching a PBS adventure show. A team of British mountaineers had clambered up some fearsome Himalayan peak that no one had ever challenged because it was even tougher than Everest, though shorter. My honey and his brother had laid down $5 bets as to which Limey would turn churlish first, as at least one mountaineer in every climbing documentary eventually does. Rick had picked—as he called him—"Barmy Fotheringay Phipps." His brother saw the gleam of destiny in his man, "Gussie Fink-Nottle." "Cyril Bassington-Bassington" was available to me, should I care to risk a fiver. (They'd both consumed reams of Wodehouse as kids.) Rick won the pot, as "Barmy" threw a tantrum in a snow cave at Camp 4 during a blizzard.

"I now have twenty bucks to my name," he announced with a flourish. "How's about we spend it on a pizza? I think, uhh, mushrooms, Canadian bacon, pepperoni, green olives, and onions?"

A favorable demonstration broke out among the delegates. His motion was seconded and passed, and before long we had the item delivered at Scott's door—a heavenly expanse of hot animal fat and nutritionless vegetable matter stretching off in front of us. The guys sipped Old Milwaukee—the favorite cheapo brew amongst Mueller men—and I gulped ice water, hoping to dilute the two martinis Denny had bought me. I told them about Bruce's call, the memorial service, and my get-together with Denny at Babes and Havana.

"I heard Babes is a pretty nice place," Scott essayed, probing the limits of political correctness.

Rick looked at his little brother with a roll of the eyes. Then Rick said precisely what he thought I wanted to hear: "I don't know, Scott, I've never been there."

We didn't stay up late because Rick had promised a buddy

that he'd assist with a very early shoot Saturday morning.

I crawled in the sack hoping I wouldn't have a hangover the next morning. Rick spooned up against me for a few minutes, then rolled over onto his side of the bed. I zoned out quickly, and slept deep and hard, in the midst of breathless dreams that rushed by like dark clouds on a windy November day.

Scott woke me up about six, with a gentle nudge on the shoulder. I hadn't even heard the radio come on at 4:30, or noticed Rick getting out of bed.

"Sorry, Marta," he whispered, "but your cell phone's beeping."

Chapter Twenty-Six

At six in the morning I hated to have anyone other than Rick see me.

But Scott was up at that ungodly hour and witnessed me stumbling into the hallway in an oversized "Daytona Beach - Fun in the Sun" t-shirt that reached down almost to my knees, athletic socks down around my ankles, and pasty, white legs. Also, stringy, limp, dirty hair. Circles under my eyes. Dragon breath. A grumble on my lips. And a broken spring in my step. Not that Scott would win a hunk-of-the-month prize in his red plaid bathrobe and blue-white striped jammies. All he needed to complete his "Beaver" Cleaver ensemble was a pair of Howdy Doody slippers and a Christmas tree to unwrap presents underneath.

Rick—somewhere on the road out to his buddy's shoot—missed the whole, awful scene.

My Nokia was sitting on the kitchen counter, next to the empty pizza box. It had ceased bleating by the time I arrived, which meant whoever had called had hung up or left word on the voicemail. Sure enough, someone had deposited a message for me in the telephonic ether. I punched the appropriate buttons and listened.

"Hiya Marta," a husky female voice quavered in a whispery tone, "this is Sue Hewlett. I, I need to see you. It's really important, but I can't talk right now. I got to get out of here. Maybe I can meet you at your house, huh? Are you there now?" She sounded like she was breathing rapidly but getting no oxygen. "Sorry to bother you so early. I'll try again later. Or call me. Maybe I'll just come over, I don't know, about nine? Uhh, bye—"

My heart began thumping and I went all clammy.

"You look like you've seen a wraith or something," Scott said, worried that I might keel over right there in his kitchen.

"It's a woman I know," I said, almost panting. "I think she's in big trouble. Her husband's abusing her. They must've had a bad night. She just got fired. Maybe he went off the deep end.

She wants me to meet her at the duplex."

Scott knew nothing firsthand about domestic bliss or abuse, apart from the idyllic childhood memories he, Rick, and their sisters shared. But, like his big brother, he did have a highly developed sense of outrage. A history buff, he was still upset about certain Civil War atrocities.

"Call the cops then, Marta. Where does she live?"

"St. Paul. But I can't go off screaming bloody hell if I don't know what's going on. I could get her in even deeper shit with her husband."

"Well, call her anyway!"

I nodded frantically. He was right. "My bag is on the couch. Would you get it?"

He fetched my satchel and I fished out my little black book. I punched in Sue's cell number and waited a few seconds. My heart—still beating an agitated tattoo—jumped a few inches when I heard the call being picked up.

"*Yeah?*"

An anger-tinged male voice—visceral, harsh.

Doug.

Shit!

I banged the disconnect with my thumb, shaking my head.

"It's the husband. She doesn't have her cell phone, then." My brain spun its wheels for a moment, then I thought of one other approach. I handed my little flip-phone to Scott, and he looked mystified.

"I want you to call Sue's landline number. If a woman answers, hand me the phone quick. It's a man? You say, 'Sorry, wrong number.' Okay?"

"Can't I hang up like you did?"

I shook my head. "Two hangups in a matter of minutes? Pretty suspicious. We don't want this guy in a worse mood than the one he's in, do we?"

Scott nervously picked out the number as I read it to him, waited, then shook his head at me. Doug Hewlett again. Stammering, Scott apologized for misdialing, and disconnected.

"Whew," he muttered, "that guy sure didn't sound like a

happy camper to me." He yanked open the door of his fridge and extracted a open quart carton of orange juice. Taking a few deep slurps, he looked at me with a certain nervous pride, the way the cornpone sidekick used to regard the sheriff just before the the big fellow stepped out for a showdown with the villain.

"So what are you gonna do?" he asked.

"I'm going to the duplex and wait for Sue there. I think I ought to grab my .38, anyway."

"Your .38?" he squeaked. "You have a gun?"

I nodded.

"Is that a good idea, Marty?"

"Hope I won't need it. But I'd feel better if I had the thing."

"Maybe we should call Rick." He peered at me to see how I reacted, but I didn't. "He's got his phone with him."

I wagged a finger at him. "No, we're definitely *not* going to bother Rick, okay? But if he calls, you can tell him what's up."

Forty minutes later I was cruising north on Cedar Avenue, past the Megamall, over 494, and into South Minneapolis—dirty hair and all. The drive from Scott's digs in Bloomington to Prospect Park takes about 20 minutes in ideal weather and light traffic. Not this morning, though. At least ten inches had collected overnight. And snow was still coming down hard. I was lucky not to get stuck somewhere.

Naturally, I kept waiting for my cell phone to beep at me, but it remained obstinately mute.

The plywood was still on the front windows, the padlock still on the damaged front door. The contractor had told Rick yesterday that our new windows and door would *absolutely, positively* arrive next week. "Yeah, sure, I bet," I muttered to Rick. I've known only one contractor in my life who did stuff when he promised, and did it right. He ended up doing a TV home-repair show on cable. Now we couldn't afford him.

I parked by the garage—which I let Grace use—and mushed in through the white stuff. I stomped it off my boots in the vestibule, went into our kitchen and flipped on the light. The place was still cold and felt weirdly alien. Grim reminders that someone wanted me six feet under, in a number of little pieces—Marta *tartare*. *Still* wanted me on the wrong side of the turf, in all probability. As I toddled past the breakfast nook, I sniffed a hint of red beans and rice.

First I listened to messages on my landline's voicemail and made notes on whom to call back. Then I wasted ten minutes hunting for the envelope Rick had left with Terry that fateful evening.

Not in the living room. Or office. Or kitchen. Not in the bedroom.

I almost thought I'd have to do without it, until I spotted the thing sitting on top of the toilet tank, next to the shampoo and skin cream. A perfectly logical place to leave it. Rick had copied at least 20 articles out of old newspapers and magazines. Standing there by the sink, I riffled through the stuff.

There was a cover story on Herb from *Corporate Report*, as well as interviews from *Ad Age* and the Minneapolis *Stribune*, as we call it. Denny had a few interviews, too. Meg got some ink for her social activism and winning a couple of Clios. Jennifer Nelson and her husband were major sponsors of a local halfway house for homeless families. The biggest stack of tearsheets belonged to Doug Hewlett, hockey hero.

For some reason my eye lit on the oldest article, an interview from the University's student newspaper, dated about the time I was matriculating there nearly two decades before: "Roseville Defenseman Haunts Gophers." That unbeloved prairie rodent was the ridiculously uninspiring mascot of the University of Minnesota.

It seems that the University had provisionally offered a hockey scholarship to Doug, then withdrew it. Doug's parents raised a stink, claiming this had hampered Doug's subsequent efforts to find a scholarship of equal value to his academic and pro prospects. They sued, but the case went nowhere. He did find a taker in Duluth State, and had a successful college hockey career up there, while building his rep as a tough guy and enforcer. In fact, he led the league in penalty minutes two years running.

The jist of the article was that Doug Hewlett always savored playing the University and, if possible, "knocking the stuffing" out of them, as he gently put it. The revenge of the spurned defenseman, you might say. His quotes contained little more than sports clichés, amplified two-fold by the sports clichés of the student "scribe."

I had to read the third and second to last paragraphs twice before I got it.

Hewlett has always enjoyed a pugnacious reputation, of course, from Roseville High onward. Not dirty, just hard-nosed. He even picked up a great nickname—a sign of particular status for a high school player in any sport.

It seems the big defenseman spent his high school summers travelling the Upper Midwest working for an uncle's road construction company. His favorite job, he acknowledges, was helping the demolition crew set explosive charges to blow out obstructing rock formations. That's why they used to call him 'The Bomber.'

"Ho-ly shit," I muttered. "Holy, bloody shit."

Before I could slap myself and issue instructions—*calm down, maybe it's just a coincidence*—my cell phone beeped from inside my satchel.

I tore the zipper open and rummaged around for it—an agonizingly long five or six seconds. With a snap of the wrist I flipped it open and stammered, "Marta Hjelm here."

"Thank God I got you," a quavery contralto voice said. "It's Sue."

"Are you okay?" I blurted.

"We had a bad night." She was almost sobbing. "A *real* bad night. He beat me up again. He says everything is fucked. He's gonna lose the bars now."

"Just because you got fired?"

"I think he was getting money from Herb. I mean, a *lot* of money. With Herb gone—"

"As an investment? Blackmail? What?"

"I don't know, Marta, I just don't know. I pushed him to tell, and he started hitting me."

I was nearly cracking the casing of the cell phone with my grip. Doug hitting another guy was scary enough, but hitting his wife—

I scolded myself: Relax, chill. Wouldn't do anyone any good busting a gasket.

"Do you think," I asked as evenly as I could, "that he could've killed Herb? Does he have it in him to actually pull the trigger?"

"I— I don't really— I don't know. Oh God, *do you think so?*"

"What did he say last time you saw him?"

"He said if I went out that door, he'd come after me and tear me to pieces."

"Where are you now?"

"I've been driving around all night, Marta." Now she sounded numbed, anesthetized. A sudden transformation. "Forgot my cell phone at home. So I'm standing here freezing my butt off in a phone booth in Uptown. I didn't even know there were any phone booths left. And it's snowing, too. Got stuck just a little while ago. A nice man helped me get out. What a goddamned great day."

No way did I not sympathize with her desire to soliloquize. But that didn't seem too constructive at the moment. "I want to get you to Grabowski, Sue," I said, like a grown-up to a kid, "down at the government center. It's the only safe place. You're safer off the street, until the cops get hold of Doug. Okay?"

She panted at me for a few long seconds. "I've gotta see you first, talk with you. I've gotta figure this out before I do anything I'll regret."

"You can figure it out downtown."

"I don't know," she pleaded, "I don't know. Where are you, Marta?"

"At my duplex in Prospect Park. Like you asked me to be."

"I'll get there, okay?"

"We could meet at your Mom's."

Truth be told, I didn't like the thought of sitting here like a ruptured duck, with Doug on the loose. Not a particularly brave attitude, but lately I'd become very fond of staying alive. Cheap heroics did not come with the $75 an hour.

"No," she gulped, the panic back in her voice. "He might lay for me there. He knows I'll go to Mom's eventually. Anyway, he and Mom don't like each other, and Michelle hates his guts. I don't want to—"

"I understand, Sue," I said. "I understand. I'll sit tight. Park in back and come in the back door."

"Okay." She made what can only be called a pregnant pause. "Do you have a gun, Marta?"

"Why?"

"I don't. And I think you should have one. Just in case."

My turn to gulp.

"Yeah," I said, "I do."

"You're a real friend, Marta." And she disconnected.

Breathing heavy, I put the cell phone back in my satchel, folded Rick's envelope of tearsheets in half and stuck them in, too.

I sprinted across the hallway to the bedroom, and before you knew it underwear and t-shirts were flying out of the middle drawer of my dresser onto the bed and floor. I dug and dug and couldn't find the revolver. Then I located the cold metal object—my Ruger .38—entwined incongruously in an ancient silk bra that Terry had bought me during our hot-to-trot Santa Barbara days. One of those items meant to be rapidly stripped from one's body in the heat of— Well, you know. Dressed up to get messed up.

Finding the ammo in the junk drawer was even more challenging, because too much haste would produce a collection of cuts, contusions, and piercing wounds to my hands. So bit by bit I extracted hammers, pliers, screwdrivers, door-lock hardware, boxes of nails, rolls of picture-hanging wire, two defunct tripod heads, and a mystery tool with nasty metal burrs on one of the edges. And there at the very back sat the single box of .38 cartridges.

Obviously, I didn't shoot the weapon very often.

I flipped open the cylinder of the revolver to double check that the five chambers were empty. Then I tested the safety, which would keep me from shooting off my big toe. The revolver apparently hadn't suffered for its sojourn in the world of intimate apparel. Without much enthusiasm, I loaded five bullets, clicked the cylinder shut, and gently lowered the weapon into my satchel.

I paced back and forth across the living room for a good half-hour. Then it struck me that killing time inside the house probably wasn't a great idea. Better to go out back and wait for Sue in the car. She could leave hers here, we could drive around in mine, have our chat, and go downtown. Then all we'd have to do is go to ground, and let Grabowski and his people collar Doug.

Buttoning up my coat and pondering that question a bit too intently, I headed out through the kitchen and pulled open the door that led out to the back vestibule.

There facing me stood Doug, smiling like a shy young guy on his first date.

He had a frosted stainless 9mm in his hand, pointed at my stomach. Meg LaGrange's 9mm.

"Hi Marta," he said, a little tiredly. "Mind if I come in?"

Chapter Twenty-Seven

"I want you to back into the kitchen," he told me, with an encouraging nod. "Real, *real* slow. Keep both your hands in plain sight, okay? I've had a really long night and I don't wanta get sloppy with this thing. Do something stupid, make any funny moves, and maybe I accidentally shoot you through the gut. Understand? I hear getting gutshot is no fun."

"No fun," I agreed.

"So Marta, we move backwards real nice and slow." He flipped off the safety and yanked back the top slide. He knew how to use the thing.

I nodded and shuffled back-asswards—as my Dad put it—slack-jawed, feeling almost nauseous, with my hands up like little bunny-rabbit paws. Muscles and tendons in my neck tautened like piano wires. I felt an intense throb of pain behind my right ear, like the sharp jabbing of an ice-cream headache. Instead of distracting me, it concentrated my attention, got me focused on getting through this.

The old noggin rapidly leafed through what my former Brit boyfriend used to say about being held at gunpoint: Do what your assailant says, *unless the weapon isn't ready to fire and he's close enough to attack.* Meg's stainless steel nine was ready for business and Doug was well out of range. Punches to the neck or nose, knees to the family jewels, boots to the shins would do me no good.

Suddenly my kiester bumped into the counter by the stove. I'd come as far as I could.

Doug shuffled in, reached behind his back, and pushed the door shut behind him. His boots were making a big puddle by the door. Strangely, that little mess on the floor annoyed me almost more than being taken hostage in my own house.

"Put your purse on the counter next to you." He suddenly sounded more business-like, less embarrassed.

I stood there staring at him like a dope.

"Put your fucking purse on the counter!" he growled, his mouth curling into a snarl

Like the man said, I put my "fucking purse" on the counter and meekly muttered, "Whatever you say."

"Now move away, over there. Backwards again. Keep your hands up." He gestured at the doorway on the other side of the kitchen with the 9mm.

"Okay," I said, "okay."

Inching away in reverse gear put me close to the hallway that leads to the living room, the hallway with walls full of work that Rick and I had shot. Our artsy images—landscapes and still-lifes, street photos and nudes. The stuff we were hoping to take to art fairs the following summer. There's our bedroom and guest room on one side of the hallway, my den/office and bathroom on the other side. If I bolted, I had no place to run, no place to hide.

Still, every instinct shouted, "Run, girl, run!" I tried to put a lid on it. My brain bellowed: "We gotta think our way outta this one, gang!"

As the ex-hockey star stole glances at me and rummaged through the satchel, priorities clicked into place.

One, get him out of here before Sue arrived. Whatever it took. Two, try to talk him out of his second opportunity to kill me. Three, wrestle the gun away from him. Memo to self: First, take down a former National Hockey League defenseman. Yeah, *right*. I would have to break his nose...hammer his knee...or crush his nuts. Then bolt out into the blizzard.

With a chuckle he extracted my Ruger .38, trailing several tissues. It looked like a toy in his hand, not even filling his huge palm. "Carrying a little sting, are we?" he said, pocketing the weapon.

"Not anymore," I said.

"Just as well, somebody could get hurt."

"Like you."

"You mad at me, or something?"

Before I could help myself I snapped, "Cut the bullshit, Doug."

"I am *real* sorry," he said, so quietly it scared me. Like a 4H kid murmuring sincere regrets to the blue-ribbon steer he'd just sold to the slaughterhouse. "You know too much. Would've been a lot easier for both of us if you'd just gotten in your car that morning. *Boom*, no more pain.

"You know," he continued, waving Meg's 9mm around in a conversational way, "I didn't think I could kill Herb. I just didn't think I could do that kind of thing, you know, *cold-blooded*. I was almost peeing my pants, Marta, driving out there. I was kind of wired anyway, after tailing you and Sue. You know, window dressing for the terrorist scam? Sue had me do that, and the thing with the syringe and the cola. We bought the Escort in Eau Claire, had it painted, got the Minnesota plates out of a junkyard. But murdering Herb? I mean, I've been in lots of fights. I've hurt people. Not just on the ice. But I never killed anybody before. You have any idea what a big deal that is, fixing to kill someone?"

"Definitely a major life move, Doug."

He frowned at me. "You know, sometimes I have trouble figuring out when people are being sarcastic, ragging on the big ol' dumb jock. But I'm gonna cut you a little slack and assume that you meant that in a way that wasn't insulting. If you didn't I can give you a little of what I gave Sue. Understand?"

"Yeah, I do. And sorry about getting snarky. But this's kind of a stressful situation."

"Apology accepted," he said, nodding, "and it's stressful for me, too."

Sue could be here any time. I had to get him out of the house.

"Listen, Doug," I lied breathlessly, running the words together, "my boyfriend's going to be here any minute, and I don't want him to get hurt. You can understand that, can't you?"

He nodded.

"He has nothing to do with this. So why don't we go out and get in my car, or yours, and you can take me someplace, okay?"

He shook his head and laughed like I was the silliest woman alive. "Do you have any idea how crappy it is outside? The snow's going sideways. We're supposed to get eighteen inches. I don't want be slip-sliding all over Minneapolis and you trying to get at the gun."

"So stick me in the trunk, tie me up in the back seat. "

"Nah, this's better."

The wheels of my brain spun hopelessly. "So why'd you do it then?" I asked.

"Kill Herb?"

I nodded, wondering gratefully why he didn't seem in any hurry to do the deed.

"It was him or me, Marta," he said, with an expression that translated into: What a dope!

"What do you mean?"

"He was gonna go the feds about my bars."

"What about your bars?"

"Funny thing was, I *really* went out there to kill him. That was the plan."

"And Meg was going to be the patsy?" I offered.

"Yeah, it was set up beautiful. But I got cold feet. I'm standing there, holding this gun on him, thinkin', 'I can't do this, I *cannot* do this!' I'm looking in his eyes— And he had scary eyes, let me tell you—he really woulda been something when he was younger. And I'm thinking *I gotta get outta here!* However big an asshole he could be, I just can't kill him. It wouldn't be right. But he sneered at me, Marta, told me what a stupid, dumb-shit jock I was."

I was practically vibrating and my voice had a terrible quaver in it. "What was it about your bars and the feds?"

The bemused expression on that big, doughy face in a blink transmuted into pure rage. "*Shut the fuck up, you stupid bitch!*"

He very nearly lurched toward me, but caught himself.

It's a challenge being attentive and sympathetic, with a 9mm automatic leveled at your heart. But suddenly I was Miss Congeniality again.

"Sorry, Doug," I mumbled, somehow dampening the quiver in my voice.

"He was sick, you know," Doug continued, calming as quickly as he had flared up. "Some kind of Alzheimer's, I thought. But I guess it was cancer. Hell, he'd come to me in the first place, after Sue and I got married. Said he wanted to invest in my bar. Surprised the hell out of me, but I sure could use it. The money came under the table. Hundreds of thousands a year. Got so it made a real difference. Couldn't have kept going, couldn't have opened the second and third places without it. Where you met Denny and Susie that night, that was the first one. It's a great place, isn't it?"

"Sure is," I mumbled, beginning to understand what the trouble was with his sports bars.

"No more money now, I suppose."

"So it would seem, Doug."

"Like I said, when I got to his house *I couldn't do it.*" Doug laughed so hard, it brought tears to his eyes. The 9mm dropped to his hip and I almost thought I could charge him. But back up it bobbed, aiming at my chest again.

"So the old man did it for me. Almost like he wanted me to take him out. Came at me with a letter opener, Marta." He broke eye contact and absent-mindedly regarded the frosted stainless automatic, as if it held the answer to all this mayhem. "Some kinda fancy brass letter opener. I shot him in self-defense. *Honest to God, he would've stuck me in the neck with that thing!* He fell on the desk and he must've knocked a cigarette outta the ashtray or something. Guess that's what started the fire. I mean, I got outta there fast as I could."

When I heard the back aluminum screen door rattle open, I nearly jumped out of my boots, and a long, dismal "*Shiiit*" unfurled itself under my breath. Doug didn't seem surprised. He looked pleased, actually, and turned to see both me and whoever came in.

A pair of feet tromped on the mat in the back vestibule, knocking snow off boots. The knob on the kitchen door turned gently and a red-parka-ed Sue Hewlett tip-toed in. She had on blue jeans and blue women's Sorel boots, with generous globs of snow in her black, luxuriant pageboy. She blinked at me, smiled, grinned at her husband and wiped the snow out of her hair.

"Hi, honey," he said. "What do you want to do with her?"

Chapter Twenty-Eight

"Let's take her to the living room," Sue answered, as coldly as any Gestapo man in a war movie. "Where's her gun?"

"Right here," Doug replied, patting his pocket.

"It's loaded?"

"Yeah, hon."

As I trod down the hallway with Doug holding Meg LaGrange's 9mm in the small of my back, I blathered an impotent phrase along the lines of: "What the hell's going on here?"

Doug knocked me down from behind with a rock-hard elbow. He hissed something about keeping my fucking mouth shut or else.

Ideas whirled through the tattoo of my banging, pounding heartbeat and throbbing head. How could Sue benefit from murdering her boss? Why would she bother to kill an investigator who'd uncovered nothing of any consequence that connected her with the case? Why would she set up her husband on abuse charges, *if* she set him up? It made no sense.

Whatever the details, I had a pretty good idea about the upshot: I'd been played for an absolute fool by a very beautiful woman. It was like I was in a classic noir thriller, only it wasn't Humphrey Bogart playing the sap. It was me. An old, old story, whatever the gender variations. When Doug had told me, sitting at his dining room table, that Sue was "the top dog around here," he wasn't kidding.

I stumbled to my feet and staggered into the living room. It was awfully dim in there, with the plywood on the windows, but you could see the space clearly enough.

"Stop right there," Sue snapped when I reached the center of the maroon Persian rug. She held her hand out. "Give me her gun, Dougie."

He handed her the Ruger, planted a quick kiss on her cheek and whispered a sweet term of endearment in her ear that I heard clearly: "Love you sweetie."

She gave him a glowing, affectionate smile and leaned toward him. "You too, hon. Is this thing ready to shoot?"

He shook his head.

"Would you fix it up for me, please?"

"Oh, sure." He took the revolver from her, clicked off the safety and pulled back the hammer. Then he handed it back. I swear she tossed him a little air kiss. Then she trained the gun on me.

"Doug, turn on a light."

He leaned over the sofa and flipped on the floor lamp behind it. Rick's oriental fan collection on the wall blossomed in the warm light, like a bouquet of giant butterflies. Our breaths showed mistily in the cool air. But I savored the oak floor that Rick and I had refinished, the antique prints, the Cartier-Bresson. One of my favorite places in the world, this room. I missed the birds and their cages, but I found myself thinking: It's good they won't see what's going to happen here. They're smart enough to understand.

As Doug hopped off the sofa, I figured I had nothing to lose by getting up on my hind legs.

"Will one of you," I spat, "tell me what's going on?"

Doug was facing me again, and Sue stood next to him. Both of them had me covered. "Soon enough, Marta," she said, still sounding eerily calm. "Soon enough."

The next few seconds seemed to last forever, and I felt relieved when Sue began speaking, instead of shooting.

"Now, Dougie," she said, "why don't you put Meg's gun down on the sofa. I can handle it from here."

He looked puzzled, but he nodded and set down Meg's frosted-stainless automatic—the bizarrely named "Ladysmith." He stood with his long arms dangling by his sides. His face seemed placid, reassured. The brains of the operation had arrived, had taken charge. He was someone who lost control occasionally, perhaps, but wasn't the crazed wife-beater. Maybe she taunted him until he burst—just to provide her with the bruises and contusions she needed.

My pal Sue turned around, backed away a couple of steps. I didn't see her aiming the revolver at Doug's mid-section.

At the first flaring explosion I imagined I felt the slug smashing into my stomach instead of Doug's.

The next shot lifted him into the air.

At the third shot I saw the muzzle flash form a corona over his chest.

I started to leap at her, but things happened so quickly that I wasn't in time.

She hopped back away from her husband, as he became a giant, limp rag doll—his eyes wide with wonderment. Then she did a half pivot and had the barrel of the .38 aimed at my chest before I could get closer than eight feet. She had two shots left, more than enough.

I lurched to a juddering stop and felt a sharp pain in my right knee. But I managed to catch my balance and limped back away from the lovely murderess.

Surely somebody would hear the shots and call 911. Then I remembered that Grace was gone, and the blizzard outside would muffle any kind of noise.

Doug had fallen to his knees on the Persian, clutching his stomach. Blood weltered slowly out from between his huge fingers. If it had been me or Rick, we would have died already. Amazing he could even stay upright on his knees. His strength and size gave him an extra moment of life.

He was looking up at Sue, plaintively. Then he crumbled onto the rug on his side, pale blue eyes open and empty, coincidentally gazing up at his lovely bride.

I slowly turned to peer at her. She looked saddened by the whole nasty, sordid affair. As if to say, "Poor Dougie, how could such a thing happen?" Then, like a switch flipping, she was all business.

"Don't talk," she said, a little testily. "Hands on top of your head. *Now!*"

I did what she said. Then I began, "So you—"

"Shut up!" she barked.

Keeping an eagle eye on me, she sidled over and grabbed the 9mm from the couch, tucked the .38 in a coat pocket and returned to Doug. She had on leather gloves. She squatted down, put the 9mm in Doug's dead, bare right hand and fired a shot in my direction.

I jumped two inches in the air, then realized I hadn't been hit.

She stood up quickly, aiming the automatic at me. "Hands on top again, lady!"

"Why didn't you shoot me just now?" I panted.

She shrugged. "What's the rush? Besides, I like you, Marta, and I need to talk to *somebody*. Might as well be you. Get it off my chest. Do you have any idea how hard it is to pull off something like this and not be able to tell somebody? Not that you're going to be telling anyone yourself. Besides, I think you've figured out a lot of it."

With my hands back on top of my head, I felt like I'd stumbled into some macabre version of Simon Says. "I wouldn't be so sure of that."

She looked surprised. She really thought I knew something I didn't.

"So what is the story?" I groaned.

She shrugged: Humor the dead woman walking. "At the very beginning? Herb was ashamed, mortified." Her voice had taken on an actorly quality, like she'd practiced this speech for a long, long time. "White guy, big wheel, knocks up 16-year-old black girl from public housing. Not good PR. *Biiig trouble.*"

My turn to look surprised. I wasn't sure I'd heard her right. "Michelle's your *daughter?*"

She nodded and smiled tiredly. "Yeah, my kid and Herb's. Love child, bastard, whatever you want to call it. Mom blackmailed him at first. She's always been practical. It wasn't just the money, though. Mom said, 'We're all family now, and family helps family.' So Herb put me through college, got me into advertising, poured the bucks in Doug's bars, helped support Michelle. We have enough in the bank to put her through college. Heck, med school or law school, if she wants. She's a good kid, she really is."

Sue paused for a few beats, trying to read my reaction. I was shooting for inscrutable, but I'm not sure I hit it.

"I married Doug to prove to Mom that she didn't own me

anymore. It was okay at first, I really did love him, but then he'd get drunk and shout at me. Was always sorry afterwards. Most of the time he was a pussycat. He never hit me until lately. No fun, I can tell you. But I began to think it might be useful. Poor little abused wife, huh? I figured after what happened to you last summer, you might be a little receptive to that."

She was taunting me, but I tried not to react.

"He was drinking too much, the bars were in tough shape, life with him was— It's been miserable the last couple of years. Except for Michelle's support, what I call Herb's 'fun' money had been going into those damned taverns of his. I mean, Marta, it was only natural to fall in love with Archie."

Inside my head I yelped: "*What the!?*" To all appearances I merely nodded agreeably. Because it might keep me breathing a few minutes longer.

"There's so much of his father in him. I'm so damned sick of the sneaking around, though. We're going to go away when all this settles down. We're thinking Saint Kitts."

"Does he know about Herb being Michelle's father?"

She looked at me like I was some kind of disgusting. "Of course not! That would be like...like sleeping with my own stepson! I'm a lot of things, but I'm no pervert. All Archie knows about is the terrorism thing."

"Even if this works out the way you planned," I said, trying to keep it together, "you're still on the hook for trying to extort Herb, for the Lexus."

"I know, I'll deal with it. If it means jail, it means jail. But it would only be for a year or two." She stared down at Doug briefly and shook her head. The hallway entrance gaped darkly behind her, dim but for a little light coming from the kitchen. Our pictures were reduced to shadowy rectangles on a dismal gray wall.

"I knew Herb had cancer," she continued. "I could tell just looking at him. His energy started to go, and that just wasn't like him. Wasn't like him not to jump at Bertram Tobacco and Hemo. You know?"

I understood just what she was talking about. I nodded

again.

"When I asked him 'round Christmastime, he denied it. Then he quit paying the money. All of it. He called my bluff, Marta. I wasn't about to reveal who Michelle was. Not in public anyway. Not after all this time. I think he knew I couldn't do it. It would ruin her life. I'm not sure whether he gave a shit anymore, or not."

"Why not just wait for nature to take its course?"

She looked cagey and tapped the side of her head with a free index finger. "Because Herb could do me one more favor before he died. And I could do one for him."

"What do you mean?"

"Simple, Marta. I told Herb that if he didn't fire Meg, I'd tell Michelle—nobody else—who her Daddy *really* was. Not some white guy that my Mom met at a bar, who vanished after a one-night stand. But a greedy, selfish bastard racist who was a-shamed of the color of his daughter's skin. A guy who'd seen her up close, seen how neat she was and still wouldn't own up."

"I thought he didn't care anymore."

"Turned out he did. On some level it mattered to him. Maybe intimations of mortality. Who knows?"

"Were you bluffing?"

"Sure. You think I want Michelle to know what I did to her, did to *us*? But I guess he couldn't tell. Or didn't want to take the chance."

"Why go after Meg?"

Her black eyes flared like torches. "*'Cause the fucking bitch took Herb away from me!*" She glared at me, still livid after all these years. "Herb, you know, I worshipped him. I really thought he might marry me, after I turned eighteen, once he got divorced. I mean, he couldn't marry jailbait, could he? And after that, he couldn't marry a black girl. That was just never in the cards. Stupid teenage dreams. But my little girl still got a pretty good deal out of it all."

"So, Herb helps you frame Meg for murder, only he doesn't realize it. He just thinks you're getting even with her."

Sue nodded.

"You calculate that Meg will rush out there to confront Herb."

She nodded again. "Part of the deal was that he tell me when he was going to e-mail her, so I could get Doug out there with her gun. I'm still amazed that everything clicked."

"But offing your hubby isn't usually part of the wedding vows. Doug told me that Herb was going to turn him in. That's how you got him to sign on." I looked down on the other poor sap in the room.

"Exactly. All I had to do was tell him that Herb had threatened to put him out of business, go the feds, tell the newspapers how the bars were going down. The double books, everything. Same as I told him you'd found out about his deal with Herb, and you were blackmailing us. I think the poor guy got frostbite, coming out in the middle of the night to rig your car."

"A very nice little plot you cooked up there, Susie. All the wheels and gears meshing."

She smiled modestly. "Thank you."

"What's the favor you did Herb?"

She huffed out a misty breath into the air and peered at me with a look of pride on her face. "I helped him go with his boots on, Marta. I saved him from a miserable, slow death. A last gift from an old lover. He would've thanked me."

"Doug told me that Herb came at him with a letter opener, that he wouldn't have shot him otherwise. Just couldn't do it."

She smiled down at her murdered husband. "Ol' Dougie, a softie at heart." She looked up at me. "Good thing Herb had the guts to push him."

Sue aimed the 9mm right at my face and regarded me dispassionately—an object in her way that needs removal. An honest-to-God pathological narcissist. Even then it struck me how gorgeous she was.

"And me? Why me?"

"I couldn't take the chance that you'd figured out where Michelle came from. No one knew but Herb, my Mom and me. Archie didn't know. Doug knew I had something on Herb, but never asked what. Michelle has no idea. No one had really dug before. You seemed headed in the right direction, maybe even knew something already. Besides, you had to kill Doug in self-defense. But you were fatally wounded in the process. Think of it as my instant divorce."

I planned to keep talking, because I could visualize the next minute or two as lucidly and breathtakingly as an incoming gut punch.

She was going to shoot me with Meg's 9mm. To accommodate the wax test she'd probably fire a wild shot from my .38 with my dead hand, just like she'd done with Doug and the automatic. Then the new young widow would stumble onto the murder scene, horrified, call 911, and cross her fingers. Perhaps clasp Doug to her bosom, to explain some of the blood on her coat. I'd be the dead hero, Doug would be the dead goat.

After a decent interval, after Sue and Archie did their time and community service, she and he would repair to that warm, hospitable clime where no one had ever heard of a tawdry murder case involving a Minneapolis ad man, an ex-NHL hockey player, and an obscure lady PI.

"I know this deal is real shitty for you, Marta. But it's like the only chance I have of getting my life—"

Out of the corner of my eye I saw a dark form creeping up the hallway, slouching along.

I tried not to give anything away with my eyes.

But Sue heard the whispery padding of stocking feet. She spun around just in time to get off one wild shot.

The bulbous, black Nikon soared out of the dim hallway, cartwheeled through the air, and lightly grazed the side of Sue's head—like a three-pound boomerang.

She flinched in surprise as Rick burst from the shadows, launched himself in a flying tackle, and dropped her to the floor with a sickening thud.

I came at her from the other side and piled on.

The two of us tried to grapple the 9mm out of her stubborn right hand. She was amazingly strong.

It was only a few seconds, but it seemed like eternity. A see-sawing, three-sided wrestling match where any loser could lose bigtime.

"Let it go, Sue," I panted.

And the gun went off, a sodden percussion that sickened me. I could feel someone other than me take the slug.

"Rick!" I screamed.

Nothing.

"Rick!"

"I'm okay," he wheezed, prying the 9mm out of Sue's perfect, begloved fingers and tossing it aside. "You?"

All I could manage was a shaky "Uh-huh."

We rolled and scuttled away from Sue Hewlett, on our hands and knees, like big old crabs in overcoats.

She lay gasping for air on her back, almost cheek to cheek with Doug, her blue sorrel boots splayed out at odd angles.

The wound was in her chest. And it had begun turning the waist of her parka a deeper hue of red. She turned her head a little and blinked up at me, her eyes clearly out of focus.

"Marta?" she whispered, like someone with laryngitis.

"Yeah."

"Don't let Michelle know, okay?"

Chapter Twenty-Nine

Slumping there in our living room, literally shellshocked, we understood that we couldn't cover up what happened in our house, the actual gruesome events.

I can tell you, it's way easier to say what you believe is true, than maintain a complex structure of deceit in the face of professional interrogators. Unless the lies are very simple and clean, *they will break you down.*

No way we could have honored Sue Hewlett's last wish. No way we could have protected Michelle Norton from the truth. Even as it was, spilling every detail we knew, we endured many hours of grilling in the days after the incident—and yet more in the months following. Rick and I were cleared of any wrongdoing by reason of self-defense.

Sue Hewlett died about three days after the shootings—in a coma in the ICU. As far as I know, she never said another word after her last word to me. A few weeks later I heard that Jennifer and her husband consolidated their control of Gottwaldt and Ryan, and hired an ad man out of Dallas to run it. "A young Herb," was how Meg described him to me over pizza and pinot grigio. After a long vacation, she returned to the agency as Chief Creative Director, bringing several hefty AmberGrain accounts with her. She told me she was "itching for action."

Emmaline Norton—who lit the fuse nearly two decades earlier—slipped the criminal-justice net entirely. Her original blackmailing of Herb in California was well beyond the statute of limitations. The money he gave her for Michelle was perfectly legal—regular gifts that she declared on her taxes. No evidence could be produced that Herb's "support" was anything but voluntary. Having received a document from the district attorney's office stating that she was in the clear, Emmaline corroborated the tale that Sue Hewlett had told to me at gunpoint. She claimed to have no knowledge of the plot to kill Herb Gottwaldt, or Sue's intent to murder her husband and me.

On the basis of Emmaline's testimony and mine, Meg LaGrange was cleared of murder charges. Subsequent investigations out in California added to the backstory of Herb and Sue, and the daughter they produced.

The only people left alive who ended up with skin in the criminal game were Denny and Archie—for making terroristic threats and for the aggravated assaults by Lexus and cola. Both of them copped pleas. The police could find nothing, though, that connected Archie to Sue Hewlett's murder plot, but plenty of evidence of their year-long affair bubbled up. Having been upright citizens until that point, the two conspirators were given brief stretches in chokey, then much, much community service—sentences yet to be served.

Naturally, the papers, the TV news shows, and news websites were full of reports—the hottest crime story of the winter. It only started fading out a few weeks later.

As for Rick and me, we visited the Apple Store at the Megamall and got ourselves a pair of the big iMacs—for our new digital studio at the Amalgamated. At West Photo we picked up some "glass" that we'd been lusting after—that's photo geekspeak for lenses. After all, I'd collected my fees and a large bonus from the agency *and* Jennifer Nelson. Quite a tidy sum.

Best of all, I found a creampuff, low-mileage Mercury Marquis in metallic gray on Craigslist. Practically new. All it lacked were the scent of ancient cigarettes and the funky bumper stickers. As a gesture of thanks to the gods and my old Pop—who were looking over me that morning—I put a remote starter in it. And an ahooga horn.

Most of our days we spent on stock photography and fineart work—when we didn't have commercial shoots. We bombed around all over the Upper Midwest in the Merc and Rick's Explorer, shooting scenics and people and history. We'd done three art fairs since Memorial Day. Not easy in this economy, but part of our plan. Rick was able to quit the museum gig. PR was never really his thing. I still took some cases—skip traces, a retail job, a referral from Jennifer Nelson.

I think Rick probably was right: For this old cowgirl there's just something addictive about getting to the bare, naked truth. I only hoped that it never would come again in the form of a frosted stainless 9mm wrapped up in terrible secrets.

• • •

Early one muggy August morning, just after sunrise, I'd gone for a hike around Prospect Park with the very same Nikon D3 Rick had heaved at Sue Hewlett. The lens had gotten smashed, but the camera body came through fine—tough as a brick.

I ended up huffing and puffing up the hill to the Witch's Hat Tower, a former water tower long since become a beloved Minneapolis landmark. Thoroughly winded, I perched on a bench and settled in to watch the new day's rays illumine the hazy downtown skyline off to the west.

I'd photographed the view a few times and sold one of the shots. You can still find it on postcard racks around town. They tell me it's a good seller. But like most shooters who return to a favorite scene, I couldn't resist climbing up on the bench and cranking off a few frames.

"Marta?"

I turned around.

It was Michelle Norton, tall and brown and beautiful, in spritely colored jogging gear and the latest Nikes with swooshes and gee-gaws all over them. Her thick, ebony hair was tied up in a exuberant ponytail. You could tell how fit she was by the muscle definition in her legs, the strength in her shoulders, and the spring in her posture.

"Well hi, Michelle," I said, clambering down without much grace, like the nearly-middle-aged, slightly-overweight woman I was. My heart started thumping. Trepidation lurched out of the weeds: I had no idea what she might be thinking of me these days.

"How you doin'?"

"You ever read Dickens?" she said.

"Not since high school."

"Well, the answer is: *Best of times, worst of times.*"

"Not surprising, I guess."

"Can I sit with you?"

"Absolutely."

We plopped down next to each other, a hazy, humid, Minneapolis laid out before us.

She tried to find the right words, and chewed on her lower lip like a kid—a gorgeous young woman making a little-girl face.

"Mom and—" She snorted. "See! *I'm still doing it.* I mean Grandma and I— We felt just so rotten you had to get yourself and your boyfriend involved in this awful thing on account of Susie and Doug."

It *was* awful, but I just shrugged. "It's gotta be totally freaky," I said, "to suddenly find out your sister is your mom, and your mom is your grandma and this old guy you barely knew is your dad. That's gotta mess up anyone."

"Like tell me about it! I mean it's a good thing I'm not into drugs or alcohol. I would be *so* screwed up by now!"

"Do you ever think it'd be better if the truth never came out?"

She peered at me. "You know, you're like some kind of mind reader, Marta. 'Cause I asked myself that question all winter. Things had been *so* nice. Everything going good. Other than the broken leg. Then, *kaboom!* The answer is: I don't know."

"How are you getting along with your grandma?"

"I still love her, I guess. But I *hate* her too. Does that make any sense? I mean, lying to me all my life! How easy is it to have a good relationship with someone, when the whole deal was based on a huge lie? So we're trying to talk it out. We're going into a therapist *three* times a week. Fortunately, I'm gonna get some breathing space. I won't be here my last year in high school."

"Whadaya mean?"

"I'm going to do my senior year at a private school out in Connecticut. My real friends've been great. But there are plenty of jerks at school, too, and it was awful having to listen to them every day. It got pretty bad. I had to get out of there. Grandma home-schooled me, some of my teachers helped and I did a lot of stuff online. But I ended up getting mostly B's and A's, so that's good. Nobody'll know who I am at my new school."

"That's gotta cost a lot."

"No kidding! But my sister— My *real* sister—"

"Jennifer."

Michelle nodded. "She's gonna help pay for me. And Mom— Grandma is okay with it."

"So you're getting along well with Jennifer."

"Yeah, pretty much. She's okay. Actually pretty nice. I mean, this hasn't been very easy for her, either. I've even been out to her house a couple times. What a place! Good to have money, huh? She took me to the symphony, too, and to a play at the Guthrie."

Finally, I asked the question I most wanted an answer to: "What are you thinking about Sue?"

She just shook her head. "The question ought to be: What am I *not* thinking? I loved Susie, now I *loathe* her. For the lying, for what she did. Killing people is an awful thing! I mean, I didn't like Doug *at all*. But he didn't deserve what what he got. Then I ask myself: If it'd been me getting pregnant at 16, and I'd had those options, what would I have done? Where would I have ended up?" Suddenly she looked almost nauseated. She shut her eyes and shook her head.

"What, Michelle?"

She blinked at me, still shaking her head—apparently in disbelief. "Think about it, Marta." Her voice was quavering. "Susie and Archie Gottwaldt! *My mother and my brother! Bangin' each other! O-M-G!*"

"Pretty gross, huh?" I said.

She nodded tiredly and rolled her eyes.

"What are you thinking about Herb?"

She shrugged. "I understand how I could've messed up his life in a lotta ways. I understand *why* the big secret. And I appreciate that he supported me, at least. I mean, there's enough money left for college, and maybe law school, too. But couldn't he have said one word? *One little word?* Like written me an anonymous letter or something? Send me an e-mail you *stupid old man!* Just something that says: I know who you are. In my screwed-up way, *I do care about you!*"

I decided it was a good occasion to tell a little white lie. "You know that Sue, right there at the end, said to me that she thought he really loved you, was really proud of you."

She glared fiercely. *"Then why the hell didn't he tell me!?"*

That's when some tears came. I put an arm around the girl and let her sob for a while. I offered her a tissue and she daubed at her eyes.

When she settled down, I asked, "So how's your leg?"

"It's fine now." She sucked in a slow breath. "Did you know that I got my first real job?"

"No. Where you workin'?"

"Hunsberger's Department Store down University Avenue. Women's sportswear. Three days a week. Now that we're not getting free money anymore, Grandma had to get a job and said I had to, too. Not easy this summer, finding work. The Great Recession, huh? But we managed."

For a while we stared out at the city. The office towers downtown, the University right in front of us, the fugly new football stadium, the sprawling neighborhoods of South Minneapolis across the Mississippi.

It was going to be a hot, muggy one, promising the upper 80s that afternoon. Not a cloud in the sky. I was already starting to sweat.

The girl sighed, long and hard. "I kind of keep asking myself why did it have to happen. You know how you go back in your mind, before something bad, and you try to see how you could have stopped it?"

"Uh-huh, I think we all do that."

"I've been trying to get some kind of handle on it. Like could I have gotten Susie and Doug broken up? What could I have said? Could I have stopped the whole thing?"

"You know, Michelle, people have to help themselves. Sometimes we can rescue them, sometimes we can't. I don't think anybody could have saved Sue. Especially herself."

She didn't respond. Her chin was down, her eyes focussed on the empty tennis courts below us.

"Hey," I said, trying to brighten my tone, "how about we hike up the road to Dunn Brothers? Get a latté and a scone. My treat. You can tell me all about this new school of yours."

She shot me a tired grin. "A nice dose of caffeine always makes things a little brighter, doesn't it?"

"Sure does," I said.

And off we tramped down the hill.

ABOUT THE AUTHOR

D. R. Martin is a writer of wide experience, with over fifteen-hundred credits in fields as diverse as book reviewing, travel journalism, music journalism, television script writing, business writing, and medical writing. He is an award-winning copywriter, the former editor of a weekly newspaper, and a semi-pro photographer. Smoking Ruin *is his second mystery novel.*

If you have questions or comments, you can contact D. R. at drmartin120@gmail.com.